Praise for Brighton Walsh

"A vulnerable but indomitable heroine and a hero who will haunt your dreams long after the last page. Raw, sexy, and unexpectedly tender, *Captive* is a powerful, gripping story."

— Kit Rocha, *New York Times* bestselling author

"A sexy, suspenseful, and deliciously forbidden love story!"

— Laura Kaye, *New York Times* bestselling author

"Walsh entices readers with the lure of romance and a hint of mystery. Sensuous detail . . . with intense heat and complex characters."

— *Publishers Weekly*

"It will be impossible to put this book down. It was so engrossing, it'll be a stupid idea to stop. Solid five stars for this one!"

— *Nerdy Talks*

"Super sexy and romantic, and I want everyone to read Brighton Walsh's books. . . . You'll be hard-pressed not to fall for Ghost and want the best for Madison."

— *Love at First Page*

"If you haven't tried Brighton Walsh in the past, you should definitely try out her books because there is just something magical about her writing that draws you in and prevents you from abandoning the book. *Captive* was a fantastic novel that made me feel all the feels!"

— *Nick's Book Blog*

ALSO BY BRIGHTON WALSH

Captive

Caged in Winter

Tessa Ever After

Plus One

Season of Second Chances

Exposed

BRIGHTON WALSH

ST. MARTIN'S GRIFFIN 🅼 NEW YORK

This is a work of fiction. All of the characters, organizations, and events portrayed in this novel are either products of the author's imagination or are used fictitiously.

www.stmartins.com

Designed by Omar Chapa

Library of Congress Cataloging-in-Publication Data

Walsh, Brighton.
    Exposed / Brighton Walsh.—First edition.
      pages ; cm
    ISBN 978-1-250-05964-2 (trade paperback)
    ISBN 978-1-4668-6502-0 (e-book)

   I. Title.
   PS3623.A4454E96 2015
   813'.6—dc23

                2015016929

St. Martin's Griffin books may be purchased for educational, business, or promotional use. For information on bulk purchases, please contact the Macmillan Corporate and Premium Sales Department at 1-800-221-7945, extension 5442, or write to specialmarkets@macmillan.com.

First Edition: July 2015

10 9 8 7 6 5 4 3 2 1

For all the Evies out there—you're not alone.

Exposed

Chapter One

EVIE

After twenty-two years, I'd come to the realization that people only saw what you let them see. Or, more apt, what they *wanted* to see. Generally the pretty, skin-deep things that didn't make them uncomfortable. They didn't look for the messy, ugly parts . . . the dark, twisted secrets hidden away. The skeletons inevitably buried in everyone's closets.

They definitely didn't see the bones I had concealed in mine, buried under years of dirty secrets and lies and the hundreds of miles separating me from the truth.

That fact was a comfort on nights like these—nights where I felt like the biggest fraud. Because I knew all these people surrounding me with their fake smiles and their pretentious small talk weren't really looking. Not at anything more than what I was wearing, how close Eric and I were standing, how many times I smiled, or how many glasses of wine I had.

At a fund-raiser for Kirkland & Caine, I smiled and laughed, engaged in meaningless small talk. On the arm of my fiancé, dressed in a sparkly dress that cost more than what my rent used to be, I did nothing more than pretend. Put on the pretense of a person I'd invented from the ground up. Not a person I ever was or ever would be, if I had the option.

Funny thing—options weren't plentiful when you were in my shoes. Not when you were running from everything you'd ever known. Not when your life was in danger if you ever stopped.

Like always at events like this, Eric didn't leave my side the entire night, letting my hand rest in the crook of his elbow as he led us from group to group, making the rounds and putting in face time. These kinds of things only came up a few times a year— this was only the third I'd ever had to attend—and even though they were relatively infrequent, they still made me uneasy. I couldn't help my eyes from darting to all the corners of the rooms, checking for the exits, scrutinizing the attendees, the waitstaff, the bartenders. Looking for anything suspicious, anything out of the ordinary. After all this time, I couldn't imagine that the people who would give just about anything to see me found and caught would grab me in a public place. They wouldn't make such a spectacle. They'd be quiet about it, maybe come for me at my house or while I was getting into my car in a secluded parking lot. Someplace the noise and commotion would go unnoticed.

They were professionals, after all.

Even knowing this, I was on edge. The whole night, I was twitchy and jumpy, waiting for something I knew wouldn't come—not here. And I couldn't even say it was because I felt something in my gut, a voice that told me something was off. Because that voice was never silent, forever by my side, forever whispering and reminding me of all the ways I'd screwed up, of all the ways I *could* screw up if I stepped even slightly out of line. If I didn't preserve this façade to the utmost detail. Of the lives I could ruin if my truth ever came out.

If I was ever found.

Eric leaned down, his lips right by my ear, his hand resting on top of the one I had clutched to his elbow. The familiar, woodsy scent of him calmed me, and I reminded myself to relax. To breathe. His voice wasn't much over a whisper, just loud enough for me to hear in the din. "Not much longer. You want another glass of wine?"

After a year together, ten months of which we'd been engaged, he'd nearly perfected being able to read me. Nearly.

A bright burst of light echoed from off to our right as a photographer snapped pictures of the crowd, and I flinched. It was the barest of movements, just my fingers tightening on Eric's arm, but he didn't wait for my response to his question before he flagged down one of the waitstaff and grabbed a glass of wine from the tray. He passed it to me with a smile pasted on his face. Had to keep up pretenses, because people were watching. Someone was always watching.

His voice was low, soothing, as he said, "We'll head home soon. Fifteen more minutes."

He'd always been considerate of how much time we had to spend at these events. He thought I had social anxiety disorder, that the reason I didn't do well in crowds was because of that. I had a prescription for Prozac that I got filled every month. A tiny green-and-white capsule I flushed down the toilet every morning.

He had no idea the real reason I was twitchy, the real reason I hated doing anything in public, was because I wasn't who I said I was. I wasn't Genevieve Meyer, recent graduate of U of M with a degree in Journalism—the one tiny piece of my old life I'd allowed to seep through. Originally from Miami and the only child of deceased parents.

Everything he knew of my life now was a lie. Every facet of it a fabrication erected from my imagination. Every ounce of it created and built through more steps than I was aware of, even now. Even five years later.

No, I wasn't Genevieve Meyer, fiancée of Eric Caine, the

up-and-coming lawyer and son of a former senior partner at the biggest law firm in Minneapolis and current Republican senator from Minnesota.

I hated yoga, though I took a class four times a week. I'd rather have a beer than drink wine, but I dutifully sipped my red. I'd be more comfortable cleaning my grandiose home than I was living in it.

But after this long, after five years—two hundred seventy-three weeks; one thousand, nine hundred and seventeen days— I'd gotten used to the lying, to the pretense of my new life.

So used to it, it was getting harder to tell what was the truth and what was a lie.

The light on the front porch shone in greeting when we pulled into our driveway nearly an hour later. It was a trek to get downtown, but this suburb was one of the best in the city, and Eric thought it would look better if we settled out here. Thought it would look better to everyone else watching one of the most eligible bachelors in the city go off the market.

He pulled into the garage, then came around and opened the car door for me, his hand on the small of my back as he led me into the house. It was clean—clean and sterile—Jane, our housekeeper, having been there earlier in the day. The house and furnishings weren't at all what I would normally choose, but it was nice enough.

And it was something Eric took pride in, which was enough incentive for me to smile and keep my opinions to myself. My successful fiancé was eleven years older than me. Someone with whom, under normal circumstances, I wouldn't have anything in common. But these weren't normal circumstances, and despite our age difference, we meshed seamlessly.

After four years of keeping my head down, keeping to myself, holding myself apart from others—a self-sustaining island—

I'd allowed him to wear me down. And that had been it. He'd asked me on a date and wouldn't take no for an answer. When I'd relented, when I'd finally gone out on that first date with him, I'd found that I'd actually enjoyed myself. We'd had fun together. We'd clicked.

Two months later, we'd been engaged. The wedding was scheduled for June next year. Deposits had been put down on locations and vendors my future mother-in-law had selected. A dress I didn't want or particularly like was on order at the bridal shop. Soon, it'd be time to look at invitations, or so I'd been told.

Eric hung up his keys on the peg next to the door and took off his coat, then came over to me, helping me out of mine. "Sorry we had to stay longer. You feeling okay?" His eyes were worried as he studied me, his hands running up and down the expanse of my bare arms.

"Yeah, I'm fine." I averted my eyes as I set my purse on the counter. "I just get nervous with so many people around." That, at least, was the truth.

"I know." He leaned forward and pressed a kiss to my forehead. "Thank you for doing that for me."

He always did that—thanked me for my part in his life. For putting on a smile and showing up with him to the important events. And they were important—I knew that. Not only to his father, but to him, too. Because eventually he wanted to follow that same path. Follow the steps his father took up the ladder at the law firm, then, when it was time, transition to politics, the same as his dad had.

And even though Eric thanked me, it should've been the other way around. I was a girl who'd come from nothing, and now I was living in a million-dollar home with a three-carat rock on my finger, engaged to be married to one of the most handsome and kindest men I'd ever met.

"You don't have to thank me. Part of the job, right?" I tried to tease, inflecting a lilt to my voice as I held up my left hand with a smile, the diamond catching in the overhead light and sparkling just like in a jewelry commercial.

He didn't return the grin like I'd hoped he would. "Yeah, well, my part of the job doesn't cause me distress. Yours does."

"It's really not a big deal." I squeezed his hand. "I promise."

He stared at me, his eyes delving far enough into my soul that I knew he could tell I was lying. Still, he didn't press. "Fortunately, we won't have another one to attend until the Christmas party."

I laughed, rolling my eyes. "Considering Christmas is less than two months away, that's not so reassuring."

He finally cracked a smile. "Okay, new tactic." He spun me around, his hands on my shoulders as he guided me toward the steps and upstairs to the en suite bathroom. "Bath?"

I exhaled, my shoulders finally relaxed. "Yes, please."

I escaped to the bedroom and into my walk-in closet, the space that was twice the size of my childhood bedroom. Off came the four-inch heels, then the conservative-yet-still-sexy dress. I unhooked the strand of pearls from around my neck, tucking them safely into the freestanding jewelry armoire in the corner. Then came the bracelet and the matching earrings.

Finally, I pulled my robe from the hook next to the door leading into the bedroom and slipped it on, then headed into the bathroom. The lights were off, a couple of my favorite candles lit, and the oversized tub was already filled to the top, mountains of bubbles heaped over the water. I shrugged out of the robe, letting it pool at my feet, and breathed a sigh of relief as I stepped into the claw-foot basin, closing my eyes as I sank into the hot water.

The door was still open partially, and I could hear Eric moving around. He raised his voice so I could hear him clearly. "I'm sorry I have to leave tomorrow, Gen. You know I hate doing that after a night out."

I leaned back and closed my eyes, running my hand through the bubbles covering the entire surface of the water as I settled my head against the high back of the tub. "It's okay. I'll be fine."

"You could still come with, you know." His voice was softer now, closer, and I cracked open an eye to see him at the door, his shoulder propped up on the doorjamb as he studied me. "I can get a last-minute ticket. Two weeks in London? Not a bad vacation. I'll have to work, but you can go sightseeing, visit the Natural History Museum . . . go shopping."

I snorted at his suggestion. "You know I hate shopping."

He rolled his eyes and turned around, raising his voice again as he went about getting packed for his trip. "I know. I just mean there's lots to do there. You won't be stuck in the hotel room the whole time if you don't want to be. Though the hotel room is actually a very nice suite and not a bad place to be stuck. Just think about it, okay? We can buy you a ticket tomorrow morning at the airport, if you want."

I hummed in acknowledgment and he let it rest, finishing up what he needed to do. And even though I pretended to be contemplating actually going, I wasn't. I couldn't.

The thought of going to London filled me with equal amounts of excitement and dread. I would love to visit, to see all the other things the world had to offer. To go all the places Eric went while visiting different branches of Kirkland & Caine. I could picture myself in New York and L.A., in Paris . . . I could picture myself there, though I'd never go.

Because if I went, that'd mean leaving my safe little cocoon. And the thought of doing that filled me with terror so real I could almost feel it clutching my throat. Even though my identification was top-of-the-line, the best money could buy—Aaron had assured me of that—I still worried about what would happen if I went through customs. If I had trained eyes scrutinizing everything I handed over.

But it wasn't only that.

It was also opening up the possibility of being seen in so many different locations. I didn't know if I'd been lucky these past five years, here in Minneapolis. Hiding in plain sight. I didn't know if it'd been other forces at work—if Aaron and Ghost had kept everyone from looking for me, using their pull within the ranks of the crew to divert attentions elsewhere.

All I knew was I didn't want to chance it. I didn't want to jeopardize everything I'd worked for. I didn't want to risk everything I'd lied for.

And above all else, I didn't want to ever go back.

Chapter Two

Early November in Chicago meant it got dark way too fucking early for my liking, all the shadows making me jumpy. That was part of this business, though, always checking over my shoulder. Since I was fourteen, even before I was really part of the crew, I'd been taught to be diligent, constantly aware of my surroundings. My brother, Gage, had made sure of that. Made sure I could look out for myself. I didn't think I had anything to worry about here, a few blocks from my apartment. This far off the beaten path, the streets were usually barren, even on a Friday night, and tonight was no different, with only a couple homeless guys huddled in an alley across the street.

Flexing my left hand, I felt the dull, residual pain from the job I'd just come from. A corrupt businessman—weren't they all?—who'd gotten a little greedy, skimming from Max. You didn't steal from Max Cavett, and any idiot who thought it was a good idea to steal from the leader of the entire fucking crew deserved every bit of what I was ordered to carry out.

The idiot who'd stolen from Max had actually had the nerve to try and deny his involvement. When I'd confronted him, when he'd been trapped with no way out, he denied it, even though I set the proof right in front of his face. When he hadn't budged, hadn't admitted his deeds, my fists had to come into play.

It was always better for everyone all around if swings didn't start getting thrown. It was always better, though it rarely happened like that. And, to be honest, I liked it that way. I didn't mind the physical aspect of the job, had never minded that. I was good at keeping people in line, at using my fists to remind assholes what they needed reminders of when words just wouldn't get the job done. It also helped that I was able to get all this pent-up aggression out, and all the better that it was done while whaling on the kind of men who'd taken everything from me.

The kind of men who'd taken *her* from me.

It was early—not even ten o'clock—and I thought briefly about going out for a bit. Hitting the bar down the street, maybe get hooked up with some company for the night and push away the memories that always came knocking when I was working a job. But before I could make a decision on whether I wanted to head straight home or go somewhere else for a while, my phone buzzed in my pocket. I pulled it out, seeing Gage's name on the screen.

Pressing Accept, I kept walking toward my apartment building as I answered. "Hey, man. What's going on?"

"Ry."

The tone of his voice stopped me dead in my tracks, halting me in the middle of the cracked sidewalk. It was the same tone he'd used for years while running jobs with the crew. The same tone he'd used when he needed people to listen. It was the tone that said shit was about to get real. "What is it? Is it Madison?"

"No. No, we're fine. But I need you to listen to me, very carefully, okay? Listen to me and do exactly what I tell you to."

I blew out a breath, my shoulders relaxing slightly. "Yeah, yeah, I know the drill. Just tell me what's going on."

"You need to go see Aaron."

My brow furrowed. It wasn't unusual for me to see Aaron, to get information I'd need for a job, so it didn't seem that odd. Didn't seem worthy of the urgent tone of voice he was using. At least not until he said, "Do you remember the place?"

He was referring to the location we'd set forever ago, one we would use only if the situation called for complete secrecy. We'd never written it down, had never spoken of it again after we'd settled on it—we'd never needed to. And because of that, I knew this wasn't a simple job.

I lifted my eyes, raking the street for anything out of place, anything out of the ordinary, because with those simple words from Gage, my tension was cranked up to a thousand.

Some serious shit was about to go down. Or was already happening—I didn't know which.

Clearing my throat, I said, "Yeah."

"Good. Aaron's there waiting for you with a bag. Everything you'll need is in it."

"Okay, but—"

"I need you to go there immediately. Don't fuck around wasting time."

"Gage—"

"Immediately, Ry. Reset your phone, clear it out, and don't use it again." Then the line went dead, and I was left wondering just what the hell was going on.

I met Aaron at the shady dive bar Gage and I had settled on back before I'd even really been a part of the crew. Back when he'd just been getting started in it. It felt like a lifetime ago. Even back then, he'd been prepared for the worst.

Glancing around, I took stock of everyone in the place,

ignoring the thinly veiled looks sent my way from some of the female patrons. After a quick pass, I finally noticed Aaron in the back corner, sipping a beer while he pretended to watch a couple tough-looking girls across the room. I knew, though, that he was doing exactly what I'd been doing—always calculating, always studying the surroundings.

I walked over to him, pulled out a chair, and took a seat. "Hey."

"Hey, Kid."

I rolled my eyes at the nickname that would, apparently, follow me to my fucking grave. "You know I'm twenty-three now, right? Not a fourteen-year-old trailing after my big brother . . ."

"Yeah, well, shit sticks with you." He shrugged as he cracked a small smile and took a pull from his beer, his eyes taking in everything in the place. He looked relaxed, leaning back in his chair, his body language giving off a laid-back vibe, but I knew better. He was on alert, ready for anything. Just like I was.

"Do you have what I need?" I asked. I knew better than to say much more than that. Knew better than to name Gage—even using his crew name of Ghost—as the person who'd sent me. Anyone could be listening. Anyone could be watching.

He tipped his head toward the empty chair between us, and in my peripheral vision I could make out the outline of a black backpack partially hidden under the table. He didn't say anything about the bag or the exchange, didn't need to. His eyes spoke volumes.

Aaron lifted his beer to his mouth again, tipping it all the way back and swallowing the rest of it before setting down the bottle on the gouged wood table. "Getting late. I better jet." He held me in place with his gaze, telling me without words that I needed to stay put for a while to avoid being seen leaving together. "See you later, Kid." He clapped a hand on my shoulder, then walked out the way I'd just come.

The next thirty minutes were the longest of my life. I ordered a beer, then sat and waited, rebuffing the couple girls who came by my table and tried to get me to take them home. I barely glanced at them. I couldn't think about anything but what the hell was going on. I watched the clueless people milling about, all the while my mind churning at a hundred miles per hour, conjuring up all the different reasons why Gage would've had to put a plan like this in place.

At the end of those thirty minutes, after I'd finished my beer, I grabbed the backpack and slung it over my shoulder, casually walking out the front door and into the night.

When I got to my place, I flipped the dead bolt behind me, then made a quick sweep through my apartment, checking to ensure I was alone. After pulling all the blinds, I sat down at the table, black backpack in front of me. With steady hands, I unzipped the bag, methodically pulling out all the contents. Inside was a small laptop, a prepaid cell phone, and a pouch with a wad of cash I didn't bother counting, but by the size of it I guessed there was several thousand dollars there.

Before I could dig for a note or open the computer to search for some information, the phone rang, piercing the silence of the room. I snatched it up, seeing that the number was blocked—not a surprise—but I answered immediately.

"Yeah."

"Boot up the computer." It was Gage's voice, hard as steel, and I did as he said without hesitation.

It didn't take long before it came to life, a login screen popping up and prompting me for information. "Password?"

Gage's voice echoed in my ear, and I typed in the random letters, numbers, and symbols he gave me, then waited until the desktop was displayed. The background was empty, save for one lone folder, labeled simply *E*.

"Open it," he said.

I did as he instructed, double clicking on the icon and inputting the new password he recited when the computer asked for one. Once the password was confirmed, a dozen other files popped up, each labeled as cryptically as the folder had been.

"I'm in. Which file?"

"Open the one labeled *STN*."

Once again inputting the password he gave me when prompted, I waited and watched as what looked like a newspaper article came up on the screen. I read the headline—"Kirkland & Caine Throw Another Successful Fund-Raiser for the Children's Hospital"—and rubbed my fingers against my forehead.

"What am I supposed to be looking at here? All I see is an article about a fund-raiser."

"Scroll down to the pictures."

There were only three shots in the article—the first and largest a photo of the entire event, round tables filled with hundreds of rich people all decked out in tuxedos and fancy dresses, their attention focused on a stage where a man spoke behind a podium. The next was a shot of two men, both in their late sixties, if I had to guess, smiling as they chatted with a group of people. I darted my eyes to the caption below it: "Senator Caine, former senior partner at Kirkland & Caine, makes an appearance at the annual fund-raiser."

"Gage, man, what am I supposed to be—"

And then I got to the third picture. In it, dozens of people milled about in the background, though the picture focused on just two people. The caption to this image read: "Eric Caine, son of Senator Martin Caine, with his fiancée, Genevieve Meyer."

The man in the photo was probably in his early thirties, his head bent toward the woman on his arm. My eyes roved over the color picture, noticing how much younger she was than him, maybe a decade or more. In a long, formal dress, she stood at his side, her hand in the crook of his arm. Her most distinguishing feature was her hair—a bright fiery red that fell in waves nearly to her waist.

But her hair wasn't all I was looking at.

After five years, I'd gotten used to glimpses. Seeing things in people I wouldn't normally. Catching a peek of someone somewhere who reminded me of a girl I'd lost a long time ago. And I would've chalked this up to a coincidence, too, because of that history and the way coming from jobs always brought her memories to the forefront of my mind. Would've chalked it up to a coincidence the way the shape of this woman's lips were identical to that of someone else . . . how her nose sloped in the same way, how her eyes were the same shade. And while those were all pieces of a puzzle, they didn't add up. Because the girl I'd once known had had short hair, and it'd been every color of the rainbow when I'd known her—every color but red.

I would've looked away, figuring it was yet another false sighting in a string of too many to count. I would've looked away if it wasn't for the small beauty mark on her left cheek, the one that I knew would disappear into the dimple that only came out when she truly smiled.

The one I hadn't seen in five years. Not since the day she'd disappeared.

Not since the day she'd died.

Chapter Three

I gripped the phone so hard I was lucky it didn't break.

Gage's voice was low and controlled when he finally spoke. "You still there?"

I didn't know how long I'd sat there without saying anything, just staring, disbelieving, at the photo. At Gage's question, I tried to speak but had to clear my throat before I could force out any words. When I finally did, what came out was nothing more than a croak, but he took it as confirmation.

"I need you to listen to me, Ry, very carefully. She's in trouble. They've found her. Someone from the Minneapolis crew must've seen the article, and word got back to Max. Aaron confirmed a few hours ago that Max is sending people for her. We don't know who, and Aaron couldn't give me an exact time, but it's going to be soon. I'd bet my balls Max won't sit on this more than a few hours."

And even though I couldn't stop staring at the picture of her, at the face that resembled the girl I'd once known, I still couldn't believe it. It didn't make any sense.

I'd visited her goddamn grave.

Because of that, the denial came effortlessly. "I don't know who you're talking about."

Almost as if he'd expected that response, Gage answered without hesitation, without exasperation. "Yes, you do."

"No. I don't. It says right here her name is Genevieve Meyer, and I don't know anyone with that na—"

"Ry. You know who it is. You *know*."

I shook my head, though he couldn't see it. I couldn't reconcile what he was telling me, what I was seeing in that photograph, with the past five years. I didn't know which was real, which was a lie.

In the silence, Gage spoke again, "I'm sorry it had to happen this way. I wish I could've told you differently, but I need you to focus. It's important. Someone could already be on the way to her. She's in trouble." He sighed and cursed below his breath. Then he said the words I never thought I'd hear again: "Evie needs your help."

EVIE

It was late when I finally got home, the house empty and hollow, Eric having left for London several days prior. I both loved and loathed when I had the house to myself. It was the only time I ever truly got to let my guard down. It was the only time I was able to truly be myself.

Except I hardly remembered who that was anymore.

Hell, I didn't know if I even *wanted* to know who that was.

Because the girl I'd left behind so many years ago was a complete fuckup with more problems than a mental institution and more baggage than an airport. And even though I didn't want to, even though I fought the flashbacks with everything I had, my mind still betrayed me sometimes. It still transported me back to my childhood home—a small two-bedroom house in a shadier part of Chicago. It'd been all we could afford, though, especially after my father had been laid off shortly after I'd started high school. And even then, it had been fine.

Until it wasn't.

Until suddenly the walls of that house felt more like a prison than a home. Until those very walls held secrets—secrets buried under years of silence and pain and avoidance. Secrets I still kept to this day.

Secrets I'd keep until my last breath.

My heart sped at the remembrance of that time. When I'd been fifteen, fumbling my way through my teenage years and totally unaware of the hell my life was about to become.

Forcing myself out of my memories, I hung my keys by the back door and walked farther into the house, shedding my coat and hanging it over a chair in the dining room. Whenever I was assaulted with flashbacks, I always had a hard time sleeping. I didn't know if it was self-preservation, keeping myself from the nightmares that plagued my sleep, or if it was simply fear of the possibility that I might be transported there against my will.

After taking a long bath and indulging in a couple glasses of wine, I settled in on the couch in the family room to watch some comfort movies—old-school cult classics, the ones that always made me laugh no matter what—knowing I wouldn't be able to sleep for a while, anyway.

When I was partway through my third movie, my cell phone rang. I glanced at the time, seeing it was after one in the morning. Eric's face lit up the screen, and I answered. "What if you'd woken me up?"

I could hear the smile in his voice when he spoke. "That'd be some supersonic hearing you had, then, since you always put your phone on Silent when you go to sleep."

The thought that he knew something as trivial as that, but not something as monumental as the fact that my parents were still alive and well in Chicago, not buried in a cemetery in Miami, filled me with the heavy cloud of guilt that was always pressed down on my shoulders.

"I'm just watching some movies. How's London?"

"Busy. I'm running all over place, and this office is a goddamn mess. There's a lot to get in order before it's suitable for clients. *Too much* to get in order." He cleared his throat, and I knew enough about him to know he needed to tell me something he thought would disappoint me.

"What is it?"

Blowing out a breath, he said, "Because of that, I might need to extend my trip."

I figured that was coming, because all the business trips he'd taken since we'd gotten engaged had run longer than anticipated. "That's okay."

"I'm talking about another week, maybe two."

"That's okay," I repeated. "Take the time you need. I'll be fine."

"Maybe they'll keep you busy at work," he said.

I thought about the office job I went to every day, the job I had absolutely no interest in, and knew that even if they did, it wouldn't engage my mind. Despite my degree in journalism, I'd never put it to use, instead getting a job at an office, filing papers and inputting data into a computer. And I dutifully went to it Monday through Friday, put on my mask, and got the job done that I needed to.

Always pretending.

Before I could answer, muffled sound crept over the line from Eric's end. There was a mumbled voice, a murmur of confirmation from Eric, then he said, "Sorry, Gen, I gotta run. I'm not sure what my hours here are going to be like, so I'll try to call when I can."

"That's okay," I said for the third time. "I'll talk to you later."

The line went dead, and I tossed my phone on the cushion

next to me as I stared blankly at the comedy still playing on the TV. My favorite part of watching movies, of reading books, was getting lost in a story that wasn't mine. A feel-good story that inevitably had a happy ending. It was the only way I was going to live one, vicariously through others.

Because despite outward appearances, a happy ending wasn't in my cards.

I woke to a noise, my eyes popping open as I lay on the couch, having fallen asleep sometime during my fourth movie. Another residual effect from my teenage years—the ability to sleep light as a feather, the softest sound enough to wake me. Without moving an inch, I quickly took in my surroundings. The TV was frozen on the menu screen, the movie having long since stopped, not a sound coming from anywhere. I lay as still as I could and listened for any movement. What I'd heard was probably nothing more than a tree branch scraping a window or the house settling, but I couldn't write it off immediately.

After minutes of listening for any further noise and finally confident that it'd just been something trivial, I sat up and reached for the remote to turn off the TV, then grabbed my cell phone from the cushion next to me and stood. I checked the screen, seeing it was close to five a.m., and breathed a sigh of relief that it was Saturday, and I had nowhere to be. The hallway light upstairs lit a muted path as my feet slapped against the hardwood, heading in the direction of my room and the bed I hoped would allow me peaceful dreams.

I was three steps from the stairs when a creak sounded from the floor at the same time a hand reached out from the shadows and connected with my arm.

Without thinking, without taking a moment to second-guess myself, I snapped into action, my foot going back and connecting with a solid mass of muscle at the same time I spun around, my other arm coming down hard on his and causing his grip on my arm to loosen. I used his surprise to my advantage, not staying to fight but instead twisting from his grasp and running toward the kitchen. Toward my keys and the door that would lead me to freedom.

I'd thought about this day countless times over the past five years. How it would happen. *When* it would happen. If Eric would be home when it did. Because I knew it was inevitable. I knew I couldn't run forever, that at some point, someone would find me. I just didn't know which bad guy I'd left behind would be the one breathing down my neck.

But in all the times I'd thought about it, in all the times I'd played this scenario out in my head, I'd always gotten away. I'd always managed to get to the door in time, managed to grab my keys and get into my car before the intruder could reach me.

Never once did I end up forced face-first against a wall, the cold drywall biting into my cheek as someone pressed along my back, my arms bound tightly to my sides as his wrapped around me, the solid weight of him holding me in place.

Even then, I didn't stop struggling. Even then, when all the odds were stacked against me, I couldn't blow out the fire burning inside of me, and I fought. Against the weight pressing into my back, against the restraints holding my arms down, I struggled to get free—always struggling to get free—but I was pinned. Trapped. With no way out.

Just like so many times before.

My breaths started coming in quick, sharp gasps, buried childhood memories creeping along my spine as I was transported back to a place I didn't want to go. A place I never wanted to go, but one my cruel mind took me to without permission.

Drawn curtains and scratchy sheets and darkness and silence. Always silence, except for the muffled sobs I couldn't seem to help.

"Stop fighting." The male voice was low and harsh, frustrated.

His breath brushed my ear, and I froze, my flashback evaporating in the blink of an eye. I froze because though I hadn't heard it in years, I knew that voice. I recognized it as sure as I'd recognize my own face. Because it was a voice I'd heard in my dreams too many times to count. When my dreams were dreams and not the nightmares that so frequently plagued me, it was his face I saw. His voice I heard. His body I felt.

It was him. It was always him.

The one person who could make me feel better, the solace to my pain. My sanctuary when I'd needed escape. And I'd needed escape more often than not. More often than I'd ever let on. Because admitting that I'd needed an escape would mean admitting the truth, and I hadn't ever been ready to do that.

I still wasn't ready to do that.

"Stop fighting," he repeated, though I'd gone still at his first words. "It's me."

My breathing was harsh, Riley's matching mine as his chest rose and fell against my back, his breaths puffing against the side of my face. And despite the situation, despite the terror that still gripped my throat, I became aware of every inch of him pressed against me.

Judging by the bulk of him along my back, he'd grown a couple inches since I'd last seen him and had filled out, no longer the somewhat scrawny kid I'd known. I always wondered if he'd changed much over the years, but I'd never allowed myself to look. I'd never allowed myself to ask Ghost or Aaron about him, thinking it was better for everyone—me especially—to have a clean break. To forget about him as best I could.

But it was painfully obvious now, as that low hum of awareness I'd always felt around him buzzed through my veins, that I hadn't forgotten an inch of his body. Hadn't forgotten the sound of his voice.

Hadn't forgotten how safe it felt to be held in his arms.

Chapter Four

As quickly as the thought had come to me, it fled, replaced by a wave of anger, my helplessness and fear transforming into aggression in the blink of an eye.

"Get off me," I said, enunciating each word and pushing as much force into my voice as I could.

"Are you going to be a good girl and not fight?"

His tone, so carefree and steady, almost patronizing, only pissed me off more. "I said," I spat, twisting my head around until our noses were only an inch apart, *"get off me."*

He stared at me, his eyes flitting between mine in the muted light spilling down from upstairs. Then slowly, oh so slowly, he started relaxing his grip on me until, finally, he stepped back, the weight and heat of his body stolen from mine. I closed my eyes, resting my face against the wall, and breathed a sigh of relief as I tried to get my bearings.

When I once again had the mask in place, I pushed off from the wall and turned to face him. And even though I'd taken the time I'd needed to get myself in character, it hadn't helped. I might as well have done nothing at all as the shock of seeing him once again after so long with only my memories to keep me company hit me full force, a roundhouse kick to the chest.

I'd been right—he had filled out since eighteen. While still not as bulky as Ghost, Riley had grown, his once lanky body transforming to something lean and muscular. His hair was longer than it'd been when I'd known him, no longer the buzz cut he'd once favored. The sides and back were trimmed close now, but the top was grown out a bit more and shaggy. His eyes, even in the dim light, were still just as piercing as they'd always been, the crystal-clear blue of the ocean reflecting back at me. His jaw was shadowed with a day or two's worth of stubble—something he'd never done back when he was a kid. It made him look older, harder, *harsher*—another thing he'd never been in all the time I'd known him. Though he'd tried, though he'd put on a front because he looked up to his brother and wanted to be like him—something I knew he'd never admit to—he hadn't ever really fit in with the crew. He was too laid back, too easygoing, too happy to truly fit in with a group of people who broke the law for a living.

And yet here he was.

How much had these past five years changed him?

Forcing myself to snap out of my musings on the kind of guy Riley was now—because it shouldn't matter; it *didn't* matter—I asked, "Why are you here?"

He was quiet for a moment, and if he was shocked to see me, he didn't let on. Had he known I was here this whole time? I wondered if, despite my attempts to keep myself hidden from him, he'd found me anyway somewhere along the line. The thought that he'd known where I was but hadn't made any effort to see me shouldn't sting the way it did.

His face was a mask, hardly different from the one I put in place every day. Finally, he said, "Ghost sent me."

I swallowed against the disappointment I felt, pushing it down, down, down. Burying it deep where it belonged. There wasn't room here, in the life I lived now, for those kinds of emotions. Especially not when they were for Riley. "Why?"

He stared at me for another moment, then blew out his breath and shook his head, a hollow laugh leaving his lips as he looked toward the floor. "Apparently my ex-girlfriend, who I thought was dead, is alive and well, living in a fucking mansion in Minneapolis." He looked up at me, his eyes locked on mine. "Engaged to a rising attorney."

He didn't let me answer, didn't even give me time to contemplate the look in his eyes, before he plowed on, "A picture-perfect life to anyone looking in. Not for long, though. You've got a bull's-eye on your back, and people are coming to collect. Soon."

RILEY

The trip here had been brutal, both because I'd been awake for nearly twenty-four hours, thanks to the job I'd just come off of when I'd gotten Gage's call, and because my mind wouldn't stop spinning. Like Gage had told me to, I'd dropped everything and moved as quickly as I could. I'd thrown a couple things in a bag, jumped on my bike, and gotten the hell out of the city. Minneapolis was a long enough trek from the South Side of Chicago—one that was, thankfully, made easier by the middle-of-the-night road trip and the fact that I didn't have a problem breaking every speed limit, but I was still edgy. Still worried I wouldn't make it to Evie before someone else did.

And now that I was here, looking at her in the flesh for the first time in so long, I didn't know what the fuck I was feeling. Over the course of the past five years, I'd run the gamut of emotions when dealing with grief, eventually ending with acceptance.

Yet here she was, standing in front of me, alive and well. A part of me wanted to simply turn around and leave, forget all of this. But then another part of me—a part that was too fucking big for my liking—wanted to grab her and shake her, brush her hair back from her face and look into her eyes, feel her under my hands and make sure she was real.

"I'm not—" she started, shaking her head and running a hand through her hair.

I still couldn't get over it—how different it was from the short, blunt styles she'd always preferred. Before, she'd dyed her hair a different color every week and had dressed in all black. Combat boots and baggy black jeans all topped off with a fuck-everything attitude. Now, she stood in front of me, her long, vibrant red hair hanging in loose curls all the way down her back, an oversized ivory sweater falling off one shoulder, not even a bra strap to interrupt the creamy, pale skin dotted with the freckles I'd once had memorized. My fingers itched to see if she was as soft as I remembered.

She looked up at me, her eyes pinning me in place just like they used to. With her jaw set and her shoulders straightened, her arms crossed right under the tits I was sure were bare beneath that sweater, she said, "I'm not going anywhere, if that's what you're suggesting."

I clenched my teeth, at both my reaction to seeing her in the flesh and her defiance. I'd already anticipated her reluctance. As much as Evie had changed—and I had no doubt she'd changed as much as I had these past five years—she wouldn't have been able to drop this part of herself completely. The part that always pushed back, the part that always had to be in control—the part that had craved it.

While I'd definitely anticipated that aspect of her, what I hadn't anticipated was the pull I still felt toward her. Shoving that aside, forcing it down where it belonged, I said, "You'd rather stay here like a sitting duck? Waiting for whoever Max sent? Whoever is coming? Because"—I stepped closer to her, lowering my voice—"don't doubt this, Evie. *They're coming.*"

She rolled her shoulders back, jutted out her chin. Defiance pouring from every inch of her. "I can take care of myself."

Raising an eyebrow, I said, "Can you, now? Take care of your-self like you did when I had you pressed up against the wall? If I was someone who wanted you dead, make no mistake, you would be right now."

Her eyes hardened even further, into the look I used to be wary of. The one that used to tell me I needed to tread care-fully. That was the great thing about no longer being together, though. I didn't have to tread for shit. "If you think Max will let you go after a talk, you're wrong. You have something he wants. Whether that's literal or figurative, I don't know. But either way, he's not going to stop with just a slap on the wrist."

With her arms still crossed, she stared at me, none of her soft-ening at my threat. Willing to do anything to get her to concede, I tried a different tactic, even though the words burned my throat as they came out. "What about your fiancé? What about keeping him safe? Whoever is coming isn't going to stop with just you, if they find him here."

It was the first time I saw any kind of emotion other than anger cross her face, and I clenched my fists at the wave of unease that washed over me. I hadn't felt jealousy in a long, long time, and I sure as hell wasn't ready to feel it now. Not for her. Not for the girl who, up until half a dozen hours ago, had been out of my life—*dead* to me—for the past five years. She wasn't mine anymore, and I had no right feeling anything other than indiffer-ence now.

"He's out of the country until the end of the month, proba-bly." She shook her head and glanced out toward the window across the room. As she did so, the softest whisper of movement from somewhere else in the house caught my attention. "I can—"

So fast she didn't see it coming, I had my hand over her

mouth, her body clutched tightly against me, chest to chest as I pressed her back into the wall around the corner. We hadn't turned on any lights, and it was still dark outside, providing the cloak of coverage we needed. Lowering my mouth so my lips brushed against her ear, I breathed, "We've got company."

She went still as stone in my arms, and I carefully removed my hand from over her mouth, clutching her harder against me and telling her without words to stay still. We stood there, waiting, watching, for what felt like an hour, when in actuality it was mere seconds.

Whoever had broken in was good, because as hard as I tried to hear something, anything, there were no noises. I peered over my shoulder and strained my eyes, looking for shapes in the shadows, and finally, just when I started to wonder if I'd mistakenly heard something, a dark form loomed on the wall across from us. Evie tensed even further in my arms. I gripped her hips and pushed her back against the wall, pressing her into it, hoping she got my meaning and stayed put while I dealt with the problem.

I didn't know who was here, if it was just one guy or a handful. And if it was the latter, I didn't know if I'd be able to take them all down while keeping Evie safe. Making sure she got out was my number-one goal. That was why Gage had sent me here, because he'd known that even after so long, after years of her absence, after accepting her death, I would still do anything for her.

Before I could focus anymore on the what-ifs, the shadow disappeared and a dark shape loomed in front of me.

I didn't even pause before I took the first swing.

Chapter Five

EVIE

One minute, Riley was pressing me into the wall, his hands telling me without words to stay right where I was, and the next I heard the sickening sound of flesh against bone, followed immediately by a grunt. I held my breath, praying the groans I was hearing weren't coming from Riley. While I tried in vain to see what was going on, I listened to the sounds of the fight, my back flattened against the wall. It was too dark, though, the shadows playing tricks on my eyes, and I couldn't tell what was happening, who was getting hits in . . . who was the one taking those hits.

I didn't know how long it'd gone on for, me standing against the wall, watching and listening and waiting, before I realized this wasn't me—the girl who stayed out of the way while a guy fought her battles for her. That was Genevieve, the girl who'd never been in fights, who'd never learned to defend herself.

The girl who'd never had to.

As much as I didn't want to distract Riley from what he was doing, I couldn't stay still any longer. I had the ability to help, and I was going to. This was *my* fight, and I sure as hell wasn't going to let someone else fight it for me.

As quietly as I could, I slipped away and toward the front entry where there was a heavy plaster figurine. I'd always hated it, this woman wrapped in flowers, her pale blond hair flowing down her back, a serene smile on her face.

With the statue gripped in my hand, I crept over to where Riley and the other man were in a full-out brawl now. One person definitely had the upper hand, getting in most—if not all—of the hits. I only hoped it was Riley. Squinting my eyes, I tried to make sense of the bodies in front of me. One was taller than the other by several inches, bigger, too. And while Riley wasn't massive, he also wasn't scrawny, not like the dark form I saw attempting to block the near-constant incoming strikes.

Confident the smaller shape was the intruder, I moved around to the other side, being sure to stay in the shadows so I didn't distract Riley from what he was doing. When I got into place, the alcove off the dining room my cover, I gripped the statue in my hands and waited.

Riley and the other man stumbled in front of the staircase and into the light spilling down from upstairs. Riley's face was more pronounced in the shadows, the hard, sharp edge of his jaw and the hollows under his cheeks making him look intimidating . . . and so different from the boy I once knew. I was so relieved to see that he was free of any cuts and bruises that I forgot what I was doing for a moment, not moving as swiftly as I should've.

Not wanting to waste any more time, I stepped out of the shadows, coming up behind the intruder. My movement alerted Riley and he looked up at me, shifting his attention from the fight in front of him to me. The look in his eyes was something I'd seen from him more times than I could count.

Pure, undiluted fear. For me.

Years ago, back when we'd been together, we'd run jobs for

the crew, the two of us a team, though no one there had ever known of our relationship besides Ghost. My job hadn't been physical—I had always been the knowledge collector, used to ferret out information. And I'd been good, but Riley had always come with, just in case. He'd been smaller then, but he'd always known how to fight, and every time he'd had to step up and fight off someone, I'd be right there next to him, helping in any way I could. And every time, there had always been a moment where Riley would look at me, his expression full of worry and uncertainty . . . full of terror for my safety.

I'd loved that look, because it'd meant someone had cared for me. Truly cared for me, for more than what I could give them—whether that was my body or my mind.

But just like before, I didn't like staying in the shadows. I didn't like other people fighting for me. Riley and I had always worked best as a team, and I was sure that would still ring true now.

I raised the statue over my head, ready to bring it down on this guy, when he used Riley's distraction to his advantage. He got a punch in, and Riley staggered back, his head snapping to the side at the same time I swung.

RILEY

A thud sounded, followed by a grunt, and then I twisted back around and watched as the guy's body slumped to the floor. Evie was standing over him, some object clutched in her hand. When she looked up at me, the dim light from upstairs casting shadows over her face, her eyes were brimming with determination.

And that pissed me off.

"Evie, what the *fuck*?" I snapped, walking over and pushing at the guy on the ground with my boot. He flopped over, his body lifeless, and I reached down to feel for a pulse.

"He's just unconscious," she said with certainty. Then with

irritation lacing her voice, she continued, "I fended him off. You should be thanking me, not yelling at me."

I stood from where I was squatting and glared at her. "You could've killed him. You've got to think, Evie. What the hell would we do if you had a dead body in your house? Jesus Christ." I clasped my hands together behind my head and spun in a circle.

"Well, I'm not apologizing for it." Her voice was hard, and if I'd been looking at her, I knew she'd be staring back at me with eyes just as hard. "Jesus, Riley, you act like I've never had your back in a fight before."

Walking up to her, I didn't stop until we were mere inches apart, her head tipped back to look at me. "A lot has changed in the past five years, me included. Starting now, we do things my way or not at all."

"Not at all it is, then."

"Are you fucking kidding me?" I pointed to the guy sprawled out on her floor. "Not at all isn't an option for you anymore, baby. Sorry. Now here's what's going to happen." I gripped her shoulders, turned her around, and pushed her toward the steps. "Go get whatever necessities you need. And I mean *basic* necessities. You've got five minutes and then we're leaving."

She breathed out a laugh. "You're kidding, right? This Neanderthal bullshit didn't work back then, and it's sure as hell not going to work now."

"Oh, it's going to work, because I'm not leaving here without you. So you can either get your shit and come with me willingly, or I can toss you over my shoulder and haul you out of here. Your choice."

Her mouth dropped open before her eyes narrowed. "You cannot haul me out of here, that's—"

"Exactly what I'll do if you don't get your ass in gear." I went over and flipped on a light, then walked back to see who the guy was. Squatting next to the unconscious form, I turned his head toward me so I could get a good look at his face.

"Shit," I muttered.

It was Frankie, a greasy, creepy son of a bitch who used to work with the crew. He'd made himself scarce since an incident involving Gage and his girlfriend, Madison. Frankie had been aggressive toward her and made some brutally crude comment about Madison. If Gage ever saw him again, I wasn't sure I'd be able to stop him from bringing a world of hurt down on this asshole. A world of hurt that would make getting knocked unconscious by a statue seem like child's play.

"See what you're dealing with? It's not going to stop with him, Evie, more are—" I glanced up at her, and her face had gone white, her eyes wide as she stared at the unconscious form of Frankie on the floor. "Evie?"

She didn't move at the sound of my voice, and I stood from my crouched position, then walked over to her, my hand settling on the bare skin where her shoulder met her neck. She flinched away from me.

"Hey," I said, my voice softer than it had been, my thumb brushing back and forth against her collarbone. "It's just me. It's okay. He's out cold."

Finally, her eyes met mine before they flitted down again to Frankie. She nodded then, swallowing and straightening her shoulders. "I'll go get my stuff."

She ascended the steps as I stood in shock at the complete one-eighty she'd done. I didn't know what had finally gotten through to her—if the thought of more guys like Frankie coming had been the thing to finally snap her out of her defiance or what—but I wasn't complaining.

While Evie was upstairs, I grabbed my phone and dialed Gage.

"What's the status?" he answered without pleasantries.

"We've got a problem."

There was a pause, then, "You didn't get to her?"

"No, I did. But we have company. He slipped in about twenty minutes after I got here."

"Who?"

I took a breath and blew it out slowly. "Frankie."

Gage growled a string of curses. "I never should've let that fucker go."

"You know if it hadn't been him, Max would've sent someone else."

"Why the hell is he back working this now? You said he was scarce after what went down with Madison in the cabin, right?"

"Yeah, I haven't seen him for months. I was wondering what would bring him back, too. Why this?"

"We'll have to look into it when you're both to safety. For now, what do you need there?"

"He's unconscious, so I'm going to need a pickup and a drop. I don't want to use one of Evie's cars to do it, and I just have my bike."

"I can have someone to the house within half an hour. Just get the fuck out of there. Who knows if others are on their way."

I glanced up as Evie came down the stairs, a small bag slung over her shoulder. She darted her eyes down to Frankie, then she lifted her gaze, her posture stiff as she walked straight toward me. Mask firmly back in place. Into the phone, I said, "We're leaving now. Should be to you in a couple hours."

"Good. See you then."

I pocketed my phone, then looked at her. "Get what you need?"

She gave a single decisive nod. "Ready."

Tilting my head toward the back door, I said, "Go wait for me. I'll be there in a second."

Narrowing her eyes, she studied me, the irritation pouring

off her in waves. I was waiting for her to spew a string of curses my way, but instead she finally relented and walked toward the kitchen. I glanced around, finding an old envelope on the desk off to the side and grabbed it, ripping off a section of it. Uncapping a pen with my teeth, I quickly scribbled a note on the piece of paper, then stuffed it into Frankie's pocket.

Telling them to try harder next time was akin to waving a red flag in front of a bull, but I was pissed, high on an adrenaline rush, and I wanted to give them the finger in whatever way I could. Sending one of Max's guys back to him, unconscious, with a taunting note wasn't quite as physical as I'd have liked my message to be, but it would have to suffice.

I walked over to Evie, putting my hand on the small of her back and leading her out the side door. She glanced back over her shoulder at Frankie. "You're leaving him in there?"

Shaking my head, I said, "I've called for cleanup. He'll be gone within the hour."

I felt her body relax under my fingers still pressed against her back. That simple movement caused my mind to go all kinds of places it had absolutely no fucking business going, a film strip of memories flipping through my head from when Evie and I had been together. The first time I saw her, her attitude drawing me in as much as her looks had. Then the first job we ran together, when we'd both been so wound up after, we'd had our first kiss— our first way more than kiss—in a seedy alley, pressed against a harsh brick wall. I could still hear the breathy sounds she made when she was turned on, could still feel the clench of her fingers gripping my arm, urging me for more.

I could still remember the taste of her lips.

Clenching my jaw, I pushed the memories away and guided her down the driveway and around the corner to where I'd parked my bike.

Once we were close to it, she halted in her tracks, her eyes

narrowing as she looked at it, then back at me. "I'm not sure how
you thought you were going to drag me out of here unwillingly
with this thing." She inclined her head toward the motorcycle.

I pulled the small bag from her shoulder and stuck it in the
luggage compartment before grabbing her helmet and holding it
out to her. "Yeah, I might've been bluffing."

She stared at my outstretched hand, at the helmet I wasn't
sure she remembered—the one that used to be hers—not moving an inch. Her arms were crossed against her chest, her foot
tapping a frustrated rhythm on the sidewalk.

"Time's a wastin', baby." And then I gave her the smile that
used to get me out of anything with her—the kind of smile that I'd
used more times than I could count when I'd gotten hotheaded
and went off on someone because he'd looked at her wrong. She
hadn't had a whole lot of patience for that then, but one smile
from me, and she'd melted.

She narrowed her eyes and clenched her jaw before snatching
the helmet out of my grasp and putting it on. Quickly, she tied
her hair back in a ponytail, producing a hair tie from whatever
magical place girls kept them, then climbed on behind me. I tried
not to think about what it felt like having her so close again, because I sure as shit didn't want to get lost in the memories of what
her body had felt like when a whole lot less clothes were involved.
Even with my reluctance, I couldn't help remembering what it
used to feel like when she'd ride with me.

My first bike had been older, junkier—a pile of shit a buddy
of mine had pulled out of the junkyard and miraculously gotten
running—but it'd been mine, and Evie and I had ridden it around
all over the city. This one was newer, sleeker, the product of working job after job for the past five years, but having her on the back
felt exactly the same as it always had. Except she wasn't as close as
she'd always been. Before, she'd climb on and wrap her arms
around me, her legs tight on the outside of mine and her chest

pressed to my back. Now she held herself away, gripping the handle behind her seat, and there was no fucking way we were driving three hours like that.

Starting up the bike, I revved the engine, then turned my head and said over my shoulder, "Better hold on tight. Gonna be a fast ride."

Chapter Six

The dark sky gave way to midnight blue, then it seemed like all at once it burst into a ball of fire, streaks of red and orange lighting up the sky as the asphalt disappeared under my tires. The weather, though warmer than usual for this time of year, was still biting as we flew down back roads to get to Gage's place. After my words of caution, Evie had pressed herself up against me as I'd told her to, wrapping her arms around my waist and clutching me tightly. And she hadn't moved since we'd left a couple hours ago.

But even with that distraction, I couldn't stop my mind from churning, going over and over and over the last several hours. And as I did, anger and resentment grew within me with each mile we passed, building until it was nearly all I could think about. There was anger and resentment toward Evie and the lies she told . . . at the fact that while I'd been mourning her, she'd been off living a life of privilege.

But more than that, more than the anger I felt toward Evie, was this overwhelming fury I felt toward my brother. A fury that was burning up my insides. I didn't have all the pieces to the puzzle yet, but from what I'd been able to fit together, it was clear he'd known about this—about Evie—for a while. The whole time? That, I wasn't sure, but regardless, he'd known. He'd known and he'd kept it from me, kept his mouth shut and gone about life as if nothing was unusual. As if the girl I used to love hadn't been alive the whole fucking time.

I'd never before felt betrayed by him, had never had a reason to. My entire life, he'd had my back. He'd been the one to look out for me when we were younger, when our mother was strung out on whatever drug she could get her hands on. He'd been the one who'd taken care of me after she'd died, the one who'd started in with the crew in the first place, just so we could afford a roof over our heads and food on the table.

Never in a million fucking years did I think I'd have a reason to doubt him.

And now I did. Now I knew he'd betrayed me in the biggest way.

I'd memorized the directions Gage had given me, and soon Evie and I pulled up in front of a small brick apartment building. It sat only a few blocks from the campus Madison attended, situated in a neighborhood that was neither upscale nor run-down. Planting my feet on the ground, I turned off the engine of the bike, pulled off my helmet, then twisted to face the building, only one question on my mind . . .

How long had he known?

I helped Evie get off the bike, then headed up the walkway and into the building toward the apartment. She didn't say a word as we stood in the hallway in front of the door marked 2C, as I stared at it for a moment before I finally knocked. Before my knuckles could connect with the wood a second time, the door pulled open, Gage on the other side. I hadn't seen him in months, not since he'd left to follow Madison here. He looked pretty much the same as he always had, except that he'd let his hair grow out a bit. But his stare was still hard and penetrating like it'd always been, his jaw set as he looked from me to Evie, then behind us, taking stock. Always taking stock of the surroundings.

And that was when it hit me. Of course he'd known the whole time. He wouldn't have had everything in place, everything ready for a retrieval like he had now if he hadn't planned for exactly that. He'd known. All along, while I'd been grieving, while I'd gotten fully entrenched in the crew *because* of Evie's death, he'd known.

His eyes locked with mine, and I saw everything I needed to in them.

Without thinking about it, without taking a second to consider what I was doing, I pulled my arm back and snapped it forward, my fist connecting with his jaw. Through the blood thrumming in my ears, I heard Evie gasp out my name.

Gage turned his head back to face me, his hand going up to rub his jaw as he stared at me. "You done?"

And that just pissed me off even more. Stepping over the threshold, I got right in his face, then shoved him hard. "Fuck no, I'm not done. I have five goddamn years of your lies to get re demption for."

"Ry, you don't—"

I didn't let him finish before I threw another punch, this time my fist connecting with his stomach. He doubled over, letting out a soft grunt, then stood up straight once he'd caught his breath. His eyes met mine once again, his intention clear in the way his arms hung loosely at his sides, his hands unclenched. He wasn't going to fight back? Fine. He didn't have to. I had enough fight in me for the both of us.

I went at him again, letting my fists do all the talking. Over my heavy breaths and Gage's grunts, I heard Evie in the background, trying to get me to stop, pleading with me, but I blocked it out as best as I could, focusing only on the anger and betrayal eating away at me. Anger and betrayal I felt at *both* of them, but Gage was the only one I could take it out on. The only way I could get this out of me.

I poured every bit of it into him, the years I'd gone thinking Evie was dead, all the paths I'd followed because of that one event—taking my place in the crew because I'd been so full of rage that I hadn't been able to think straight. I'd been so full of contempt at unanswered justice that I'd wanted to do anything I could to keep these assholes off the streets. The assholes like the one who'd killed Evie.

The crew had been told it'd been a confrontation gone bad. That Evie had gone with them on the boat—the one the crew used as a scare tactic to get shady bastards to talk under the threat of dropping them into Lake Michigan miles upon miles from shore—and everything had gone to shit. Some accountant who was skimming from the top, stealing from Max, had grabbed one of the guys' guns and shot Evie, multiple times. She'd fallen overboard. They'd never found her body.

Yet even without the body, I'd believed every bit I'd been fed, every morsel of the story because Gage had seemed to believe it, too. But above that, he'd had Evie's locket. The locket I'd given her, the one she never took off. He had it, broken chain and all.

"Ry," Gage said, ducking away from a swing. "Riley, Jesus Christ, chill the fuck out."

"Fuck you."

"I don't want to have to fight you, but I will."

"Then do it already!"

I took another swing, aiming for his kidney, but he dodged it, and then he started fighting back instead of just blocking my hits. His fist connected with my jaw, snapping my head back. His voice filled the space around us between the hits, telling me to stop, to calm down and listen. Both Evie and Madison were trying to break it up—I could hear them in the background, somewhere beyond the pulse thrumming through my ears—but I couldn't think past the red haze clouding my vision.

I came at him again, but before my fist could connect with his flesh, Evie stepped between us, her eyes hard, her arms outstretched, separating us.

I halted my advance on Gage immediately, not wanting to accidentally hurt her. "Evie, get the fuck out of the way," I said, wiping the back of my hand across my mouth. It came away wet and smeared with blood, but I still wasn't done. I didn't want to stop.

I *couldn't.*

"No, I'm not going to get the fuck out of the way. I don't take orders from you, remember?" She dropped her hand from in front of Gage and turned to me, shoving me hard in the chest. "You're pissed, I get that. But you're pissed at me, too. Quit using your brother as a punching bag when this is as much my fault as it is his."

I clenched my jaw and stared at her, then looked over her shoulder at Gage. His lip was busted, a bruise already forming on his cheekbone, and even with proof of the damage I'd done, he didn't look pissed at me. Not even then.

And yet I still had this rage, this *regret* thrumming through my veins, and I didn't know how to get a handle on it.

I shook off the hand she had resting on my forearm and spun around, stalking out of the apartment and through the halls to the front door.

I needed some space.

Chapter Seven

EVIE

I watched as Riley stormed out the door, closing my eyes as it slammed shut behind him. Taking a deep breath, I tried to piece together the bits of information I knew from having been in contact with Ghost sporadically over the years, as well as what Riley had told me when he'd shown up at my house. All of it added up to one conclusion.

I spun around and stared at Ghost, shaking my head in disbelief. "You never told him?"

He crossed his arms and fixed me with a heavy stare. It was strange looking into his eyes—near replicas of Riley's yet still so different. Ghost had always had a haunted look to his heavy gaze, one Riley's had never been filled with. Even now, even after thinking I'd been dead this whole time, his didn't carry the heaviness present in Ghost's.

"Did he ever show up at your door?" he asked. "Thought that pretty much would've already answered the question for you."

I blew out a breath, closing my eyes and pressing my fingers to my forehead. "Jesus, Ghost, no wonder he's pissed. You've lied to him for five years!"

He uncrossed his arms, one dropping to his side while he held the other in front of him, his finger jabbed in my direction. "*You've* lied to him for five years. *I've* protected him. Do you have any idea what Max would do if he knew what kind of history you two had? If he'd known Riley had any kind of interest at all in this whole thing? I did what I did to keep him safe. No thanks to you."

I furrowed my brow as I stared at him. "What the hell is that supposed to mean?"

His jaw worked back and forth as he clenched his teeth, anger radiating from the set of his shoulders. Finally, he said, "Riley was only ever in the crew because you dragged him down with you."

My eyes grew wide, my head pulling back in shock. "What? No, *you* were in the crew well before I was. Riley was there when I came in."

"He was there, but did you ever see him running any jobs before you pulled him along on your first one?"

I opened my mouth to respond, then snapped it shut, because he was right. It was true that Riley had always been around, but he'd never done any jobs. He'd only been there because Ghost had been there. And then I'd come in and dragged him along to every single job I had, pulling him under with me.

I swallowed, asking quieter, "And after he was told I was dead? Why didn't he go straight then? From the looks of it, he's in deeper now than he ever was when I'd been there."

Ghost took a deep breath, exhaling as a girl entered the room—the same one who'd come rushing in earlier while Riley and Ghost had been fighting. She was tall, her long brown hair swept back in a ponytail, a look of concern filling her eyes as she studied Ghost. Her arms were full of supplies—cotton balls, a bottle of hydrogen peroxide, some first-aid cream, and various other items. Ghost glanced at her, and without her even having to say a word, he followed her to the couch and sat down, relaxing patiently while she wiped a wet cloth over his cuts. I didn't know who she was, hadn't even gotten her name yet, but she obviously thought a lot of Ghost. And from the look he gave her as she cleaned him up, it was clear the feeling was mutual.

When she turned away to get a clean cloth, Ghost fixed his stare on me again and answered my earlier question. "He did it for retribution. He wanted justice for your death, and that was the only way he knew how to get it."

I carried the first-aid supplies with me as I went off looking for Riley, hoping he'd stayed close. I didn't think he'd go off half-cocked on his bike, but I didn't really know him at all anymore. I had no idea what kind of man he'd turned into over these past few years. Except it was clear, just based on his contact with Frankie at my house and the fight with Ghost, that he was a lot more hardened than the teenager I'd once known.

More hardened than the boy I'd once loved.

But then again, I'd lived a hundred lifetimes in the five years since I'd been gone, so if anyone could understand change, it was me.

My instincts had been right, and I came across him sitting on the front stoop of the apartment building, his back hunched as his forearms rested on his knees. Without saying anything, I sat down next to him and looked out at the early November morning, the wind blowing enough to send a waterfall of fire—orange and yellow and crimson leaves—raining from the trees. Riley didn't make any movement, didn't even look my way, just continued to stare straight ahead.

Clearing my throat, I racked my brain for something to say, finally settling on, "It looks like Ghost isn't exactly the same guy I used to know. He's been busy."

Riley snorted, shaking his head and finally glancing over at me. "I haven't even officially met his girlfriend yet. The first time she sees me, I'm whaling on Gage."

"*Gage?* That's new, too."

"Yeah. He doesn't like to be called Ghost anymore. Not since a few months ago. Not since Madison, actually."

Madison must've been the girl inside the apartment, fawning all over Ghost—*Gage*. The one who'd stared at him like he was her whole world, the looks passing between them making me so uncomfortable, I'd finally excused myself to the bathroom.

I shifted on the cold concrete step, tucking my hands between my thighs. "So he's out now?"

"Yep. Since March. He moved here over the summer. He's taking art classes now, if you can believe it."

I couldn't, actually. The Ghost I'd known would never make a move like that. "Well, I never saw that day coming, to be honest. I thought your brother would be a lifer."

"Yeah, me, too."

He got quiet again, and after several moments of silence, I grabbed the wet washcloth I'd brought out and scooted closer to him. "Turn this way. I'll get you cleaned up."

Glancing at me out of the corner of his eye, he didn't say anything. He didn't have to. His eyes spoke a hundred words between us, and I couldn't stop the memories from assaulting me—of all the times I'd done this for him after we'd come from a job together. He had a short fuse back then, determined to prove his worth, and that ended in more bloody lips and black eyes than I could even recall.

But every time, I'd been there.

We'd go back to the apartment he shared with Gage, and I'd clean him up, tenderly looking after him even though I didn't do anything tenderly in my life.

For years I'd tried to block those memories out. Anytime I was conscious, I refused to think of that time in my life, and that included Riley, believing it'd somehow be easier, this hollow feeling in my chest. But my subconscious made up for it a thousand times over in my dreams. Blocking him out there was a whole other battle. One I never won.

Riley always, *always* came to me in my dreams.

And now that those memories had worked their way into my mind, had crept in after I'd fought them for so long, I had to wonder . . . who'd cleaned him up since I'd been gone?

Tentatively, I reached up and pressed two fingers to his stubble-roughened chin, guiding his face toward mine. We were so close, I could feel the heat of his breath against my lips, and as much as I told myself not to react at the feel of him around me—his air in my lungs and the brush of his skin against mine—it didn't matter. That hum of awareness I'd always felt in his presence was real and alive and all-consuming.

To distract myself, I darted my eyes around, taking stock of all his injuries, falling into a series of remembered movements, ingrained deeply from having done it more times than I could count. I tried to focus only on the cuts and bruises forming, only on the parts of his face I needed to clean up, but he made it damn difficult.

He'd always been something to look at, cute in a boyish way, but since then, he'd changed from a boy into a man, his jaw sharper, the contours to his face more defined. His eyes were just as mesmerizing as they had been so long ago. Framed in dark, thick lashes, they were as clear as the water right offshore, breathtaking and bottomless. Through the scruff blanketing his jaw, there was a cut at the corner of his mouth, just below his full lower lip. Before I could get too lost in what those lips had once done to me, I grabbed the washcloth and brushed it over the cut. Riley didn't flinch, didn't even move, and I had to remind myself to get it together. Five years was a long time. Who knew what had happened with him over that time, if he was involved with anyone now. Besides that, I was engaged, for fuck's sake.

I was *engaged*.

My hand froze against Riley's cheek as thoughts of what the hell I was going to tell Eric bombarded me. He'd never known about this part of my life. And he never would, if I could help it. I just didn't know how I was going to get out of this—how I was going to get out of this with my life, and with the lives of those I cared about. Which, sadly enough, I could count on one hand and still have fingers left.

With Eric being in London till the end of the month, that would buy me some time. Though I knew it wouldn't buy me forever, and sooner or later, Max was going to come to collect the one thing I've made sure to carry with me at all times since that day I fled. The one tiny little piece of technology that, ironically, could be my ticket to freedom as much as it was my death sentence.

RILEY

With her hand frozen on my jaw, Evie stared at me, though she wasn't really looking at me. No, she was staring right through me. It was something she used to do all the time—get so lost in her thoughts, so focused, she'd block out everything around her.

I didn't mind, though.

While she was staring through me, I stared at her. Looking at her now, it was hard to believe I'd ever doubted that it had been her in that picture in the newspaper. Yeah, her hair made her look different, but her face was just the same. Her skin was still pale, the bridge of her small, straight nose dotted with freckles, even more spilling onto her cheeks, which were splotched with color, no doubt from the chill in the air. Gray eyes stared unseeing toward my chin, her full lips parted and so fucking taunting.

Those lips, the lips of a woman—seductive and made for sin—didn't belong with the rest of her face. She'd always looked so innocent, even with the rainbow array of hair colors she'd sported. That fresh-looking face was what had gotten her so far when she'd been working jobs for Max. She'd had this wide-eyed innocence to her that had allowed her to sucker more than one person. Now, though, with her long, fiery red hair, and a jaded, angry glint to her eyes, she hardly resembled that innocent teenager I'd known.

She blinked and, just like that, she snapped out of the trance she'd been in. She'd paused in her soft, brushing strokes with the washcloth against my skin when she'd zoned out, so she started up again, her eyes flicking up to mine once, then back down to her task.

Her voice was soft when she spoke again. "You remember when I always used to do this for you after one of our jobs? When you'd go off on someone for stepping even a bit out of line?" She glanced up at me, finding my eyes still locked on hers. Clearing her throat, she lowered her gaze again and said, "I always thought it was because you thought you had something to prove with me."

It had never bothered me before to talk about how far I'd come in the past five years. I'd filled out, finally hit a growth spurt at nineteen and bulked up from working out, and people tended not to mess with me anymore—not that they had then, either, but still. Back then when I'd been scrawnier than everyone else in the crew, smaller, I'd always thought I'd had something to prove. Especially with her. Though I'd never admit that to her in a million fucking years.

"A lot's changed in five years," I said. She lifted her eyes to mine, and I could see in her gaze, just as clear as I was sure she could see in mine, that the time away had changed her as well. "I've been cleaning up my own shit for a long time now."

She nodded and lowered her head, setting aside the washcloth and focusing on prepping a cotton ball with some hydrogen peroxide. As she dabbed it on the cut, she asked, "So you're in still? With the crew?"

She wouldn't meet my eyes for more than a fleeting second, instead focusing on my mouth and the cut there. I wanted her to look at me so I could get a read on what she was really asking.

Evie didn't do small talk. She dug for information—she always had and always would. I just couldn't tell if she was hoping my answer would be yes or no.

And I honestly didn't know how to answer. As of twenty-four hours ago, I'd had a purpose within the crew. Vengeance and justice for the girl I'd loved. In the past few hours, all my reasons had been blown to dust. And the man I worked for, the one for whom I'd executed more jobs than I could count, was after her.

Instead of going into all that, rehashing the questions I hadn't even begun to really delve into myself, I gave her the simplest answer, nodding stiffly when she finally glanced up at me. And if I hadn't been studying her so intensely, looking specifically for any kind of reaction, I might've missed the brief flash of disappointment that was there in her eyes.

She grabbed a tube of ointment and put some on her finger, then reached up, stopping just before touching my skin and glancing up at me. And then her eyes were focused again on my cut, and the fingers of one hand steadied my chin while her others were brushing against me in a way they hadn't in so long. It was too much and not enough, and I had to get out of here.

"Riley . . . I'm sorry. For what it's worth, I'm sorry. I'd like to tell you what—"

I turned away from her hand, letting it fall by my side. "Doesn't matter. You did what you had to do. I don't hold that against you." I grabbed everything she'd brought out and stood from the stoop. "Let's head in and talk to Gage, see what the plan is."

And I hoped to God he had a plan, because I had nothing.

I had no idea what lay in front of us, why the guys in the crew—in *my* crew—were after her, but if I knew Max, he wasn't going to stop just because I'd sent one of his guys back a little roughed up. If anything, that was only going to light a bigger fire under him.

Because of that, I knew with utmost certainty that our fight was just beginning.

Chapter Eight

After Evie and I had come in from outside, Madison had taken her to the bedroom to get set up for a bit so she could try and get some rest. I didn't know when she had last slept, but I was coming up on almost thirty hours, and I was dead on my feet.

I couldn't sleep yet, though—too much shit to deal with.

While Madison and Evie were in the other room, I sat down at the dining room table across from Gage. His forearms were resting on the battered wood, his head bowed toward the cup of coffee in front of him. He glanced up at me when I sat, and I got a good look at his face for the first time since the fight. He looked worse than I did, since he hadn't fought back right away. A large, angry-looking purple bruise was blooming on his right cheek and another on his jaw, his bottom lip split near the corner.

I cringed and closed my eyes, rubbing my fingers over them. In all the years we'd been on our own, running the streets and being part of the crew, we'd never gotten into a fistfight. We had our issues, sure, but for the most part, we got along fairly well.

He was the only person in my life who'd always been there for me, unconditionally.

Which was why his betrayal stung all the more.

"Sorry about your face," I said.

Gage snorted and shook his head, leaning back in his chair. "Yeah, sorry about yours, too. I didn't want to have to fight back, but Madison seems to like my mug how it is and you weren't stopping, so . . ." He shrugged.

I reached for the cup in front of me, taking a drink of the still-steaming coffee. Even though the fight had allowed me to get my aggression out, I still had questions. "Why did you do it? Why didn't you ever tell me?"

He was quiet for a few moments, his fingers running along the handle of the coffee cup. Clearing his throat, he looked up at me. "Because I knew you'd go after her—hunt for her and not give up until you found her. And I thought it'd be safer for both of you—I thought it'd be safer for *you* if you didn't have the choice."

I shook my head and tugged at my hair, letting out a frustrated growl. Gage had always only seen me as his kid brother, even though I was only a year younger than him. "Fuck, man, you can't do that shit. I'm not a little kid anymore. You can't make decisions for me. It's the same thing as when you tried to get me to stop running jobs a few months ago. I'm going to do them until I don't want to do them anymore, period. I've been an adult for a long time—a lot longer than just the years since I turned eighteen. You know that better than anyone."

Gage stared at me for a moment, then gave a short, sharp nod. I knew that'd be the only acknowledgment I'd get from him on it. And even having that didn't mean that everything would be perfect immediately. But it meant he'd try.

After a couple minutes, he cleared his throat, then leaned toward me, his arms still braced on the table. "I was able to get you guys set up in a loft above a bar not too far from here. Luckily, I have a buddy who's out in California for a couple weeks, said it'd be cool if you crashed there for the time being. It's not big, but it's furnished and it'll be better than everyone staying here."

Nodding, I said, "That's good. We'll head over there after sunset."

"Yeah, that's what I was thinking." He crossed his arms against his chest. "Listen, have you talked to her about any of this?" he asked, inclining his head toward where Evie and Madison were.

"No. She tried to tell me a bit outside, but I stopped her. Figured I didn't need to know." I didn't think I needed to go into all the details with him of why I didn't need to know—namely, so I could still keep my head in the fucking game. I didn't need to give him any more reasons to see me as incompetent enough to warrant his babysitting.

Too bad Gage shot my reasoning all to hell.

"You need to know. You're in this now, whether you like it or not. She never told me or Aaron the details of why she needed to disappear—we all thought it'd be better the less we knew. So I don't know what she's dealing with, what Max has on her, but you know if it was enough to send her running, it's some serious shit. And you also know he's not going to stop until he gets what he wants." He fixed me with a hard stare, his eyes serious and grave. "Or until she's dead."

EVIE

We left Gage and Madison's place under the cover of night, wanting whatever protection the darkness provided. Neither Gage nor Riley had reason to suspect anyone knew where they were— Aaron and Riley had been the only ones in the whole operation to know where Gage had gone to when he'd left after the situation with Madison—but we wanted to take all precautions.

The loft Gage had gotten for us was above a dive bar in an area that I would guess passed as their downtown, three parallel streets full of rows of brick and plaster buildings all lined up together. A couple bars and restaurants, a drugstore, a few boutiques, and a used bookstore among the mix.

We rumbled to a stop on Riley's bike around the back of the building in a little alley. It was nothing like the alleys back home— *home* being Chicago or Minneapolis. It was dark back here, shadows breeding in every corner and behind the groupings of trash bins lined up along the walls, but it didn't feel seedy or ominous.

It had been easy enough to transport the couple bags we'd gotten earlier in the day, Gage and Madison having gone out to get some necessities for us, since Riley had left with nothing, and I hadn't brought much more than him.

Riley used the key Gage had given him to unlock the back door, which opened immediately to a looming staircase that allowed us to avoid the bar completely and go straight into the apartment. At the top of the stairs, Riley slid the key into the lock on another door, then pushed it open and held it for me, gesturing for me to go in ahead of him.

He was silent, just as he'd been much of the day. We'd spent most of it resting, me in Madison and Gage's bedroom and Riley on the couch in their living room. I didn't know how much sleep he'd been able to get, but I hadn't gotten any, because whenever I'd closed my eyes, dozens of images flew at me—so many different memories from the past five years bombarding me, flashes and snippets of a life that didn't feel like mine, but was.

A year or so after I moved to Minneapolis, I'd allowed myself to be lulled into a false sense of security. It had been long enough away from all the horror I'd faced in Chicago that I'd let myself relax. I'd been browsing at a used bookstore close to campus during a break between classes. A man had stood outside, pacing in front of the large window, shooting glances over his shoulder into the store. It'd felt like he was staring right at me. Right *through* me. I could still remember details about him—the bulk of his shoulders and the color of his shirt, the cut of his hair and how it shone under the sun, the sunglasses that had hidden his eyes from me.

Watching him watch me, I'd been certain that was it. Genevieve was no longer, and someone had finally come for Evie. I was going to go down amid dusty books and cracked spines. A cold sweat had broken out as I'd checked for any other exits, as I'd tried to find a way out, realizing I'd somehow let down my guard enough to be unaware there *was* no other exit. That if I wanted out, I'd have to walk right past this man whose gaze was boring right through me.

At that moment, I'd hated Genevieve. I'd hated the girl I'd transformed into, because in a few short months, I'd gotten complacent. I'd allowed myself to get comfortable in the lies I told, in the life I supposedly led. And I was going to pay for my oversight.

As I'd been contemplating what I could use as a weapon to get away, another girl who'd been browsing next to me had walked out with her purchases in hand, hooked an arm through the man's, and headed across the street.

I'd stared out the window, my eyes trained to where they'd disappeared, shaken to my very core.

After that, I'd enrolled in every self-defense class I could find. I'd taken up kickboxing. I'd religiously carried mace with me wherever I went, no matter how innocuous. I'd made sure to take stock of my surroundings, to be aware of every nuance of a place, of the people around me . . . to be two steps ahead of everyone else.

Because despite all my precautions when I left Chicago, all the tales I wove of another life—a false life—I'd known all along this day would come.

I just never thought I'd have Riley on my side while I fought.

Thinking about how close I'd come to having to fend off Frankie by myself sent a shudder through me. Even though I'd gotten out of his grasp once before and I'd kept up on my self-defense, was diligent in taking as many classes as my schedule allowed, I wasn't sure how I would've stood up against him now, especially in a surprise attack. Riley hadn't even really been trying to restrain me, and he'd had me pressed against the wall in less than a minute. It made me realize that all the training I'd done hadn't been enough. Not against the people I was running from.

The little sleep I'd gotten since Eric had left for London combined with my last twenty-four hours and the fact that I hadn't been able to sleep today meant I was a zombie, but I didn't see how rest was possibly on the horizon for me. Not with what we were facing.

I stepped around Riley and into the space that was going to be our home for the next who knew how long, glancing around as I shrugged out of my coat. It was clear a guy lived here normally, the furnishings minimal, decorations obsolete. It was a cool space, though, the walls exposed brick broken up only by huge, arching windows, the beams and ductwork visible in the open ceiling. It was one giant room, like a studio apartment, though a bit larger. Pillars broke up the space, separating the rooms as much as they could.

There was a queen bed in the back right corner, no headboard, just the mattress and box spring on a bed frame. A simple gray comforter covered it, two pillows tossed haphazardly toward the top of the bed by the wall. A dresser made out of worn wood stood next to it, one of the drawers off its track leaving a gaping hole at the top, and another drawer missing completely. A battered TV tray was on the other side of the bed, providing a makeshift nightstand, a digital clock atop it.

The living area was just to the right of the front door, the compact space housing a faded green couch that had seen better days, its back to the bed that sat directly behind it. A TV was stationed on a stand against the wall in front of the couch, just to the right of the front door.

On the left side of the loft was a small L-shaped kitchen, and a door leading to what I assumed was the bathroom was just beyond it.

Riley closed the door to the apartment behind us, locking the dead bolt and hooking up the chain. "Home sweet home," he said as he walked in, tossing a bag and his jacket on the couch before making a sweep of the place. I knew he was probably checking to make sure the space was clear—a habit Gage had ingrained in him long ago. Seeing him do it now brought back so many memories of when he used to do it when we'd been younger.

After every job, his was the place we'd seek refuge in. We'd go to get cleaned up, and then to fumble in the dark, getting lost in each other for a while, both high on the adrenaline of the chase . . . of the fight.

I'd gone there at other times, too, when the things I'd been running from had nothing to do with Max or the crew. Riley had always been my home when I'd needed a reprieve from my life, though he'd never known why. And through it all, through every time I'd gone to him and every time I hadn't needed to because he'd already been there, he'd been looking out for me, protecting me.

Too bad he couldn't protect me from everything.

RILEY

The apartment Gage had set us up in wasn't as small as I pictured from his description, but it was wide-open. That actually worked better for me—less places to hide, less space to comb to make sure we were alone. The bathroom was the only room in the whole place that offered any kind of privacy, which was going to be real fucking interesting, to say the least.

I'd been expecting a minimized version of a standard bathroom based on the rest of the apartment, but everything in here was full size. A vanity sat adjacent to the bathtub and shower, a door to the left of it opening to reveal a small closet filled with towels and sheets just shoved inside. The guy who lived here did laundry like I did, apparently.

When I was satisfied the place was clear, I went back out and found Evie sitting on the couch, her shoulders straight and tense, nearly up to her ears. Her hands were pressed together and hidden between her knees, her eyes focused on the black TV screen.

Even after all these hours of being with her, it was still surreal to look at her. To look over at her and see so much of the girl I'd thought was dead only twenty-four hours ago. Even more bizarre was to look at her and see a girl I didn't know at all. Her long hair was pulled back into a low ponytail, and she looked tired—exhausted, really—the bruises under her eyes more noticeable than they'd been earlier. "You didn't sleep today, did you?" I asked.

My voice startled her, and she jumped, glancing up at me. She shook her head, tucked an imaginary strand of hair behind her ear. "Not much."

"That makes two of us." I tipped my chin toward the bed right behind where she was sitting. "You can take the bed. I'll crash on the couch."

"Riley . . ." Her voice was hesitant and weary, and I knew what was coming before she said another word. "We should talk. Before you get too far into this, you need to know the whole story."

"I'm not sure now's a good time."

"Then when is? Because I don't see how this is gonna end

anytime soon, and more than that, I don't see how this is gonna end without a bloody fight before it's all said and done. You deserve to know what you're getting into. What you've already gotten yourself into."

I blew out a breath and closed my eyes, tugging at my hair. She was right—so was Gage. But I also knew that hearing this, whatever she was about to tell me, wasn't going to be easy. If it'd made her run in the first place, it was some serious shit, because Evie Masterson didn't run from anything.

Knowing when to concede, I nodded and dropped next to her on the couch, leaning back into the corner, and glanced over to her, waiting for her to start.

Finally, she took a deep breath. "Earlier . . . back at my house, that wasn't the first time I'd ever seen Frankie."

Furrowing my brow, I stared at her, wondering what she meant. Frankie had come into the crew right around the time Evie had . . . Well, died wasn't really apt anymore, but that had been when he'd started running jobs for Max, shortly after everyone had been informed of her death. "How did you see him before that? You run into him somewhere or something?"

She wrung her hands in her lap, picked at her fingernails—something that was so *Evie,* it took me aback. Blowing out a breath, she brushed her hair back from her face, tucked some escaped strands behind her ear, and said, "The last time I saw him, before earlier at my house, was the night he tried to kill me."

Chapter Nine

EVIE

Silence descended around us after those few words left my lips. Riley's eyes were narrowed, his jaw clenched hard, every muscle in his body taut, like he was ready to pounce or flee at any moment.

Finally, his voice rough and scratchy, he said, "I'm going to need more information than that, Evie."

It was still odd to hear my name from his lips—hear my name from *anyone*—having been so long since I'd been called that. Gage and Aaron had always been diligent to use Genevieve anytime we'd had to speak over the years, making sure we'd lived up to every bit of the elaborate hoax we'd all created.

I took a deep breath and nodded, then twisted my body on the couch to face him, tucking my left leg under me. I rested my hands in my lap, fidgeting as I picked at my nails. "Do you remember me mentioning an accountant back then? Ned Richards? Who was supposedly skimming from Max?"

"Yeah." Riley's jaw clenched hard, his nostrils flaring. "We were told he grabbed the gun off one of the guys on the boat and opened fire. Story was that you were shot in the chest twice and fell overboard."

I shook my head, heat blooming in my cheeks at how easily my life had been swept under the rug for them. To maintain compliance in the ranks of the crew, Max wouldn't have told everyone the truth. Not the actual truth that I knew, or the lies disguised as truth that Frankie had no doubt told him. And the reason I knew Frankie had told Max some distorted version of the truth was that if Frankie had copped to me escaping, he'd be dead right now.

I'd never had a doubt there'd be a story of some sort—a spin on the truth—but I'd also never known what everyone had been told. I'd never asked Gage, not wanting those details. Not when I was trying to forget about that part of my life. Not when I was trying to start fresh as Genevieve Meyer.

"When Frankie got me on the boat, Ned was already dead."

Riley froze, every inch of him going still. "He was *what*?"

I nodded, swallowing. "That's what started this whole clusterfuck. Ned . . ." I shook my head and glanced down at my lap, then back up at Riley. "Roughing him up had been Frankie's first job for Max, but no one else in the crew had known about it. I'd been the only one who'd known he had been brought in. The only one who'd known he was working that job."

Thinking back now, I should've seen it coming. Should've realized something shady was going down—shadier than the shit we dealt with every day. Because Max only hid something if there was a reason for it. And there were quite literally a million reasons for him to hide this.

"Ever since Max had me digging up info on Ned, getting evidence of his betrayal, of him skimming money from Max, I thought something didn't add up. So I did what I do best—I dug some more. And I found that Ned wasn't actually the one skimming the money from Max. *Max* was skimming the money from Blaine Pruitt, and Ned was helping him cover his tracks."

"Goddamn . . ."

I nodded. Blaine was a widely known and hugely successful businessman in Chicago. As such, he made a lot of friends. Made a lot of enemies, too, and because of that, he was one of the top guys who kept Max in business.

"Wait," Riley said, "if Ned was covering Max's tracks, why the shakedown? Why was Frankie hired at all?"

"Because Blaine had somehow found out that *someone* was skimming from him. Max had me dig just far enough that I'd see all the transactions Ned initiated. Once I dug only that far, Max had been satisfied, told me to quit looking, that he could take that to Blaine. He'd had me get just enough evidence so he could set it up so Ned would take the fall for the whole thing."

Riley shook his head, his brow furrowed. "That still doesn't explain why there was suddenly a dead guy, and it sure as hell doesn't explain what the fuck you were doing on that boat."

"I knew something wasn't adding up, so even though Max had told me to stop digging, I didn't. I went further than he knew, and what I found proved I was right—I got the evidence showing that it was *Max* who was skimming from Blaine . . . for more than a year. I'm talking upward of a million dollars when everything was added up."

"Holy fuck."

Nodding, I continued, "I got cocky, thought I could remain unseen. Even though the evidence was in black and white right in front of me, I needed more. I needed to be certain. I didn't know who I could go to with the information, *if* I'd even go to anyone. I only saw as far as the day ahead. So I found out when the shakedown was going to happen, and I followed them—"

"Jesus Christ, Evie, you went there by yourself?" he asked, his voice bleeding with disapproval.

I rolled my eyes. "It's a little late for scolding now, don't you think?"

He took a deep breath, jaw ticcing, and ran a hand through his hair, the muscles in his biceps flexing against the harsh black line of the short sleeves of his T-shirt with each motion.

I took his silence for acceptance and continued, "That had been Frankie's first job. Max had pulled him into it, not wanting any of his other guys to sully it, I would guess. I don't think he counted on Frankie getting trigger-happy and killing Ned. And he definitely didn't count on me witnessing everything."

"You saw it happen? All of it?"

I nodded and swallowed, the images of that night blinking through my mind like a flip-book, one bloody image after the other. "Yeah. I saw it, and then I ran. I couldn't hear what they said after that, but I ran as fast as I could. Got away for a while. I was able to hide the evidence I'd found damning Max, but Frankie caught up with me shortly after that. He kidnapped me, got me out onto the boat with Ned's dead body, and took off onto the lake."

"None of that explains how you got away. Or how Max ended up with your locket."

My hand went up to my clavicle, automatically searching for something that hadn't been there in years, something I hadn't taken off since Riley had given it to me more than a year before my disappearance. I could remember everything about that night. How he'd pulled the box from his backpack, tossing it into my lap like it wasn't a big deal. How he'd feigned disinterest while I'd opened it, covering his nerves and uncertainty with apathy. As if I wouldn't love anything he'd given me.

Hearing about it now brought the same pang to my heart that was always present whenever I thought of it. It was the only gift Riley had ever given me. He'd saved for months to be able to buy it for me for my sixteenth birthday. It was a silver locket in the shape of a heart, an old-fashioned keyhole right in the center. I'd love it. *Cherished* it. Whenever I'd worn it, I'd felt invincible. It'd made me feel safe, just like Riley had always tried to do.

I'd never taken it off.

I swallowed, closing my eyes and reliving it like it had been yesterday. "Once Frankie got me out far enough onto the lake, he came over and uncuffed me from the railing, and I tried to get away. He grabbed whatever he could, but I kicked and punched. Then he got ahold of my necklace. I was struggling so hard, he ripped it right off my neck as I took off, then he pulled his gun from his jeans, and I didn't think. I jumped."

"Into the lake? Holy shit, Evie, how far out were you?"

"I could still see the lights of the city, but it didn't matter. If I didn't jump, Frankie would've killed me anyway. At least that way, I had a chance. And, as you can see, it was a chance well taken. As it was, he got a shot in. It wasn't fatal, obviously, but he must've thought it was, otherwise I have no doubt he would've gone after me. Fortunately, it was already dark and I was easily lost to him in the water."

Riley was quiet for a minute, then when he spoke, his voice was rough. "Where?"

"Where what?"

"The bullet . . . Where did he shoot you?"

I paused for a moment, then dragged the neck of my sweater down, showing the small scar on my chest near my underarm. Riley stared at it, his eyes unblinking, his entire body taut. I wanted to reach out to him, wanted to comfort him now like he'd always comforted me before.

But it wasn't my place anymore. If the years between us didn't prove that, the ring on my finger certainly did.

After what seemed like forever, he said, "How long before you contacted Gage?" His voice was hard, accusatory, his hurt bleeding through in his tone.

Though I'd always wondered how he would take the fact that I'd chosen to go to his brother over him, I never thought I'd get my answer. But I got it now, in the hard set of his jaw, the narrowing of his eyes, the stiff set of his shoulders. He was pissed. But more than that, I could see hurt in the depths of those eyes. Hurt that I'd inflicted because I'd gone to someone else. At that point in time, though, I hadn't had a choice. And even if I had, I didn't know that I would've chosen to go to Riley, if for no other reason than to protect him.

"Not long," I said. "I don't remember everything that happened. I remember jumping overboard and swimming for what seemed like forever. Next thing I knew, I woke up on the shore, then I ran. I contacted Gage as soon as I could get to a phone. By that time, everyone had already heard the news about me. He gave me a place to meet him, and I went. He'd gotten a guy to patch me up, good as new." I nearly laughed at that phrase, because that was about as far from the truth as I could get. That was the last day of my life I'd be anything resembling good. I twisted the engagement ring around my finger and stared at Riley. "That was the last day I was Evie Masterson."

RILEY

Even having known Evie from before, having known how tough and unruffled she was, it was still hard to believe the petite woman sitting in front of me had gone through all that and somehow made it out on the other side.

"So you just left everything behind." I hated that frustration bled through in my tone, that I was letting her have a glimpse of exactly how much her leaving had hurt me. And now that I knew it truly had been her choice, it was like pouring salt into an open wound.

"I had to, Riley. If I didn't . . . if I hadn't left, it would've only caused problems for everyone, you included. It was better all around that Max think I was dead."

"Better all around?" I couldn't believe she was saying that.

"That's bullshit. How, exactly, was it better, Evie? I'd really love to know, because it sure as shit wasn't better for me."

"What the hell did you want me to do? Hide out in your apartment? Be reasonable, Riley. Running was the best and only option."

"The girl I knew didn't run from anything."

She met my eyes for a moment before she looked away, brushing a flyaway strand of hair back behind her ear. "Yeah, well. I ran from this. I'd never been up against anything this big before."

"What about your parents?"

Her shoulders tightened, her spine going rigid, and that was enough of an answer without her saying a word, though she said, "What about them?"

"They still think you're dead, don't they? You never told them . . ."

"No, I didn't. And I'm not going to." Her voice was hard, brooking no argument.

I furrowed my brow, scratching the scruff on my jaw. Evie hadn't exactly gotten along with her parents back then, but this was on a whole other level. There was teenage angst, that whole butting-heads-with-your-parents thing, and then there was this. Letting them think she was dead? That seemed a little extreme.

"Never? But why—"

"I said they don't know and they're never going to. End of discussion." She stood from the couch and walked into the bathroom, closing the door behind her and effectively shutting out any response I'd have.

Before, Evie hadn't ever liked talking about her parents, had avoided it at all costs, but that was nothing compared to the way she'd just slammed the door on my questioning.

The fact that she shut it down so forcefully made me wonder how worried she was . . . if concern over her parents' well-being was what had made her run in the first place.

Chapter Ten

EVIE

Despite my exhaustion, sleep still wouldn't come. Riley had crashed on the couch a bit ago, and in our near proximity, I could hear his smooth, even breathing. Listening to it brought back memories of a time so long ago, a time when I'd crash at his place—anything so I didn't have to go home—and he'd curl himself around me, the two of us smashed on the couch because he and Gage had only been able to afford a one-bedroom apartment. Like it was yesterday, I could remember the feeling of having him pressed up behind me as he slept, his arms the only solace I'd ever known, all warmth and comfort wrapped up in a lanky kid.

He wasn't that lanky kid anymore.

He was anger and aggression and determination, the past five years having changed him so much from the boy I'd once known.

It was nearing dawn, the earliest whispers of light brushing against the sky and filling the loft with pale light. I stared at the ceiling and thought about my and Riley's last interaction, right before we'd crashed for the night. When he'd brought up my parents. Brought up the two people I had no desire to think of ever again.

Riley had always been astute, especially when it came to me. He'd always been able to read me, knowing my signs, sensing my emotions. But with my parents, he'd assumed it was standard adolescent angst, just run-of-the-mill teenage bullshit, and I'd never corrected him. He'd never known the issues I'd had with my parents. I hadn't told him, and he hadn't pushed.

He'd never pushed me in anything—not back then. He'd always let me take the reins, let me lead in our relationship. Now, though, that was something else that was different. Something else about him that had changed. He would never be satisfied letting someone else lead, that much was clear in the little bit we'd interacted.

And that worried me, because if he pushed on this . . . if he didn't take my short answers at face value, wasn't satisfied with them like he'd always been before, a whole host of shit I didn't want to talk about—especially with him, *never* with him—was going to be staring me down, looking me right in the eyes.

And I'd have no choice but to tell him. To reveal the secrets I'd worked so hard to hide.

The secrets I'd tried so hard to run from.

RILEY

With the loft being so open, it was hard to hide out, but Evie had managed to do it all morning. She'd woken up, headed into the bathroom, showered, and changed into different clothes. Then she'd parked herself on the bed, phone in hand, doing whatever it was she needed to do. Whether she was reading a book on there or surfing the Web or, more probably, talking to her fiancé, I didn't know.

The thought of that guy—Eric—made my jaw tighten, my shoulders tense. It'd been five years, and I certainly hadn't abstained from relationships during that time, though *relation-ships* wasn't exactly accurate. After Evie . . . after learning of her death, I'd slipped into an easy pattern of fuck and flee, and I'd never really gotten out of it. All the women I'd been with had been aware of how I worked, were in it for the same thing I was—physical release. Because after Evie, I'd figured I'd already used up my one chance to connect with someone so much. I'd had it and lost it, and that was it for me.

Seemed she didn't quite think the same.

When the silence that had filled the loft all damn day finally got to be too much, I asked, "What have you told Eric?"

She snapped her head up, her eyes wide as she looked at me. I didn't need any kind of answer from her, because her eyes said it all—that panicked stare focused directly on me.

"None of it?" I raised my eyebrows.

Averting her attention to the bed, she avoided my gaze again, but I was tired of being shut out by her. We were stuck here together until we figured a way out of this fucking mess she'd gotten us in, and I wasn't about to spend it talking to a goddamn wall.

"So he has no idea your real name is Evie Masterson."

"I'm not Evie. I'm Genevieve."

"Bullshit you are. That's a role you play, simple as that."

She laughed then, a hollow sound, too dark and sinister coming from such a sweet mouth. "Oh, Riley. I've been playing a role for a hell of a lot longer than five years."

"What the hell's that supposed to mean?"

Ignoring—or avoiding—my question entirely, she said, "No, he doesn't know any of it. And he won't, not if I have a choice in the matter."

"And what if you don't? What if Max takes that choice away from you?"

She blew out a breath, sank back to the pillow propped against the wall at the head of the bed. "Then I guess I'll figure it out if that happens."

I turned around on the couch, hanging my arm over the back, and faced her more directly. "Does he even know where you are?"

"He knows I'm away from home . . ." She trailed off, her gaze going to the window next to the bed. "He just doesn't know where or why."

"And he doesn't ask?"

Shaking her head, she said, "Our relationship isn't really like that . . ."

"You're engaged to marry him, but you don't tell each other where you are?" Granted, I'd never been engaged, so what the fuck did I know? But it just seemed to me that was exactly what two people desperately in love with each other would do. In fact, people desperately in love usually couldn't stand to be away from each other. Which raised another question entirely. "Why aren't you in London with him? Why'd you stay behind?"

She crossed her arms, her chin jutting up, eyes hard. "I'm not sure it's really any of your business what I do and don't discuss with my fiancé or why I do or don't do things with him."

I stared at her for a minute, at that defiant glint in her eyes, the hard set of her shoulders, and clenched my jaw, my fists tightening. I didn't know why her avoidance of my questions bothered me so much. More than that, I didn't know why I wanted to know the answers so damn bad in the first place. No good could possibly come from delving into her life like that, finding out what made her tick now. Or from learning detailed accounts of what she did and didn't do with her fucking *fiancé*.

Giving her a short nod, I said, "You're absolutely fucking right. Forget I said a word."

I turned my back on her, though I wanted to do more than that. What I wanted was to storm out, slam the door, and go for a long ride on my bike. Or hit a punching bag until I'd exhausted

myself. Or go for a hard, grueling run until I'd cleared my god-
damn head. Or fuck out every ounce of aggravation and irrita-
tion and frustration I had thrumming through my veins . . .
Instead, I was stuck here, in this too-small loft, with the one girl
I never thought I'd see again, the one girl I'd loved and lost . . .
The one girl who'd always managed to turn me inside fucking out.

One thing I was certain of: if I sat here stewing, I'd be miserable all night—hell, I'd be miserable however long we'd be stuck
here. Just because I'd gotten used to burning off my aggression
in other ways didn't mean I didn't have the best piece of equip-
ment with me. I got up and walked across the room, grabbing
the bag of stuff I'd had Gage pack for me yesterday and pulling
out an A-shirt and basketball shorts.

Evie had dismissed me the second I'd told her to forget I
said a word, burying her nose in that goddamn phone again, so
I didn't give it a second thought when I reached back and pulled
my shirt over my head, quickly slipping into the white A-shirt.
I unbuttoned and dropped my jeans, pulling on the basketball
shorts over my black boxer briefs, then shoved everything else in
the bag.

When I spun around to head toward the kitchen to get some
water, Evie's eyes weren't focused on her phone like I'd expected.
Nope, they were focused right on me, those gray eyes hidden partially behind eyelids at half-mast, her lips parted, a blush dotting
her cheeks.

I stopped in my tracks, narrowing my eyes at her. Though it'd
been years since I'd seen it, I recognized that look on her face,
had seen it a hundred times before. Evie was turned on. It could've
been my frustration coming out, or it could've been pure curios-
ity, but I couldn't help goading her. "Something you need?"

My voice startled her, and her eyes lifted to connect with
mine, telling me she'd been staring right at my chest. She shook
her head. "No. Um, no. Just wondering what you were doing."

"Well, you've pissed me the fuck off, so I'm gonna run some drills."

She glowered at me, the lusty—and, yeah, it'd been lust on her face; I'd bet my balls on it—look wiped clean in the blink of an eye. Instead of commenting on the first part of what I'd said, she asked, "By yourself?"

"Not a whole lot of options . . ." I filled a glass with water, then set it on the counter before going over to the couch and pushing it forward, sliding it to sit right in front of the TV. The space in here wasn't overly large, but it was big enough to go through some routines. Ones I hadn't been through in a while—months, if not a year or more. Gage and I always used to do this, back when we couldn't afford any other method of keeping in shape—no gym memberships for us. And in our business, you had to keep in shape. If you didn't, you were flat on your back—or worse—before you could blink.

I stretched briefly, warming up with some jumping jacks, push-ups, and sit-ups to get my heart rate up. When I was ready to really get into it, see if I could remember the series of movements Gage had taught me years ago, Evie was standing in front of me. Her hair was pulled back into a ponytail, a light gray tank top and the tiniest pair of shorts I'd ever seen the only things covering her body.

"I'm an option," she said, her hands resting on her hips. "I always did think it was more fun doing it with someone else."

I raised an eyebrow at her words and let my eyes take in every inch of her, traveling up from her bare feet, her toenails painted a boring pale pink that so wasn't Evie, to the creamy smooth expanse of her toned calves and thighs, pausing momentarily at the tiny scrap of material that counted as shorts—or panties, more likely. I knew if she turned around, the cheeks of her ass would be visible out the bottom of that little band of fabric, and I *ached* to reach around and feel it for myself.

My cock roused in my shorts, twitching to life, and it didn't settle down as I continued my appraisal, ghosting over the flat plane of her stomach and the sliver of bare skin where her tank top didn't quite meet the band of her shorts, then darting my gaze up to the creamy expanse of her shoulders, speckled with freckles and nearly bare except for the straps of her tank top. The thin straps that made it clear she, once again, wasn't wearing a bra. Not that she needed to—her breasts were small, tiny really, but perfect. The thought of them, of what they'd looked like, especially as I allowed my gaze to finally drop and take in the hard points pressing against the fabric, made my mouth water. Made my hands twitch at my sides to reach out, pull the strap from her shoulder, yank down the front of the tank top, and put my mouth to those perfect little tits, suck her nipples into my mouth, and see if I still knew how to make her moan.

See if, this time around, I could make her scream.

Chapter Eleven

EVIE

I'd sat, staring mesmerized as Riley had stripped. Right there in the open for anyone to see, like he hadn't a care in the world, and I couldn't even catch my damn breath. When I'd said he'd filled out, I'd had no idea. *No* idea.

I'd watched the muscles in his bare back flex with each movement he'd made. He'd somehow managed to make reaching for his tank and tugging it over his head look like an art form. Too focused on his broad shoulders, the defined cut of his arms, I hadn't noticed he was shucking his jeans until he'd already nearly had the shorts he'd been changing into over his ass, but I'd still managed to catch a glimpse of skintight black—boxer briefs, if his old preferences were anything to go by. And I hated that I remembered what kind of underwear he wore.

If I was honest with myself, though, I knew that the remembrances of our time together didn't start and end there. I remembered everything.

Riley wasn't someone easily forgotten.

Sitting there watching him, I'd wanted to freeze the moment

and stare at it forever. Stare at *him* forever. But more than that, more than just sitting and watching, I'd wanted to go to him. I'd wanted to be the kind of girl who could stand up from the couch, walk up to him, put my hand around the back of his neck and tug him down to me, and press my lips to his while I pressed everything else against every hard inch of him.

And the thing was, I *was* that girl. I'd never had problems taking control of that part of my life, making sure I was the one in charge in the bedroom. In fact, that was what I preferred. And not just what I preferred, but the only thing I allowed.

Except now, I wasn't that girl. I couldn't be, because I had this ring on my finger and a fiancé in London, and I wasn't allowed to stare at my ex-boyfriend like I wanted to drag him to the floor and ride him until neither of us could see straight.

So, of course, I'd done the next most logical thing. I'd stripped from my yoga pants and hoodie, going over to him in my tank top and boy shorts, offering to be his sparring partner. Because that would certainly abate the heat that was burning inside me.

"Since when do you spar?" he asked, his eyebrows raised.

Crossing my arms against my chest, I said, "Since five years ago when I started running from people. I had to figure out a way to protect myself. Just in case."

He nodded, and if I wasn't mistaken, I saw the glint of appreciation in his eyes when he looked back at me. "Do you normally work with a partner?"

"That's how I learned."

"Okay." He appraised me, his gaze landing on every inch of me, and I tried to control the shiver that ran up my spine, but by the smirk on his face, the heat in his eyes when he locked them with mine, I wasn't successful. When he'd finished his perusal of my body, he took a step forward, bringing his toes within an inch of mine, and leaned down, his face so close the heat from his breath whispered across my lips. I wanted to close my eyes and breathe him in. Wanted to lean forward and see if his lips were as soft as I remembered. See if he still tasted the same. Wanted to run my hands over his chest and shoulders, see how different he felt now. Wanted to get lost in him. Wanted to be found.

Instead, I just stared at him while he stared at me, and then he broke the silence. "Let's see what you've got, baby."

RILEY

She was good. Better than I thought she'd be. Her instincts were sharp, her movements practiced and precise, and soon, despite what she was wearing, despite the hard-on I'd been rocking at the beginning, I got into the exercise of it. Matching her movements, blocking her kicks and hits, pushing her and challenging her, while doing the same for myself.

She was shorter, smaller, but that made her quicker and sleeker, able to twist out of the way more easily when I came at her. And watching the determination on her face, the concentrated look in her eyes, was hot as hell. She took this seriously, as seriously as anything, and that was damn sexy.

As if I needed another thing to find attractive about her.

That heat between us was unmistakable. Despite the years we'd been apart, despite all the shit piled up between us now, there was still chemistry. And I'd have to be blind not to see it in Evie's eyes when she looked at me, too.

Breathing heavily, she stepped back and brushed the hair that had fallen out of her ponytail back from her face, ending that sequence. She walked over and grabbed her water, then downed it before setting the empty glass back on the counter. With her hands planted on her hips, she stood and stared at me.

I glanced at her out of the corner of my eye as I followed her lead and went to get some water, guzzling it in a few swallows, then filling the glass again. Before I drank that one, I asked, "What?"

If I'd thought she'd had steely determination in her eyes before, it had nothing on what I saw there now. She rolled her shoulders back, jutted her chin up. "I want you to show me how to get out of that hold. The one you had me in at my house."

I paused with the glass halfway to my mouth, assessing her, then gave a slow nod. Trapping her like I'd done, besting her in less than sixty seconds, was something that would eat away at her. She'd always thrived on being in charge, and being forced into a submissive position like that would piss her off.

I downed the water, then set the glass on the counter before walking over to her. Crossing my arms against my chest, I stared down at her. "You want to go over it from the beginning?"

When she nodded, I spun her around and didn't give her warning before I went at her the same way I had in her house. We replayed everything, exactly the way it'd happened. Her walking away, me grabbing her arm, and the ensuing struggle. And every time, just like at her house, I had her pressed up against the wall in under a minute.

This time, though, we had the heat of unmistakable chemistry bubbling between us instead of just the fear I knew Evie had been consumed with that night. Feeling her against me every time I pinned her, the curve of her ass pressed against the dick I was barely managing to keep at half-mast from sheer will alone, wasn't helping the situation. Neither was the fire in Evie's eyes every time she got bested. Seeing her hatred of being dominated made me want to do exactly that, but with far less clothing between us. And seeing her determination every time she spat "Again" didn't douse the fire. She was sexy as hell like this, all worked up and frustrated, slick with sweat and smelling like pure, undiluted Evie.

I wanted to pin her like this, shove down those tiny fucking shorts, and see if she was slick everywhere.

Giving her a wide berth to get into position, I couldn't help taunting her. "You gonna get out of it this time?"

"Shut up and start." She spun around, turning away from me and presenting me with her back. Her hands hung loosely at her sides, but I could see the tension in her shoulders.

Stepping up right behind her, I leaned in close, the dampness of her shoulders brushing against my chest as I pressed my lips to her ear. "You're all bark and no bite, baby. You think you can boss the bad guys around until they walk away?"

"Fuck off and—"

I cut off her rant by grabbing her arm, just like I had every other time before. And just like every other time, she spun and came at me with a kick—one I easily dodged—and then I had her on the defensive instead of on the offensive like she needed to be. She was too busy blocking my movements, not worrying about me herding her toward the wall.

And as much as I loved sparring with her like this, getting out the sexual frustration I'd felt since I'd seen her again in the only way I could, I wanted her to be able to do this on her own. "Think, Evie. How can you get out of this? Use my strength against me."

She didn't acknowledge me, just continued to respond to my strikes with more of her own. But soon, the wall was inching closer and closer, and she didn't have anywhere else to go. With one hand, I gripped one of her wrists and pulled her arm around, spinning her to face the wall as I captured her other wrist and held them both easily in one hand while I pressed her into the wall with the force of my body.

"Goddammit!" She was red faced and breathing hard, her body trapped between mine and the brick wall. Her arms had been in a slightly different position each time I'd pinned her, as she tried different things on me. Stretched over her head. Flush against her sides. With how I had her now, both wrists encased in one of my hands and pressed into the base of her spine, it forced her to arch her back. My other arm lay flush between her breasts, my hand wrapped around her neck, tight enough to make her think twice about allowing herself to be put in this position but not hard enough to hurt. Her breathing was harsh, the rise and fall of her chest pronounced, the position she was in doing nothing to hide it.

And I couldn't bring myself to look away.

"Let me go." Her voice was hard, her words low and controlled.

I pressed against her a little harder, pushing her limits, doing exactly what I knew I shouldn't. And when her hands twitched in my grasp, the side of her palm brushing lightly against my ever-growing cock, I cursed under my breath and let up, allowing her to push free.

I blew out a breath and walked in a circle, needing to get myself under control. If I was going to help her get out of this, truly help her figure this out, I needed to get my goddamn dick under control.

She paced in the open space, her jaw clenched. Frustration bled into her voice when she snapped, "Why the hell can't I get this?"

"Because you're thinking too much."

She turned to me, her face bright red, her eyes hard. "Knowing what moves I need to make is the only way I'm going to get out of this."

I was shaking my head before she'd even finished. "No. Knowing the right moves *helps* you, but sometimes you have to go with what feels right. You have to break the rules and do something you think might not work. Sometimes you have to take a gamble. See what happens if you let me get a little closer before you go on the defensive." I stepped closer to her, ready to try again, forcing myself to ignore the labored rise and fall of her breasts, the sheen of sweat over her shoulders trailing down her chest into the shadow of cleavage at the top of her tank. Forcing myself to ignore everything but helping her figure this out, despite what my dick wanted. "If you're gonna gamble, at least gamble with me. You know I'm not going to hurt you. You know you're safe with me."

EVIE

His words shot straight to my heart, sparking it in a way it hadn't been for so long. Every word made me crave him even more than I already did.

Made me crave him a hundred times more than I ever should've.

And with the need . . . the want currently coursing through my body, it was a bad combination. Bad, but one I didn't want to stop. After blocking off my emotions for so long, it was a rush to actually *feel* again.

"Ready?" he asked, his voice pitched low.

I nodded, looking up into his eyes, and then he reached toward me, gripping my shoulders and spinning me around again, repeating the same movements as every other time. Even though we'd done this nearly a dozen times, it didn't stop the bolt of awareness I felt at his hands on me. That heavy warmth that settled low in my belly when his large hands cradled nearly every inch of my shoulders within his grasp. His strength was apparent in the grip he had on me . . . as was his restraint. I wasn't unaware of the fact that if he wanted to, he could have me pressed against any surface in this apartment in fifteen seconds flat. And that pissed me off, making me want to fight that much harder.

His thumb ran lightly down my spine as he pulled away, a contradiction to the harsh grip his hands had had on my shoulders, and I tried. I did. I tried hard to ignore the shiver that worked its way through my body, but it was no use. My nipples pulled taut against my damp tank top, goose bumps popping up along every inch of my skin, and I was helpless to stop it.

I wasn't even sure anymore if I wanted to stop it.

Forcing myself to block out thoughts of what he felt like against me, what it felt like being under his hands again, I moved on autopilot. I got into position, shifting away from him and closing my eyes. He reached out, his hand connecting with my arm, and as hard as it was, I pushed down my first instinct to kick back, instead breathing, just breathing, and for once, giving myself permission to screw up. Giving myself permission to trust my instincts instead of everything I knew to be right. Because sometimes right just didn't work.

I allowed him to pull me close, his hand gripped around my arm. He didn't stop until I was pressed back against him, his forearm across my chest, my shoulder clutched in his hand as he held me tightly to him. I could feel every hard-muscled inch of him towering over me from behind, could feel the power thrumming under those hands anchoring me to him. His chest rose and fell against my back, the matching rhythm in the puffs of air from his mouth hitting my cheek, running down the bare expanse of my chest above my tank top.

And as much as I wanted to revel in the feel of him, I shoved all awareness of him away and forced myself to just breathe. Forced myself to focus on the act of what we were doing instead of how he set every nerve ending in my body on fire. I took a moment to close my eyes and concentrate on what I needed to do, knowing I could get out of this. *Knowing* it.

And I did. I took three deep breaths and dropped my weight, forcing him off balance. And then I sprang into action, my teeth clamping down on the arm he had across my chest at the same time my heel came down hard on his foot and my elbow shot back, jabbing him in the stomach. Though I didn't put as much force into any of them as I would have if this had been a real attack, it'd been enough to startle him, make him drop his arms to protect himself, and then I spun toward him and did what I needed to in order to get away.

In the end, when he was on the ground breathing hard, and I was still standing in front of him, my eyes wide and crazed, adrenaline coursing through my veins, he gave a nod of approval and didn't even try to disguise the heat blazing in his eyes as he said, "Again."

Chapter Twelve

Each time we replayed it, I did something slightly different than I had the time before, always keeping Riley on his toes. And though I hadn't been able to get out of his hold every single time, I'd gotten out more times than not. And that was thrilling. Not just the fact that I'd actually escaped, but that I'd done so by following my instincts instead of the path I was supposed to traverse.

Breathing hard, we took another quick break, each gulping some water, before we met back in the middle of the room to go through it one final time.

"Ready?" he asked.

Shaking my head, I said, "Don't ask, just do."

He cocked an eyebrow, then his gaze dropped to take in every inch of me. I felt it as sure as if it'd been his hands doing the caressing—along my shoulders, down my bare arms, whispering against my breasts and thighs, trailing over my stomach, taut with excitement. And that low hum of awareness that had been buzzing through my veins the entire time we'd been doing this sparked brightly. When he lifted his eyes to meet mine, his lids were heavy, the soft, pale blue of his irises eaten up by his dark pupils. He looked hungry, and it didn't take a genius to figure out what, exactly, he was hungry for.

Without saying a word, I turned my back to him, closing my eyes and letting myself be vulnerable. It went against every instinct I had, everything I'd taught myself, everything I'd put into practice since I was fifteen. But I did. With him, I did.

I tried to slow my breathing as I waited what seemed like forever for him to come up behind me. And when he did, when I finally felt the heat of him there, I couldn't hold in the shiver that ran up my spine. His fingers blazed a trail up the sensitive skin of my inner arm, starting at my wrist and not stopping until he got to my elbow. Gripping it lightly, he held on to it and then stepped closer, so close, until he could wrap his other arm around me, going around my chest and cupping my opposite shoulder. The heat of his skin burned into my back, the hard planes of his chest brushing my shoulders, the fronts of his legs flush against the backs of mine. And when he pressed closer, there was no mistaking the hard bulge digging into my lower back.

My breathing quickened, my nipples tightening, excitement bubbling in my veins, and God help me, I didn't want to stop this. Despite what my life looked like, despite what Riley thought I had waiting for me at home, I didn't want him to stop. I wanted to see what he was going to do next, if this was just another sequence, or if it was more.

It felt like something so much more.

When he lowered his head, the air from his lungs sweeping down my neck and across my shoulder, I knew I'd been right. Because three breaths later, his lips pressed against my skin, and that was it. I exhaled a noise that could only be called a whimper, though I couldn't remember ever making a sound like that before, and dropped my head back against his shoulder.

It'd only been only a day, one measly day, and this heat between us had already reached a crescendo. And I didn't want to be responsible. For the first time since I'd left Chicago, I wanted to let go and not think about every possible outcome. Not worry about the consequences. I didn't want to do the right thing.

I wanted to feel him—under me, around me, *inside* me. Wanted to see if it was as good as I remembered.

Riley kept kissing me, the hand that was clutching my elbow moving to my hip, squeezing and then sliding around to press flat against my stomach, tugging me back into him. He was hard, so fucking hard against my back, and I wanted to reach behind me and feel him. I wanted to tug his shorts down, slip my hand into his boxers, and wrap my fingers around his cock. Feel the heat and smoothness of him, feel the steel that I knew was a direct result of me. I wanted to push him down onto the couch, tug my boy shorts to the side, sink down on him, and ride him until he couldn't think.

Until neither of us could think.

Before I could put my thoughts into action, Riley lowered the arm he had across my chest and palmed my breast, his thumb strumming the hardened peak as he breathed my name, and that was it.

I snapped.

Whipping around, I grabbed his face and tugged him down to me, meeting his lips in a bruising kiss. It was all teeth and tongue, his sweeping into my mouth until we both groaned. He gripped my face and walked us backward until I felt the harsh bricks of the wall against my back. Cradling my head in his hands, he pressed his thumbs under my chin so he could tilt my face the way he wanted it, and I let him play for a minute. I let him think he had control of this before I pressed forward, my hands against his chest, and flipped our positions so he was against the wall.

I tugged on the hem of his tank top, pushing it up as my hands ran along the contours of his body. Holy God, this man's body was remarkable. He was etched like stone, the ridges of his abdomen hard under my wandering fingers. When I'd pushed it up as far as I could, he reached back and tugged at the neck of his tank before he whipped it off and tossed it to the side.

And I stared. Gawked, actually. His shoulders were broad, muscles sculpting their perfect curves, the barest whispers of black ink peeking over from his back, and I wanted to see them, *know* them, the designs he'd had stamped on him forever. At one time, I'd known his body intimately, and now it was like looking at a totally different person.

He reached for me, his arms flexing as he tugged me by the hips until I was pressed against the front of him. I couldn't stop myself and ran my hands over his skin, tracing those glimpses of ink . . . the dips of his sculpted muscles . . . Feeling under my fingers the body I'd dreamed about for so long.

If I hadn't been touching him with my own hands, I wouldn't have believed it was happening. After five years, after countless dreams, he was standing in front of me, a different man from the one he'd been, absolutely. And yet even with all those differences, he was still Riley.

Suddenly, he reached for my tank top, tugging it up and off, and I didn't have time to blink before he bent down and captured a nipple in his mouth. He sucked hard before he pulled back, swirling his tongue around the peak, then repeating it all over again. And I wanted to cry and scream and praise every deity in the world that he'd remembered what turned me on, what got me off. After all these years, he'd remembered exactly what I liked.

He gripped my other breast in his hand, taking turns pinching my nipple and swirling his thumb around it. And then he switched positions, placing his mouth where his hand was, and went to work on my breasts in reverse. I gripped his hair, loving that I finally had something to hold on to while he was doing this to me, something to keep him exactly where I wanted him.

When his teeth scraped against me, and he captured my nipple between them and tugged, I moaned. "God, Riley."

The look he shot me—one part arrogance, one part satisfaction, all parts man—nearly sent me to my knees. He pulled back long enough to say, "I remember what you like, baby. You wanna see?"

I could only nod, my lips parted and breaths heavy. He dropped to his knees, tugging my underwear down my legs until I could kick them off and to the side. Then his mouth was right against the place I was aching for it, his breaths sweeping across where I was wet and needy for him, and I couldn't breathe.

He pulled away and tapped his fingers on my inner thighs. "If you want this, you gotta spread these legs more. C'mon, let me see that pretty pussy again."

I breathed out a moan and leaned forward, resting my hands against the harsh bricks of the wall, my forehead pressed against the back of my hand. And then I watched. Riley was sitting with his back to the wall, his legs extended out on the floor between mine, and I couldn't look away as he gripped my ass and tugged me forward to his mouth.

He licked a line up where my thigh met my body, then he moved in, sweeping against my outer lips. The brushes of his tongue were light, feathery . . . nothing like what I needed right then. He was teasing, taunting, and it was everything I hated.

"Thought you remembered what I liked," I said between panting breaths. "Teasing isn't it."

I felt his chuckle against me in puffs of air, and then his thumbs were holding me apart, baring me to him completely, and there wasn't any teasing at all. He licked up the length of my slit, his tongue flicking against my clit, before he sucked it into his mouth with a moan of approval, and I almost shot off right there. I breathed out a curse, and Riley lifted his eyes to connect with mine, hunger and determination in his gaze, and I had to close my eyes to block it out. Stop looking at him, because if I didn't, if I kept staring into those ocean eyes, I'd come, and I wanted to ride this out. I wanted to bask in the feeling of his lips on me, his tongue stroking me, because it'd been so long. So long since I'd felt this connection with anyone. Too long.

If I could, I'd make this last all night.

Riley had other plans, though, and didn't let me draw it out as long as I'd wanted to. He swept one hand down my slit, playing, touching me everywhere while his tongue was relentless against my clit. And then he slid two fingers into me, curling them toward where his tongue was and stroking the place inside me that got me off immediately every single time. This was no different, and I clamped down on his fingers, nonsense falling from my lips as he threw me off the cliff, giving me my first non-self-induced orgasm in over a year.

I'd forgotten how good it felt, letting someone else get me there, and I wanted him to do it again. And again. And again, again, again. I wanted him to make me come until I couldn't think, couldn't breathe, couldn't do anything but crave more of his touch. Because that'd always been how it was with him. The want, the need, the constant craving, those brief, powerful moments when all thought fled and all I could do was *feel*. And I'd missed it more than anything. I'd missed it more than I'd ever let myself remember or acknowledge.

There was no stopping it now, though.

I was barely cognizant, still trying to catch my breath, still trying to reconcile what this meant that he'd awakened this within me after I'd tried for so long to suppress it. I didn't know how long I stood there, eyes closed, my forehead pressed into my hand while I panted against the wall. I didn't know how long Riley had been gone from between my legs before I felt him standing behind me, his bare skin pressed against mine. He ran the tip of his cock up and down against my slit, and I couldn't utter a word of protest before he found my entrance and pushed in. I was so wet, all it took was one smooth stroke, and he was fully inside me. Our joined moans mixed in the otherwise quiet loft.

Except this wasn't how it was supposed to be. I didn't like it like this, with him behind me, me pressed into the wall, and he knew it. I didn't like him—or anyone—behind me or over me at all. All I ever felt was trapped. Out of control. I hated all of it, especially during sex, and if he'd remembered how I liked my nipples played with, then he sure as shit remembered this.

"Riley, no, not like this."

He shifted his hips, bending his knees and tilting my ass up, and then he slid in even deeper, and we both moaned. He didn't move then, just sat deep inside me, his cock pulsing. Then he leaned forward, his lips brushing my shoulder. "You sure? Feel how deep I am. You've got all of me in you like this, baby."

He pulled back the barest fraction and pushed inside again, and I sobbed out a breath.

"Evie, tell me. Okay?" His voice was strained, barely controlled, his hands shaking as they gripped me. All that power restrained once again for me.

It helped to know he was as far gone as I was.

I closed my eyes at the feel of him behind me—both terrifying and arousing—the feel of him inside me, owning me, and I couldn't bring myself to tell him to pull away. Couldn't bring myself to do anything but breathe, "More . . ."

"Like this?" he asked as he pulled out and slid back in. Slowly, so slowly, he pumped in and out of me, letting me feel every single inch of him, the head of his cock dragging against that spot inside me that sent me spinning, but it wasn't fast enough. Wasn't hard enough. Wasn't anything but torment.

I reached back, dug my nails into his thighs. "Don't be an ass. *Fuck* me, don't tease me."

He growled, then gripped my hips, pulling me back to him

as he drove deep, and I moaned loudly, curses falling from my lips. Over and over and over again, he thrust into me, fucking me exactly how I wanted it. He reached up, wrapped my ponytail around his hand, clutching it in his fist and tugged, pulling my head back and to the side, and I choked out a moan, closing my eyes at the sensory overload. And then his teeth were on me, tugging on my earlobe, scraping the column of my neck, pressing into the juncture of my shoulder, and I pulsed around him, my second orgasm breathing down my neck.

"Fuck, Evie, I've missed this. Missed feeling you come on me. Squeeze my cock, baby. Let me feel it again. Let me feel you."

And then his fingers were strumming my clit, and he navigated my body so expertly, it was like no time at all had passed since we'd last been together. He took me where he wanted me to go, played me how I needed it—fast then slow then faster yet. Played me how he needed it, too, so he could bring us to the edge at the same time. And then I was screaming and coming around him and he was groaning my name as we both fell into that blissful void together.

Chapter Thirteen

RILEY

Even though I didn't want to, even though I wanted to stay inside her, wait until I got hard again and fuck her all over again, I gripped the base of my cock, holding the condom in place— thanking God I'd had one in my wallet—as I pulled out of her, groaning at the loss of her heat.

After placing a soft kiss on her shoulder, I walked to the bathroom to get cleaned up before heading back to her. She'd moved away from the wall, but her back was to me, her shoulders stiff and practically up to her ears, and she was already tugging on her tiny little shorts. Before she could get her tank top over her head, I reached out and wrapped my hand around her arm, turning her toward me. Her skin was soft and I wanted to reacquaint myself with it. With her. I wanted to run my hands over every inch of her body, memorizing the things I'd forgotten and learning the ways she'd changed. She tensed under my hand, pausing in her movements as her tank top fell to the floor once again, but she wouldn't look up at me, and *fuck no,* that wasn't how this was going to go down.

With my other arm, I reached out, curling my hand around the back of her neck, using my thumb under her chin to tilt her face toward mine. That mask was in place again, that shuttered look in her eyes, and I wanted it gone. Erased. I wanted it to be like I'd seen when I'd kissed her. When I'd had her back against the wall, then again when she'd reversed our positions. When I'd been on the floor, my mouth on her pussy while she'd stared down at me.

That was my Evie. The woman here, looking at me with her blank eyes, was Genevieve, and I didn't want her in my space. In *our* space.

"This shouldn't have happened," she said, but her voice lacked conviction.

The old Riley would've let it drop. But the old Riley wasn't here anymore, and I was going to push to find out where her head was, because something didn't add up. Something about her relationship with her fiancé didn't make sense.

If Evie was my fiancée, if she'd agreed to marry me, if I'd had her in my bed, I sure as shit wouldn't be satisfied with a few fucking texts while I was across the ocean, thousands of miles away.

I tightened my fingers around the back of her neck, pulling her closer to me. Bending my knees so I was eye level with her, I said, "That's bullshit and you know it."

She twisted away, out of my grasp, and glowered at me, crossing her arms over her naked breasts. "How is that bullshit? I'm engaged, Riley. *Engaged*." She held her hand up to me, the too-big ring glinting obnoxiously on her slender finger. Like I needed that piece of jewelry as a reminder that she'd promised herself to another man. Tucking a loose strand of hair behind her ear, she said, "And I just let my ex-boyfriend fuck me up against a wall. What part of that seems like a good idea to you?"

"I don't know, the part where I was inside you seemed like a fan-fucking-tastic idea to me. And one I'd like to do again very soon."

She rolled her eyes, shaking her head, and turned to grab her tank top once again. "I'm not discussing this with you. It was a mistake, plain and simple. And it's not going to happen again. It's over. It has to be."

I went up behind her, gripping her upper arms, and pressed my cheek against hers. "This isn't over, baby, and you know it. You want it as bad as I do." I brushed my thumbs up and down her arms. "In fact, if I pulled you over to the couch and sat down, I bet I could tug you right on top of me, spread those legs, and get you to fuck me exactly how I want you to. Get you to ride me until you came as many times as you needed."

She didn't make a noise—she was too stubborn for that—but her teeth were digging harshly into her lower lip, and her breaths were getting more rapid, her chest heaving with each one. Her cheek was hot against mine, and I knew if I was facing her, if I could look into her eyes, I'd see the heavy swell of desire in them.

"You want that, don't you? You want my cock all over again." I turned my head and kissed her neck, and she let her head drop back against my shoulder, just like she'd done earlier. I swept my lips along her skin, swirling my tongue around her pulse point, and then continued until my mouth brushed her ear. "You want me, you loved every minute of that, and yet you've got that ring on your finger. I know as sure as I know my name that you'd never cheat. Not even with me. So I think it's time you told me what the fuck is going on."

EVIE

Riley's body behind mine, against mine, his breath on my neck, being held safe in his arms, felt like coming home. Though not like any home I'd ever known. He felt like comfort and peace and happiness and safety, and I wanted to wrap myself up in the feeling, wrap myself up in *him*. I wanted to go boneless, let myself sink into his body, let him lead me over to the couch and proceed to do exactly as he'd described.

But I couldn't.

Despite the need coursing through my veins, I'd made a promise to someone who meant a lot to me, and I couldn't break that. Not even for Riley—the one person I've ever truly given the most of myself to. He hadn't taken my virginity, but he'd been my first in all the ways that counted.

That night all those years ago, fumbling in the dark of his apartment, the rough material of the couch against my legs as I'd straddled him, staring down into his face, hadn't been perfect, but it'd been perfect to me. Because with whispered words and grappling hands and that *look*—that heavy-lidded look that said I was his everything—he showed me that sex could be about more than just control.

And because of that, my relationship with him had been the one I'd compared everything else—every*one* else—to.

In all honesty, nothing had even come close since him, not even Eric. In between my relationships with them, I'd never involved myself with a guy for more than a few hours in an anonymous bed somewhere—long enough to get that satisfaction I needed. Long enough to feel that power rushing through my veins, to feel like I was still the one in control of my body. *My* choices and only mine were what had led me to those beds, to those men.

I hadn't felt that release in so long, though, and it was wearing on me. It would be easy to blame the fact that I'd slipped, that I'd allowed Riley inside me, on that, but that wasn't it. And I wasn't sure I was willing to write off our connection as a momentary lapse of judgment. I'd been cognizant of every decision I made, and this had been no different. I'd wanted him—*still* wanted him.

Clutching the tank top to my bare chest, I swallowed and closed my eyes. "I can't tell you that."

Riley stilled behind me, his hands tightening almost imperceptibly on my arms. Then he exhaled, his soft breath washing against my bare skin, and I shivered. "You can tell me anything. *Anything.* You know that."

And I wanted to cry at his words. I wanted to turn around and press my face into his chest, breathe him in and exhale with every secret I'd ever been harboring. Because I so desperately wanted that to be true, for so many reasons. But I couldn't trust that.

"It's not my secret to tell."

"What the fuck is that supposed to mean?" he asked, dropping his arms and coming around to face me. His eyes were hard, his jaw clenched, and he should've looked ridiculous standing there in front of me, all pissed-off man, buck naked and radiating anger. Instead he looked like everything I wanted to get lost in. "Whose secret is it? What the hell's going on, Evie?"

When I didn't say anything, didn't open up any more, he stepped forward, bringing our bodies together. He cupped my face in his hands, leaning down until our noses were barely an inch apart, his eyes darting between mine. And they were so full of fear, so full of anxiety—for me.

For *me.*

"Are you in trouble? Is it more than this? Is something else going on? Baby, please. Tell me." His thumbs stroked my cheeks reverently, like I was delicate. Like I'd break at any moment. Like he was scared I'd float away right in front of him or vanish into thin air.

The worry in his voice was what finally broke me. Riley had always been sincere, wearing his heart on his sleeve. And it was almost his detriment. It was also the one thing that got to me every time, broke down any walls I'd ever tried to keep between us.

All but one.

Shaking my head, I said, "I'm not in trouble. No more than you already know, anyway."

His muscles relaxed the barest whisper, but his body was still coiled tight, the uncertainty still sitting heavily on his shoulders. "Then what? You can trust me, Evie. It'll stay between us. I *swear*."

I blew out a breath, seeing the honesty in his eyes, hearing it in his voice, and knew with my entire being that I could trust him. "What do you know about Eric?"

Chapter Fourteen

RILEY

"Has he hurt you? I swear to Christ, if that bastard's hurt you, I'm going to kill him."

"No, no . . . he'd never hurt me, Riley. Ever." Her voice was sincere, her eyes clear. She reached out and brushed her hand down my side, resting it against my hip. "You don't ever have to worry about that. But I need to hear what you know about him."

I thought back to what Gage had filled me in on, the two of us going over the files he'd had while Madison and Evie had been in the back bedroom. Reaching up, I rubbed my thumb and forefinger over my eyes as I clenched them shut, trying to remember all the details. "Eric Caine, thirty-three, never been married. Son of Republican senator Caine. Followed in his dad's footsteps when he enlisted in the army at eighteen. Then continued in his dad's shadow as he went to law school once he was out and now works for the firm his father started—one of the biggest in Minneapolis. But he has plans to eventually go into politics. Again, just like his father." I dropped my hand and raised an eyebrow. "How'd I do?"

She nodded. "You hit just about everything."

I thought back to the files, going over all the pertinent details in them, and couldn't remember anything that I'd left out. "What'd I miss?"

"I need you to promise me this stays between us. You can't repeat it."

I nodded, the sincerity in her voice telling me she wasn't bullshitting. "Of course."

"Not even to Gage."

"Just between us. I can keep a secret, Evie. Especially one from you."

She looked at me for a minute, her eyes darting between mine, then she took a deep breath and exhaled. "Eric's gay."

I could only stare at her. When the shock wore off enough for me to speak, I said, "He's what now?"

She sighed and stepped back, finally tugging her tank top over her head—a shame to see her breasts covered up, but it was probably for the best, considering what had just come out of her mouth. I followed her lead and grabbed my boxers from the floor, stepping into them, then walked behind her to the couch. She sat sideways, one leg curled and tucked under the other, and I sat facing her, waiting for her to explain what the hell was going on.

She blew out a deep breath and said, "We met last year at a coffee shop. I was still in school full-time, so I worked part-time as a barista there for extra cash since I didn't have much. Aaron had managed to work my new records so I was able to get a full scholarship, but that didn't cover everything."

Tucking a loose strand of hair behind her ear, she glanced down at her lap, at where our knees touched, then looked back up at me. "Eric would come in every day and talk to me. He was so nice, not like some of the creeps who'd come in and hit on me, harass me, really. And one day, after about a month of nearly daily conversations, he asked me to dinner."

Even after hearing Eric was gay, that didn't stop my stomach from clenching while listening to the details of Evie going out on dates while we'd been apart. I hadn't imagined she'd been abstinent in all that time, but knowing she hadn't been and actually hearing about it were two very different things.

She rested her elbow on the back of the couch, settling her cheek against her hand, and continued, "Like I said, money was tight. He happened to catch me on a week when it was *exceptionally* tight, and I figured if nothing else, I could get a free meal out of it. So I went. And I was more surprised than anyone that I'd actually had a good time. The entire evening, he'd never tried anything physical with me, and it was refreshing. That was our first date, at least in the eyes of the public, and what started our dating life.

"We'd go out to dinner, smile and laugh—despite the lie our engagement is based on, we do have a real connection, so that was never faked. After four years of being alone, it felt nice to have someone to talk to again. And I'm not going to lie, it felt nice to not have to worry about money for once. I'd never had that, not once in my entire life, and not having to worry about it was this giant weight lifted off my shoulders. But there was never anything physical between us. Nothing more than brief kisses on the cheek—always inside my apartment, never in public. While we were in public, though, he was affectionate, just not sexually. He'd hold my hand, put his arm around me, lean in close when I was speaking, but there was no kissing, no PDA like that. And that had been when I'd started to get suspicious that something more was going on."

I knew why she'd be suspicious. Evie was a fucking bombshell, especially now with her waves of red hair, with the features that had sharpened in the years we'd been apart, and she oozed sexuality, so for a man to have no interest in that . . . yeah, something was up.

She continued, "It all changed one night when we were out to dinner. I'd been in the bathroom and came out to see our waiter leaning toward Eric, slipping him a piece of paper. When I got to the table, Eric played it off, but I saw something when the waiter looked at him. Combined with how he acted around me, things were clicking into place. I had a pretty good idea what was going on, especially after he'd told me how strict his upbringing was, how conservative his parents were, and the role his father played in guiding his decisions. So I confronted Eric in the car before he dropped me off."

"And he told you? Just like that?"

She nodded. "He took a chance. Told me he'd managed to keep the secret his entire life. And now, with his father a conservative senator and him looking to follow in his footsteps, he didn't think he could come out. That was where I came in. He knew about my past—well, the past I created. But he knew I was alone, that I was struggling. He gave me an answer to that. We both got something out of it."

My brow furrowed, because from where I was sitting, Evie didn't get shit out of it. Eric was the one who got the picture-perfect trophy wife, all the while living a lie behind closed doors, which he would've done with or without her. All she got was trapped in a loveless relationship. "What the hell did you get out of it?"

"Security. I got the kind of life I never had growing up."

"Yeah, but at a whole fuckton of sacrifices. You were willing to give up your life, your happiness, for someone else?"

"I didn't give up my happiness . . ."

"Can you honestly tell me you're happy with him? You're happy in your life?"

She shook her head and looked at me, her eyes so heavy and sad, exhausted. "I haven't been happy in a very long time, Riley.

I didn't think this made much of a difference. It was the best option I had, and it's not all bad."

I reached out and grabbed her hand, holding it between mine. "What do you need to be happy? What do you want?"

EVIE

His words settled over me, sank into my bones. It was something I hadn't ever really let myself contemplate, but now that Riley was asking it, I faced the question I'd never truly considered. The question that would only ever bring pain, because to say what I'd want to make me happy would be admitting what made me sad, what made me ache, and I'd been trying for so long—*years*—to forget it, to push it back, bury it. Force it down and leave it in the past, where it belonged.

"I don't know," I said, averting my eyes and glancing out the window.

Riley reached out and gripped my chin between his forefinger and thumb, giving me no choice but to turn and face him. "That's bullshit." He leaned forward, staring straight into my eyes, and lowered his voice. "Now tell me what would make you happy."

I blew out a breath, read the sincerity in his gaze, and let myself go down the path I'd avoided for so long. "I want to be safe." Above anything, I always, always wanted to be safe, and I hadn't truly been safe for so, so long. "I don't want to have to look over my shoulder anymore. I want to be free to be Evie, not Genevieve. I want to be able to go into whatever kind of career I want, instead of one I hate simply because it will keep me under the radar. And I want to feel content and comfortable, be able to afford a nice life—not anything lavish, like I have now. That's so much more than I ever needed, but I want to be comfortable."

I'd managed to get that all out without even a single lie.

Lying had become second nature for me, something I'd been doing for so long, it always surprised me when I was able to talk about anything involving my life and manage not to weave the truth and lies together into a convoluted version of what my reality was.

Riley was quiet for a while until he finally asked, "What about love?"

His question startled me enough that I could only blink at him in response. When I finally found my voice, I asked simply, "What?"

"Love," he repeated. "That wouldn't make you happy?"

Shaking my head, I dropped my eyes, not able to maintain contact with him. Because in them, I saw a thousand possibilities I'd lost when I'd walked away from him. "It's not a matter of whether or not it'd make me happy. It's a matter of whether or not I think it's even a possibility for me." I glanced up at him then, at the boy I'd loved so long ago, the boy I'd given my very soul to. The boy I'd walked away from. "I had it once. I don't think it's in the cards for me to have it again."

Chapter Fifteen

RILEY

Through unspoken agreement, we'd migrated to opposite ends of the loft, spending some time alone after our talk—or as alone as we could be in the wide-open space. After the sun had set, we'd ventured out to the grocery store down the street, grabbing a few bags of things. I'd managed to toss a box of condoms in when Evie hadn't been looking, because now that I knew the truth behind the Eric façade, I wasn't going to back off. Not when I heard the absolute truth ringing in her voice when she said she didn't think love was in the cards for her again. She honestly believed that, and I wanted to prove her wrong.

Evie was in the kitchen, boiling some noodles for spaghetti, the sauce from a jar already heating in a pan on the stove. It was easy and quick—and being cheap didn't hurt, either. I sat on the couch while she stirred the pasta, pretending I wasn't watching her, when in reality I couldn't take my eyes off her, remembering all the times she'd done this for us in the past.

In the years we'd been together, she'd spent most nights at my and Gage's place, all of us migrating there after whatever shit we'd gotten up to after school. Seeing her being so domestic after watching her on the streets, taking no shit from anyone, was something I'd craved. Mostly because I'd known I was the only person to ever see that side of her. It proved just how comfortable she was with me. Just how strong our connection was.

And seeing her like that now, especially after she'd landed me on my ass only hours ago through sheer will and force of her body, was sexy as hell.

"What're you staring at?"

Her voice snapped me out of my thoughts. Unashamed, I shrugged. "Your ass."

She snorted, turning around again and giving me another view of her spectacular backside. Now that I'd had her, had been inside her, it was taking everything in me not to go up behind her, reach around and cup her tits, kiss her breathless, take her to the bed and sink deep inside her body. But she'd pulled back since our talk, and as much as it was killing me, I wanted to respect that. I just didn't know how long I'd last before I snapped.

"Well, stop staring and come eat," she said, setting plates down on the counter and dishing up. I stood from the couch and headed into the kitchen area. I grabbed forks while she piled one of the plates with heaps of noodles and sauce, then put a more respectable amount on the other plate.

I grinned at her and grabbed the one she'd barely put anything on. "Feeling hungry tonight?" I asked, gesturing to the other plate still in front of her.

She rolled her eyes, but a smile flirted at the corner of her mouth, and I wanted to see her truly smile. The smile I hadn't seen in so long—the one where her beauty mark would disappear in her dimple, and I'd get a surge in my chest because I'd been the one to make her happy. Getting Evie to smile—truly smile—had always been like sinking the eight ball on the break. A little bit of luck, a little bit of skill, complete satisfaction. I could still remember the first time she'd turned that dimple on me. I'd felt like I won the fucking lottery.

After I had both our plates, I walked over to the couch, waiting as she trailed behind me with two bottles of beer, the necks clutched between her fingers. Once she was settled, I set the plate she'd dished up for herself in her lap, then took the bottle of beer from her with a tip of my head and sat on the other end of the couch, facing her.

It was quiet as we began to eat, but even with the silence, I studied her.

Without looking up at me, she said, "You're staring again, and since I'm sitting on my ass, that's not what has your attention."

I finished chewing the bite of spaghetti and then took a swig of beer. "I was just thinking about what it used to be like, when we were in high school. You remember when you'd cook like this for me and Gage?"

She stared at me for a moment, her eyes darting between mine, then she averted her gaze. "Of course."

After long enough of her not saying anything else, I filled in the silence. "We were ungrateful assholes then, probably never saying thank you, but I always loved when you did it."

She huffed out a laugh and rolled her eyes. "Why? It wasn't like I was a gourmet cook. We ate boxed mac and cheese or ramen or sandwiches on stale bread."

I shrugged. "I don't know. It wasn't so much what you made, but that you were making it, period. It felt like I got this glimpse of Evie that no one else would ever see. Where you let down your guard."

It was subtle, the way she tensed, but I could see it. And it made me wonder just how much of her I'd ever actually seen.

When we'd been so young, I hadn't ever considered why she spent so much time at our place, just happy my girlfriend was able to be there as often as I wanted. Now, though, I couldn't help but wonder what kept her there. "Why didn't you ever want to go home back then?"

If the tension in her shoulders was subtle before, now it was like Mt. Everest rested on them. Still, she played it off, shrugging those stiff shoulders. "Rather hang out with you guys than my parents. I was a teenager. Isn't that pretty standard?"

That wasn't the truth—not the whole truth, anyway—but if there was one thing I knew about Evie, it was that people didn't get her to do what she didn't want to do, so I didn't push. Instead, I finally voiced the question that'd been eating away at me. "How could you just disappear?"

She cringed, the pink in her cheeks deepening. "I'm sorry, Riley. I know Gage gave you his reasons for keeping it from you. As for me, I thought it would be better if we had a clean break."

"Better for who?"

Her eyes darted between mine, trying to read something in them. What, I didn't know. With a sigh, she said, "For both of us."

Shaking my head, I took another bite of pasta and said around it, "Just more bullshit. When are you going to learn that I know you better than anyone? Five years might have gone by, but I can still read you like a book."

EVIE

He could, too, and that was what I'd always been worried about, one of the many things that had kept me up at night. Because if he could read me, then surely he'd know, surely he'd find out the truth. And then how would he look at me? Would he see me differently? See me as tainted or dirty? See me as a liar or a tease? See me as someone other than Evie, *his* Evie?

I couldn't handle that. Not from him.

With everything he'd been through in the years I'd been gone, everything I'd put him through, he deserved this portion of my truth. I could give him this much. Nodding, I said, "You're right. That is bullshit." I swallowed down the unease creeping up my throat and pushed through. "I thought it'd be easier for me. I couldn't do it, couldn't move on with a new life, if I knew you were still waiting for me. And I know you would've waited. I didn't want that for either of us."

He stared at me for a long moment, calculating, always scrutinizing, and then he tipped his head in my direction. "Fair enough," he said before he took another deep pull from his beer.

And then he let the line of conversation drop, though just like he knew me, I knew him equally, and as such, I was absolutely certain this wasn't the end of that. He might not bring it up today, or tomorrow, but he'd be thinking about it. And when the time was right, he'd ask me again. It was inevitable.

"You mentioned Eric doesn't know anything about your past. How'd you manage that?"

I shrugged, relaxing back into the couch, thankful for the reprieve, for as long as it'd last. "It was easy. I studied the profile Aaron had created for me inside and out. I used it for so long, it became mine. It *was* me, despite how false it was. Instead of breaking and entering or getting in fights, I was going to gallery openings and sipping champagne because Genevieve was an art buff. Hell, I minored in Art History just to keep up the façade. I changed the way I dressed, the way I looked, the way I carried myself. Gone was the girl who scrounged for information for a living and knew how to fight; in her place was someone who got weekly manicures and tried the latest shade of lipstick. It was my new reality, and it was easier to feed that to him than to saddle him with the truth."

Riley studied me, watching me with appraising eyes. "And what's he going to say now? You don't plan to keep this from him, do you?"

"I guess it depends on how it all plays out. If I'm dead at the end of it, there won't be much point in worrying about what I'll tell him."

His shoulders went taut, his jaw clenched as tightly as his fists as he pinned me with hard eyes. "Jesus Christ, Evie. Don't say shit like that."

"Riley, I've been living like this long enough to know that tomorrow isn't a guarantee. Anything can happen from one day to the next."

"Anything can happen, except when you're with me. No one is getting to you when I'm here. *No one* is getting through me. I'd have to be dead first."

His eyes were hard, his voice strong and confident. He believed the words he said. If it came down to it, if there was a situation where my life was in danger and Riley was there to stop it, he would. At the cost of his life.

And that was exactly what I was terrified of.

RILEY

The thought of someone coming for her filled me with an all-consuming rage I hadn't felt in years, not since I'd learned of Evie's death. Not since I'd set out to keep as many corrupt businessman off the streets as I could . . . in whatever way I could. I knew it was an unconventional way of going about it—aligning myself with criminals to do some good, any bit of good I could— but it'd been all I'd known. And now that my truth had been shaken, now that I knew what actually had gone down on that boat . . . that it hadn't been a corrupt businessman to take Evie's life but the very man who I'd aligned myself with, who I worked for, it filled me with a regret so intense I nearly couldn't see past it. How doing the one thing I'd been good at—the only thing I'd ever known—was like spitting on Evie's grave.

The feelings swirling around inside were more than just the rage I felt at the idea of someone getting past me and getting to her. That very thought filled me with a terror I'd only ever known where she was concerned.

She'd always been able to bring out the purest, most undiluted reactions from me.

Evie let the conversation drop, standing up and putting her dish in the sink, tossing her empty beer bottle in the trash. Then she came and collected mine, all the while I sat, a hundred different scenarios flipping through my mind on everything that could possibly happen. Someone from the Minneapolis crew finding us, Aaron being tortured until he gave up our location, having Frankie slip in undetected and getting to Evie while I was sleeping. All of it, every instance, had my heart pounding heavily in my chest, my muscles tight with fear and anxiety. Not for me, but for her.

Always for her.

When she came back to the couch, I didn't let her sit down, instead reaching out and grabbing her wrist, tugging her to stand in front of me. She stumbled, a squeak of protest leaving her lips. She steadied herself with a hand on my shoulder, her head tipped down toward me, her brow furrowed. I could spend hours right here, just looking at her.

But right now, I needed more than to just look. I needed to *feel*. Needed to remind myself that she was okay.

I let go of her arm and reached up, gripping her hips. She'd slipped back into her tight cotton pants and a fitted long-sleeve T-shirt after taking a shower earlier, and I wanted them gone. I wanted those pants that hugged her ass so spectacularly around her ankles while they rested on my shoulders. I wanted that shirt across the loft, out of the way so I could feel her smooth skin under my hands.

I pulled her closer to me, situating her between my spread knees, and leaned forward, resting my forehead against her stomach. All that stood between me and her skin was a shirt, a thin piece of cotton, and it didn't take much at all to lift it with my thumbs, and then my lips were on her. Her skin was smooth like silk, and she smelled like heaven. I brushed my lips back and forth against her, just the barest of whispers, but she felt it. I knew she felt it, because her stomach fluttered under my touch, goose bumps covering her skin, and her hands tightened on my shoulders.

"Riley," she breathed. "What are we doing?"

I glanced up at her, meeting her hooded eyes with my own. "Exactly what we both want to."

Chapter Sixteen

She didn't say anything, didn't tell me to stop, and I couldn't help myself any longer. I leaned forward again and let my tongue taste her, licking a circle around her belly button, then trailing down to the waistband of her pants. I wanted them gone, wanted to feel every inch of her bare before me. I wanted to taste her pussy, sink inside her again, make her scream. She didn't protest when I hooked my thumbs in the waistband and tugged down enough to expose those tiny fucking shorts again, blue this time. She didn't utter a plea for me to stop when my hands kept going, pushing her pants over her hips and down her legs, didn't stop me when, once they were pooled at her feet, I went to work on her panties, shoving them down as well.

I kissed a path across her abdomen, down to her hips, getting closer and closer to the tiny strip of hair leading to her pussy. Despite having tasted her only hours ago, I wanted it again. I wanted to lie back on the couch, make her straddle my face, and lick her until she screamed. Evie had always liked to be in control in the bedroom, and I hadn't minded. Hell, what seventeen-year-old guy would? But doing that, eating her out, had been when

I'd always felt in control, even if she hadn't been the one on her back. She took what I gave her, never able to direct the speed, the movement, and I'd fucking loved it.

Now, though, I wanted something more than those tiny scraps she used to give me. In the last several years, I'd realized that while being bossed around once in a while could be hot as hell, I preferred to be the one in control. But I also knew that Evie had given me something earlier when she'd let me take her up against the wall, so I'd give something back to her. I'd do it her way this time.

Just like I knew she would, she got impatient with my teasing and yanked her shirt over her head, then leaned forward and reached for mine. I didn't put up a fight as she tugged it from me, then straddled my thighs, pressing her knees into the couch and reaching into my running pants to pull out my cock.

Letting out a groan, I dropped my head to the back of the couch and closed my eyes, resting my hands on the bare skin of her thighs. She stroked me exactly how I liked it—hard at the base, lighter over the head, her thumb sweeping the underside at every pass, and when she reached down and gripped my balls, I nearly shot off the goddamn couch.

Growling, I slid my hands up her thighs, tugging her hips toward me and lifting my head enough to capture a nipple in my mouth. She let out a moan, her stroking pausing for a moment, almost like she forgot herself. And I fucking loved that I could do that to her. Could make always-in-control Evie lose herself at my hand . . . at my mouth . . . however brief it was.

She resumed stroking my cock, then reached up with her other hand and ran her fingers through my hair, tugging it. She pulled hard enough that I eventually leaned back, letting her nipple slip from my mouth, and looked up at her. And then she crashed her mouth down on mine, her tongue licking against the seam of my lips, and I groaned as I opened to her. I gripped her ass, pulling her closer to me, feeling the heat and wetness of her pussy against my cock, and it would be so fucking easy to slip inside her. To slide her against me, tilt her hips the right way, and drive deep. And I knew if I didn't get a condom on really goddamn soon, I would, too. I'd be too far gone to stop myself.

I let her grind on me, her hips swiveling as she rocked back and forth against my erection, the head of my cock hitting her clit with each pass. She could come like this, I knew she could, and I wanted her to. I wanted to see her come undone above me before I even got inside her.

"You gonna come, baby?"

"Uh-uh." She shook her head, her eyes closed. "Want you inside me when I do."

Except I wasn't going to give up that easily. I might be surrendering a bit of control, letting her lead, but I wasn't going to bend on this. "You're going to come when I'm inside you, but gimme one first." I guided her hips harder, faster, against me and listened with anticipation as her breathing grew quicker, little moans slipping out from between her parted lips. When she was almost there, when I could tell she was on the precipice, her legs clenched tight to my sides, I leaned forward and captured her nipple between my teeth, then I tugged.

"Riley, *shit*!"

She threw her head back and moaned through her release, her movements losing rhythm as she rode out her orgasm. I'd missed seeing it, missed feeling it, and I wanted to feel it again. Wanted to feel her wrapped around me, tight as a vise grip, when she went off the next time.

While she was still breathing heavily, trying to get her bearings, I reached into my pocket and pulled out one of the condoms I'd gotten at the store earlier. As fast as my fingers would allow, I ripped open the package and covered my cock, then lifted her up, my hands under her ass. Before she'd completely caught her breath, she reached behind her, circling my erection in her hand and sliding me back and forth against her slit. Pausing at her entrance, she sank down an inch, then lifted up and repeated the torture all over again.

And this was just another thing that hadn't changed over the years. She didn't like torture or teasing . . . unless it was on her terms. Unless it was me begging for more.

I groaned at her fifth pass, making a note to return this favor the next time. Turn the tables on her and make *her* beg for more. Right now, though, all I could think about was all her heat surrounding me, and I wanted it now. "Christ, baby, sit on my cock already. Fuck me," I said, my fingers digging into her hips, forcing myself not to use my strength . . . not to use my power to do exactly what I wanted to. It would be so easy to grip her, tug her down onto me, or flip her around, lay her on the couch and pound into her, but I wanted to give her this. Wanted to give her a reminder of how it'd been between us.

How good it'd always been between us.

EVIE

Not able to torture him any longer—not able to torture *myself* any longer—I sank down onto him. I went slowly, so slowly, feeling every inch of him as he filled me up. We'd always fit together so perfectly, despite our disparities in size—disparities that had only increased in the past years, him filling out in more than just the breadth of his shoulders.

I'd never felt as full as he made me feel . . . never felt as whole, either.

"*Jesus,*" he breathed. His fingers dug into my hips, the muscles in his arms twitching with restraint. It was clear he wanted so badly to guide me, to move me how he wanted, to control the tempo, but he didn't. He sat there, head against the back of the couch, eyes at half-mast as he watched me ride him.

When he was seated fully inside me, I didn't lift myself off him and start the rhythm I knew he craved. Instead, I slid back and forth, rubbing my clit against him and reveling in the feeling of his thick length so deep inside me. God, I'd missed this. As much as I didn't want to admit it, as much as I'd tried to avoid my feelings, there was no denying it. I'd missed this . . . missed *him*.

And not a day had gone by since I'd left when I hadn't.

Finally ready to put us both out of our misery, I leaned back, braced my hands on his knees, and lifted up, riding him in long, deep strokes, lifting almost all the way off him before sliding down again. He was sprawled out, looking like he was relaxing and enjoying the show. I might've believed it, too, if it weren't for the clench of his jaw, the tautness of his shoulders and arms as he held my hips in his tight grip. It was taking a lot for him to give up the power and let me lead, and it only made me want him more. He'd always been sexy, but now . . . the guy in front of me was all man, any shadows of the boy he'd once been long since eradicated. His body was something I didn't think I'd ever get sick of looking at. Nor would I get sick of the way *he* was looking at *me*.

He stared, taking in my face, then my breasts, then focusing on where he was disappearing inside me. I tipped my head, too, looking down to watch as my body opened around him, spreading wide for the thick head of his cock, then engulfing his entire length, taking him all the way inside.

"*Fuck* . . . You feel how good we are together? How good we fit?" And then he reached forward, his open hand wide against my lower stomach and hip, his thumb pressing just above my clit. And he didn't move.

I groaned, removing one of my hands that had been braced on his knee, and reached for him, trying to move his thumb down to where I needed it. But he wouldn't budge, and when I looked at him, the smirk he sent me said more than words ever could have.

"Tell me. You feel it?" His voice was all scratchy and low, the sound shooting a wave of need straight through me, because I'd been the one to make him go all crazy with want. "You like having my cock this deep inside you?"

I did. I *loved* it. Loved every bit of us being together. How he made me feel craved and wanted and beautiful. "Yes," I breathed, closing my eyes and hoping my answer would satisfy him enough to move his thumb to where I wanted it most.

Instead, he didn't budge, just kept his hand planted right where it was. Not needing him to do a job I'd been doing for myself for a long time, I slipped my hand between my legs, just about to touch my clit, when his other hand suddenly gripped my wrist, holding me away.

"Ah ah . . ."

My eyes flew open as I gave a frustrated growl. "If you're not going to touch me, I'm going to do it myself."

"I am touching you."

"No, you're *teasing* me."

He slipped his thumb down, coming in contact with my clit for the barest second, and I relaxed, my muscles melting as I sank down on him. And then he pulled away again.

"Goddammit, Riley!"

"All you have to do is tell me what you want, baby. That's all."

"I want you to touch my clit."

He moved his thumb down, pressing against me, and held it there. I growled again, increasing my tempo as I rode him, trying to get friction against it in any way I could. "Don't be an asshole."

"You said you wanted me to touch your clit."

He was getting way too much pleasure in this game, so I stilled above him, keeping only the head of his cock inside me, and then I stared at him. He kept that smirk on his face until I reached behind me, tickling my fingers against his balls, so lightly it was barely a breath.

"Jesusfuck," he breathed, his eyes closing. "Harder."

"Rub my clit," I countered.

He opened his eyes, staring at me, both of us at a stalemate. He looked at me for what felt like hours, a challenge in his gaze, and I knew he could see the same thing reflecting back at him.

But instead of sitting still like he'd done a hundred times before when we were younger, he moved both of his hands to grip me hard on my hips, holding me in place while he lifted his hips from the couch and pumped into me. The sudden, harsh thrust against me caught me off guard, stealing my breath. Before I could catch it, he was bucking up into me at a breakneck pace, the sound of our skin slapping together mixing with my panting breaths and his rough groans.

"Fucking love your pussy . . ." he mumbled, his eyes focused on where he was disappearing inside me. And then he looked up at me, slipping one of his hands up and around my neck to pull me toward him, taking my mouth in a deep, fast kiss. Wild and reckless and utterly consuming.

It didn't take long after all the teasing for both of us to take each other exactly where we needed to go, chasing our releases until we were breathless and boneless heaps against the couch.

As I lay there, spread out on top of him, my cheek resting against his shoulder, I realized I'd never felt so comfortable with another person. Even when he'd stripped me of my power and took it for himself, he did so without making me feel weak, without making me feel threatened. And I never wanted this to end, this feeling of completion I always seemed to have when I was with him. Never wanted to have to leave him again, not when he made me feel like this. Made me feel like everything would be okay. Made me feel safe.

But I knew I didn't have a choice.

Chapter Seventeen

RILEY

It was late, the loft shrouded in darkness except for the glow coming from the TV. Once again after sex, Evie had retreated into herself, distancing herself from me, and I hated every fucking second of it. I loved being with her like that, being inside her, but I wasn't sure it was worth the aftermath every single time. Worth me having to fight my way through once again just like the first time.

Now we sat on opposite ends of the couch, pretending we were watching the TV. After nearly an hour, I'd managed to coax her legs out straight, her feet in my lap as I kneaded her arches, trying to get her to relax even further. Every once in a while, she'd glance over at me, catching me staring at her, but she wouldn't say anything, and neither would I. I also wouldn't look away, not ashamed at having been caught looking at her. I think she realized I wouldn't stop, that I liked looking at her now when I'd been denied it for so long.

And maybe that was why she didn't push, didn't tell me to stop.

The ringing of a phone sounded from her side of the couch, and Evie shifted, grabbing her cell from the pocket of her hoodie and looking down at it. She lifted her eyes to meet mine as she answered. "Hello?"

I knew without her saying a word exactly who it was. She wouldn't answer the call from anyone but Eric—as far as I knew, she didn't have anyone else in her life who'd call her anyway. And even though I'd been inside her twice over the course of the last several hours, had tasted her on my tongue, felt her pulse around me, it didn't stop the wave of jealousy from sweeping over me, nearly consuming me. It didn't matter that Eric wasn't a threat to me, that he didn't want her sexually. Because he'd lived with her for the past year, had been a part of her life when I'd thought she was dead, and I hated him for it.

Evie's body went stiff, her eyes wide as she looked at me. "When?"

The tone of her voice and her body language set me on edge, and I sat up from my reclined position, leaning forward. Despite straining toward her, I still couldn't hear his side of the conversation. Not caring what kind of breach of privacy it was, I grabbed the phone from her hand and pressed the speaker button, causing Eric's voice to fill the space.

"—call from the security company. I went back and checked the time the alarm had gone off, then watched the recorded feed of it happening. The whole house has been trashed. They didn't take anything. The TVs, electronics, jewelry, paintings—everything is still there, from what I could tell. It looked like they were digging for something specific."

My hand tightened on her foot, and I narrowed my eyes at her. There was only one conclusion about who, exactly, had broken in. That wasn't hard to figure out. But what I wanted to know was what the hell they'd been looking for, and why she hadn't told me there was something to find in the first place.

"Did you see what they looked like?" she asked, her voice tight.

"Yeah, but I don't think it's going to be much help. The footage is grainy, and the guys who did it were nondescript. Average weight, average height, average build, from what I could tell, both of them in dark clothes wearing baseball hats. Not much to go by."

She raised her eyes to me, and I knew what she was thinking.

Even with the generic description we knew exactly who'd been there.

When Evie and I had been quiet for a minute, Eric asked, "Gen? Are you still there?"

Hearing him call her a different name—the name she'd been when she wasn't mine—sent that sharp jolt of jealousy straight through me. I fucking hated that the time had been stolen from us. That she'd been stolen from me.

By the very man I'd pledged my loyalty to.

"I'm—" Her voice cracked at the brief word, and she cleared her throat and tried again, "I'm here."

Eric paused, then said, "And where is *here* exactly?" His voice was heavy with skepticism, and I knew Evie heard it as well as I did. With her eyes still connected with mine, she opened her mouth several times to respond, but nothing came out. The question was clear in her gaze: How much should she tell him? How much was enough to pacify him without telling him more than necessary?

When it was evident she wasn't going to answer, Eric filled the silence. "The security company suggested I go back and view the footage over the last several days. Just to see if any suspicious activity had happened before the break-in. Anything that would give us a clue as to who did this."

I thought about what that video no doubt showed—me grabbing Evie, our altercation, then Frankie coming into the mix and our ensuing fight. From the look on Evie's face, she was thinking the same thing.

"I haven't yet . . ." Eric said. "I haven't gone over the video, because I wanted to talk to you first." He took a deep breath, then blew it out in a slow stream. "It just seems odd that all of this would happen in such quick succession—this break-in and you going on a mysterious girls' weekend. Odd because you've never once gone on a trip anywhere since we've been together. And as far as I know, you don't have any girlfriends, none that you'd go away with." He paused and I watched as Evie held her breath. "So before I go over the feed from a few days ago, is there anything you want to tell me?"

She swallowed as she fidgeted in her lap. "Eric . . ."

If he knew Evie at all, he knew that tone. It was the tone that said she wasn't going to tell you shit, despite any pleading from your end. And with his next words, he confirmed that he knew it just as well as I did.

His voice was resigned as he said, "You know, I always knew you were keeping something from me. The entirety of our relationship . . . I've always known you weren't being completely honest. And I was willing to let that go, because it was obvious it was important to you for me not to know. I could live with that then, but now? After all this? Enough is enough. I think we've crossed a line here, don't you agree? The lies have got to stop, Gen. I need to know what's going on."

Her eyes were wide with fear, and I knew it was fear for him. For what he'd be dragged into if he knew the details of what was happening.

When she hadn't said anything for long moments, I finally spoke up. "It's better if you don't know the details."

Utter stillness radiated from his end of the line until he said, "Who the hell are you?" His voice was hard, then turned panicked when he continued, "Gen, are you still there? Are you safe? Are you hurt?"

"I'd never hurt her," I snapped at the same time Evie reached out and put a hand to my knee and said with complete sincerity, "I'm fine, Eric. But Riley's right. It's better if you don't know. It's safer."

"Safer for whom, exactly? Someone better tell me what the *hell* is going on." His voice had risen with each word until he was nearly yelling into the phone, and that shit wasn't going to fly with me. I didn't give a fuck if he was her fiancé—*fake* fiancé—or not.

"Look, man, I know you're probably pissing in your pants right now considering the shit going on and that you're across the ocean while it's all going down, so I'm going to give you a little leeway on the way you're talking to her, but if you snap at her again, this conversation is over. Understood?"

He didn't say anything, didn't respond to me, and I was about to end the call altogether when he finally said, "This him, then?" Evie's eyes widened, and without her saying a word, I knew she was trying to figure out what Eric had managed to piece together of her history despite all her lies. Before Evie could say anything, Eric blew out a laugh, the sound resigned, not taunting. "I can practically see you squirming, Gen. Don't worry, you never slipped. You never said anything, but you didn't have to. It was clear from the second you agreed to everything between us that there was something from your past you weren't telling me. Why else would a beautiful woman in her early twenties agree to this? I just assumed it was a guy. Looks like I was right."

Evie relaxed back on the cushions at the confirmation that he didn't really know anything about her past. "It's more than just a guy, Eric. And I'm sorry, but I can't tell you the details. It really is safer for you the less you know. And it's probably a good thing you're out of the country."

"What about my family? My parents . . ."

I shook my head and spoke up. "They wouldn't go after a

senator and his wife. Too high profile. They're safe. If anything changes to make me think otherwise, we'll get someone there to protect them."

Eric was quiet for a minute, then said, "Riley, is it?"

"Yeah."

"I trust you're capable of keeping her safe?"

I looked at Evie, at the girl I thought I'd lost and who, despite all circumstances, had somehow come back into my life. The girl who'd sent my world spinning at seventeen. The same one who sent it spinning at twenty-three. The girl I'd do anything for to make sure she was safe. And I said the only truth I knew: "I'd die to protect her."

Chapter Eighteen

EVIE

Riley hung up the phone with a promise to keep Eric informed as much as possible. And now his gaze was fixed on me, those eyes narrowed and questioning, and I knew why. He wanted to know what the hell they would go digging around in my house for. But more than that, I knew he'd want to know why I'd kept this from him.

If only he knew this wasn't the only thing I was keeping from him.

"What were they looking for, Evie?" His voice was low, smooth, despite the tension that sat heavily on his shoulders.

And I knew there was no point in keeping it from him any longer—not this secret.

I blew out a breath and got up from the couch, then went to grab my purse. Fumbling into the side pocket, I pulled out a zippered pouch that to anyone else would look like a makeup bag filled with various cosmetics. It was the same bag I'd carried with me all the time, no matter where I went, despite wearing very little makeup.

I walked back over to Riley with the bag and settled it into my lap when I sat down, then rummaged around inside it until I found what I needed and pulled it out.

Riley's forehead was furrowed when I handed it over to him, and he rolled the small black tube around in his fingers, flipping it forward and back, looking at it from all angles. With his eyebrows raised, he looked at me. "They're after your lipstick?"

Tipping my chin toward it, I said, "Open it."

He uncapped the top, and instead of finding the tube of color he no doubt expected, he found the end of a USB drive. Pinching the base of the lipstick case between his thumb and forefinger, he raised his eyes to mine. "What's on here?"

"All the evidence I found when Max had me dig into what Ned had done." I paused and swallowed. "Plus all the evidence I found proving it was actually Max who was stealing from Blaine, and Ned was only doing as he'd been told."

As much as I saw frustration gleaming in Riley's eyes, no doubt at the fact that I'd kept this from him, I also saw what looked like appreciation. "How old is this information?"

"I got it all right before . . . before everything happened. So five years, give or take."

"Does Max know you have this?"

"I can't imagine how. You're the first person I've ever told and the first one to see it."

He raised his hand to his jaw, the sound of his fingers scraping against his harsh stubble loud in the otherwise quiet room. "If you were Max Cavett, would you really go to all this trouble for evidence on something that had happened so long ago? On something that was buried and done?"

Furrowing my brow, I said, "I don't follow . . ."

Riley narrowed his eyes at the flash drive, then capped it again, gripping it in his fist before looking up at me, his arm propped on the back of the couch. "If you were Max and had gotten away with stealing a million dollars without being caught, would you stop after someone had—successfully, in his eyes—taken the fall? Especially when the only person who knew what you'd been doing was dead?" He fixed me with a hard stare. "Or would you keep stealing?"

I raised my eyebrows at him. "You think he's still doing it."

"I'd bet money on it."

It made sense. Max was a businessman above all else—a corrupt businessman, yes, but one who would find the most effective way to make fists of money. And stealing from someone without that person being wise to it was the quickest and easiest way for him to do so.

"He's a paranoid fucker, and given the kind of shit he's pulled in the past . . . well, it'd make sense that he thinks you have something more on him. Something other than what you'd found five years ago." He tossed the flash drive to me. "How long had he been skimming off the top when he accumulated that million?" Riley asked.

I tucked the drive back into the bag and zipped it up while I thought back to what I'd found so long ago, the information that had been burned into my brain. "Um, not quite a year. Nine months, give or take a week or two."

"So imagine how much he could've racked up in five years."

Riley stood from the couch and paced in the room, his fingers tugging at his hair. He was like a caged animal, all coiled energy, his lithe legs eating up the length of the room in five quick strides. "Maybe we've been looking at this all wrong. We've been on the defense the whole time, but maybe it's time we went on the offense."

"How do you mean?"

"Is there a way for you to dig into what Max has been doing the past five years, look for what you found last time?"

"I . . . I don't know. All the records should be computerized, so maybe. I'd need Aaron's help, though. I know where to start looking, but I'd need his hacking expertise to get me in."

Riley nodded and reached for his phone. "I'll make a call."

RILEY

I should've known Evie had some sort of evidence in her possession to pin on Max. She was smart enough to know that any bit of information she could get could potentially be used to cover her ass. And that she'd carried it with her this entire time in a fucking tube of lipstick was so ingenious, so *Evie*, I had to smile.

I walked into the kitchen, thumbing through my phone until I got to Gage's name.

"Riley," he answered after only a single ring. "Everything okay?"

"We're all right, but something's happened."

"I'm listening."

I told him about the break-in, about the evidence Evie had against Max. After letting him know our plan to see what else Max had been involved in these past years, Gage was going to get in touch with Aaron and get a laptop to us tomorrow morning. The thought of sitting idle while waiting for him, knowing Max was actively hunting Evie, had me edgy as fuck, but there wasn't anything else we could do.

After hanging up with him, I slid my phone into my front pocket. Evie hadn't moved from the couch, her jaw working back and forth as she bit at her fingernails, her gaze focused out the window.

I walked over and settled on the couch next to her. "Gage will be by in the morning with a laptop for you to use. And he's gonna get in touch with Aaron. See what he can do from his end."

She nodded, dropping her hand from her mouth and looking at me. "Good. That's good."

I reached out and wrapped my hand around her leg, running

my thumb along the smooth skin of her ankle. "We'll find something."

The look she fixed on me was so full of fear, it gutted me. Then she said, "That's what I'm afraid of. What I found the first time was enough to put a bull's-eye on my back. It was enough to send a guy to *kill* me. And now? If I find this when you and Gage and Aaron are all involved, too?" She blew out a breath and closed her eyes, shaking her head. "What's Max going to do when he realizes I have even more evidence on him? It's going to put everyone else in even more danger, just by being aligned with me."

The thing she was forgetting was that I'd stand by her, protect her till my last breath if that was what it took. "That's why we're doing it this way—on our terms. If we go after him first, he won't have a chance to come after you, because we'll already be at his fucking front door."

Chapter Nineteen

Sunlight poured into the loft, the brightness outside a contradiction to the mood within these four walls. Evie was restless, pacing back and forth in the space, while we waited for Gage.

I was in the kitchen, fixing a cup of coffee, when my phone buzzed in my pocket. I slipped it from my jeans, and after a quick glance at the screen confirming it was him, I answered. "Yeah."

"We've got movement."

I stiffened, my arm freezing as I brought the cup toward my lips, my entire body going rigid at his words. Evie noticed, her pacing having stopped once I answered the call. She moved over to stand by me, her eyes focused intently on me. I met her gaze as I asked, "By who?"

"One of the guys—not anyone high up—just asking questions. I think Max is covering all the bases, trying to get a lead on anything, and tracking down all the people who'd known Evie is where he'd start."

Setting the coffee cup on the counter, I asked, "How'd they find out where you are?"

"Anyone could find me if they looked hard enough. We never went under the radar."

Not like Evie had.

With my eyes connected with hers, I asked into the phone, "What'd you see?"

"Chuck was over by the campus when I dropped Madison off today. With all the shit that's happening, I didn't want her walking by herself. He was twitchy as fuck, not at all covert. Fumbled his way through some bullshit excuse about why he was asking about Evie."

I blew out a breath, scrubbing a hand over my face before shoving my fingers through my hair. "Fuck," I bit out, consumed with worry. Knowing I hadn't been able to protect her last time only fueled the fire currently burning up inside me. "Okay, so what do we do?" I asked.

"We wait," he said, which was the last fucking thing I wanted to do. Sitting and waiting wasn't in my nature. I was a doer, and I wanted to fix this, right the fuck now before Evie could get hurt. "We'll continue with what we talked about last night. Evie can dig for info, and let's hope she finds something. Something big that we can use against Max, because this shit isn't gonna blow over. It's only been a few days, and they've already tossed her house and sent guys out beating the streets, tracking down info."

"You still think it's a good idea for you to come this way?"

"Better than you two being out. If I'm seen, it's no big deal. I live here. Someone sees you strolling around town, and flags are gonna be raised. I'll circle around, weave in and out, make sure I'm not being followed. I'm waiting to hear back from Aaron, but I've already got the laptop. I'll be by in a couple hours."

I nodded, knowing he was right. Despite every instinct I had telling me to go out and *do* something, it was safer for everyone— safer for *her*—if we stayed put. "Sounds good. See you then."

"Later. And Ry? Keep your eyes and ears open."

The line disconnected, and it took everything in me to calmly slip my phone into my pocket. Because what I wanted to do was throw it across the room, smash it into the brick wall. I wanted to stalk out of this too-small apartment and hunt down everyone who was after her. I wanted to grab her and hold her, protect her from it all, because they were coming for her. No matter what I did, no matter how well I hid her, I wouldn't be able to keep her safe forever.

And it fucking killed me that after everything she'd already been through, she still had to deal with this shit. It was never going to end for her.

With a muffled curse, I braced my hands on the counter and hung my head. Evie's footsteps sounded behind me, then her fingers were on my back, lightly tracing, and I wanted more. I always wanted more with her.

"What happened? Are they here?" Her voice was low, resigned, and I hated that she'd already accepted this as her future.

I would do everything in my power to keep it from being so. *Everything.*

I turned around, leaning back against the counter and tugging her between my spread legs. With one finger hooked through a belt loop on her jeans, I kept her close to me. I raised my other hand and brushed her hair back from her face, pushing it behind her shoulder. She was in that oversized sweater again, the one she'd been wearing the night I'd seen her for the first time in five years. And just like that time, her shoulder was bare and so fucking taunting. All that creamy skin, so silky and smooth. I hadn't had my lips on enough of her yet.

I didn't take my eyes off the freckles that decorated her pale skin as I said, "Not Max. Some guy low in the ranks was poking around, trying to get a read on Gage. Gage thinks it was to see if he knew anything about your whereabouts."

She shivered as I brushed my thumb over her skin, ran it up the column of her neck, rested it against her pulse point which, despite the circumstances, was steady. "But Gage is still worried," she said.

"I wouldn't say worried." My brother didn't do worried. He did prepared. "He's cautious. Thinks there's a reason Max is moving so swiftly with everything and wants to make sure we have our shit together if anything goes down. How long will it take you to find something, assuming you can?"

"I . . . I don't know. It all depends on how well he's covered his tracks. If he's pulled in others to help him, or if he's still running it by himself. Maybe a couple of days?"

I stared at her, my eyes speaking everything that I wasn't prepared to say aloud yet, but the way she inclined her head to me, the softness around her eyes, told me she heard me anyway and knew as well as I did.

We might not have a couple of days.

Needing that reminder that she was here, she was safe, I wrapped my fingers around her neck and pulled her toward me. Lowering my face, I swept my mouth across hers, and I went from half hard to hard enough to pound nails when she melted right into me. She rested her hands against my chest, and a breathy little sound left her lips when she connected them with mine, her tongue licking along my bottom lip.

I dropped my hands to her ass, cupping it and hauling her up against me, letting her feel exactly what she did to me. With a moan, she tilted her head and opened her mouth to me, sliding her tongue against mine, and I wanted her. Right then.

While it had always been good between us, it'd never felt like this. I was a junkie needing a fix when it came to her now. I didn't know if the change was simply the time that had passed, how we'd both changed as people, and what that meant for the chemistry between us . . .

Or if it was something else, something more. If the fire between us sparked so brightly because we both knew how it was
without the other.

We knew exactly how much we both had to lose.

It was a couple hours later when the intercom buzzed and crack-
led, the sound breaking over the speaker by the apartment door.
Evie was on the couch, her back straight as a board as she looked
to me. After the phone call earlier from Gage, after our brief but
intense make-out session, she hadn't said much of anything in the
hours we waited, too lost in her head.

Glancing out the window, I saw it was Gage standing at the
back door, and I walked over to buzz him in. His boots thudded
up the stairs, then he knocked twice before I opened the door.

"Hey." He entered the loft, a bag slung over his shoulder, and
I shut the door behind him, locking up before following him into
the room. He tipped his chin in greeting at Evie.

"Anyone follow you?" I asked.

Gage turned around and leveled me with a stare, his eyes hard
and his jaw set. "I might've been out of this shit for months, but
I'm not a fucking idiot, Ry. Jesus." He shook his head, running
his thumb along his jaw.

I gave a nod of acknowledgment. I knew he wasn't an idiot,
but I couldn't take chances with Evie. Gesturing to the bag he
had with him, I asked, "You bring the laptop?"

"Yeah." He shrugged it off his shoulder and placed it on the
floor by Evie's feet. "I had no idea what kind of specs to get, but
hopefully you can do what you need to with it."

"Thanks," she said as she unzipped the bag and unloaded the
laptop, powering it up a second later.

Gage turned to face her fully, his arms crossed. "I know you
kept everyone in the dark because it'd be safer, but that time's
passed, Evie. We need to know what we're going up against here.

I need to see exactly what kind of dirt you have on Max so we can try to figure out our endgame."

"Well, that's just it. If—when—I find this other evidence, what then? What are we going to do with it? Knock on his door and hand it over in exchange for freedom?" She shook her head. "I don't trust him to do that, so it doesn't leave us with a whole lot of choices."

Gage glanced over at me, and I could see every unspoken word reflected back at me in his eyes. We'd do whatever it took to make sure Max couldn't threaten any of us. "Don't worry about that now. All you need to worry about is finding whatever you need, and finding it as quickly as fucking possible, because the clock's ticking faster every day. And Max isn't going to stop until he gets what he wants."

Chapter Twenty

EVIE

I'd only been running jobs for Max for a couple of months when I'd run into my first problem. By then, Riley had been going with me to every single job, making sure I had cover. At first, I'd dragged him along because I'd liked him. It'd been as simple as that. I'd wanted him around. Wanted to flirt and laugh and talk, pretend for a minute that I was a normal fifteen-year-old girl. Of course, I hadn't been a normal fifteen-year-old girl. I'd been one who made bad choices and got myself into shit situations all because I hadn't wanted to go home. But Riley had been with me nonetheless, and on that particular night, I'd been thankful for it.

It had been my hardest job to date—a dirty cop who was sliding drugs under the table to Max. The only problem was that Max found out the cop wasn't being entirely honest. Max had it on good authority that the cop was pocketing almost half of everything he got off the dealers and turning around to sell it and keep the profit for himself.

The job had looked simple enough on paper. Slip into the

cop's apartment, retrieve whatever drugs I could find, and bring them back to Max. Get in, get out, don't get caught.

And it had almost worked. Riley and I had nearly made it out in the clear, but the cop had come home early. There'd been a moment where Riley had looked at me, both of us knowing it was up to us to get out of there, because all we were to Max was two disposable kids. He'd be more upset about the lost drugs than he would about some dead low-life teenagers.

Even to this day, I wasn't under the illusion that we got out by anything other than pure luck. The cop hadn't had time to draw his weapon, and we leapt. Riley had fought dirty, had done everything he could to make sure that if we both couldn't get out, that at least I would be able to.

And that had been the first night I'd jumped into the fray, wanting to save him as much as he wanted to save me.

With the drugs stashed in my coat pockets, I'd grabbed the only weapon I could—a heavy lamp base—and swung widely, hitting the cop square in the nose. It'd been a messy blur of panting breaths, grunts, and blood—so much blood—and more of a struggle, but then Riley and I were running with everything we had, our hands clutched tightly together as we disappeared into the night, getting lost in the dark streets of the city.

Seeing him fight for me, struggle against someone bigger, someone stronger, just to make sure I'd be able to get out, to get to safety, had made me fall for him. That had been the night I'd realized the special thing between us hadn't been just teenage lust or a crush. That had been the night I'd realized I'd fallen in love with him.

And now that we were facing another situation not unlike that one, where our opponent wasn't stronger in the traditional sense but in the sense that he had a power we couldn't touch, I couldn't stop the worried ache gnawing at my gut . . .

What if we didn't get away this time?

It was well after midnight, but sleep still eluded me. After a day of talking to Aaron and both of us brainstorming, of hacking into whatever we could—and coming up with dead ends each and every time—Riley and I had finally both crashed on the bed. Since we had slept together twice, I didn't see a point in keeping up pretenses. Riley had fallen asleep quickly, no doubt exhausted from the last several days. He was on his side facing me, his arm wrapped around me while I lay staring at the ceiling, trying to figure a way out of this mess.

Riley shifted, tucking his arm farther around me and tugging me enough so he twisted me onto my side, my back against his chest. "Your thinking woke me up." His voice was scratchy and rough, heavy with sleep, and hearing it transported me back to when I was sixteen, curled up on the couch in his and Gage's apartment. My sleeping troubles had started not long before I'd met Riley, and although it'd been comforting being in his arms, it hadn't helped. Even with his warmth behind me, his arms protecting me, I'd still found it difficult to sleep. Except at that time, what had kept me awake was something altogether different from what was causing my insomnia now. Something equally terrifying—at least to me—but something that hadn't affected anyone but me.

Riley gripped my hip, his thumb slipping under the cotton of my tank top and rubbing a soothing circle against my stomach. Pressing his nose to my hair, he inhaled deeply, then moved the loose strands out of the way so he could brush his lips against my shoulder. "You okay?"

And, really, what could I tell him? No, I wasn't okay. I hadn't been okay for a very, very long time, and now I didn't see how I ever would be again. I didn't see how I could possibly get out of this alive, but more than that, the fact that I didn't see how the people I loved would get out of it alive was what truly terrified me.

Mustering up as much sincerity as I could, I said, "Just couldn't sleep."

Riley didn't say anything in response, and just when I thought he'd call me on my lie—because I had no doubt he knew I was lying—he pressed his hand flat against my stomach and pulled me back to him, curling around my body. "I could probably do something to help you with that . . ."

He didn't wait for me to respond before slipping his hand completely under my tank and reaching up to cup one of my breasts, his thumb whispering a circle around my nipple. And I knew this wouldn't help anything, just like it hadn't any other time we'd slept together. But it'd let me get lost for a bit, allow me to feel something other than hopelessness and the fear that had been eating me alive for so much longer than just the past five years.

I shifted, tilting my hips so my ass rubbed his cock. He was hard already, his length pressing against me, and I reached back and slipped my hand into his boxers. I gripped him, ran my thumb over the silky smoothness of his thick head, down the length of his cock, and gave him a couple quick pumps.

His answering groan echoed into my ear, his lips resting against the shell, his seeking fingers pausing on my breast while I tried to drive him out of his mind with teasing strokes. And though this wouldn't solve anything, wouldn't get me any closer to the end of this mess, it would give me back something I'd had stolen from me so long ago. Something I craved with every ounce of myself.

Power.

I loved it, needed it. And here, in the bedroom, had been the one and only place I'd gotten it on my terms. That control in knowing I was the one calling the shots, that I was able to lead us however I wanted. Knowing, too, I was the one who could make it stop in the blink of an eye.

And knowing, beyond anything, that Riley would stop. Without question, without pressure or groaning or coercion, he'd stop. And that gave me the freedom to keep going.

"Touch me," I whispered, reaching up with my other hand and guiding his lower, down to where I was already getting wet for him. He took my plea, slipping his hand into the front of my boy shorts and not stopping until he came in contact with my clit. Before being with Riley again, I'd forgotten how good it felt to be touched by someone who knew my body almost as well as I knew it myself. Who knew how fast I liked to be stroked, what parts I liked to have focused on, the exact rhythm I needed to get off.

And Riley was an expert at playing my body.

He propped his elbow on the bed, lifting himself and leaning over me, bending down to steal a kiss while the hand he had in my panties drove me crazy. He didn't play, didn't tease or draw out the torture. He traced his fingers down my slit, slipped one inside me, and then slid it back up, stroking the wetness around my clit. I moaned, squeezing his cock harder in my hand, and I wanted to make him go as weak as he always seemed to make me. I wanted to make him drop to his knees and beg for more.

RILEY

Her hands were like heaven, stroking me, her thumb playing with the head of my cock, and I wanted so badly to pin her to the bed and drive inside her. Hook her knees over my arms or prop her ankles on my shoulders and fuck her until she screamed. Make us both see stars.

Before I could do just that, she rolled over and placed a hand on my bare chest, guiding me onto my back. And when she slid down my body, pulling my boxers off before she wrapped her fist around my cock and licked a line straight up my length, I certainly wasn't going to say no to a blow job, especially from her.

"Christ," I groaned, my head falling back to the pillow, pressing into it while I squeezed my eyes shut. She licked the head of my cock, swirling her tongue around it a dozen times, before she engulfed it in her mouth, sucking on just the tip while she pumped my shaft with her fist.

I reached out for her, gathering her hair in my hands and holding it away from her face so I could watch her lips stretch around the head of my cock. As much as everything else with her was familiar, especially sex, all it took was the simple act of holding her hair back to remind me that everything *wasn't* familiar.

While the way she was swirling her tongue around me and the rhythm of her strokes were both things I remembered intimately, the mass of hair I held in my fist was so at odds with the memories I had. Before, her hair had always been short. Blunt styles that I'd loved because it made her look like the badass girl she was, the girl who took no prisoners, who got what she wanted, when she wanted it. But Evie now? She was such a contradiction—her innocent-looking face dotted with freckles combined with her bombshell body, her fiery red hair—and I loved that I knew who she was behind the illusions of her outward appearance. I loved that she looked like nothing more than a pretty girl to others, but she could drop you in thirty seconds. I loved that she knew how to fight, how to take care of herself. That she could get any bit of information out of just about anyone, knew all the tricky ways to get what she wanted, and wasn't afraid to do so.

I knew what she was like behind closed doors, behind that mask she put on for the world. Only me, and I fucking loved it.

Evie flicked her tongue against the underside of my cock, then blew a gust of cold air against it, and I wanted back inside. I wanted to feel the warm wetness of her perfect little mouth, wanted to feel her tongue massaging my shaft. Gripping her hair just tight enough that she lifted her eyes to mine, I said, "Open up. Take me inside again." My voice was scratchy and low, and when she didn't acknowledge me, I thought she didn't hear.

But then she gave me a wicked smile, the corner of her mouth lifting before she drew out the torture even longer. She drifted her lips up and down the length of my cock, her tongue fluttering and teasing, her fingers stroking my balls, but she wouldn't give me the hot suction of her mouth.

"Evie." Sitting up, I propped myself on one of my elbows while holding her hair back in my other hand. "Give me your mouth." I guided her up my shaft until her lips were poised over the tip of my cock and applied pressure to the back of her head. She opened her mouth against me, but instead of engulfing me like I wanted, she let her teeth drag over the head, and I hissed out a curse.

As much as I wanted her mouth on me, wanted her to go exactly where I directed her, I couldn't deny that this power play between us was hot as hell. Part of the reason I loved Evie was because she didn't take shit from anyone. She stood up for what she wanted and wasn't afraid to take control. The thought that she was my equal in every way only made me hotter for her.

I looked down my body at her, seeing that mass of red hair fisted in my hand, her lips pink and wet and waiting for me. And then she was doing exactly what I wanted, surrounding me with her mouth and sucking me inside. And seeing her lips spread wide around me, taking all of me in, made my cock jerk inside her mouth.

"Fuck," I breathed. "Your mouth is so good . . . so good."

She glanced at me then, her eyes connecting with mine, and Jesus Christ, I'd missed this.

Evie and I clicked, meshed together perfectly, and that had been obvious even as young as we'd been. And despite the time apart, despite the years between us, it wasn't something either of us could deny now.

She pulled her mouth off my cock, flicking out her tongue to tease the underside, and I groaned out a low breath, loving that she still knew how to tease my body, get me worked up so fucking much I couldn't wait to bury myself inside her.

I let her hair fall from my grasp as she pulled away and sat up on her knees, removing the rest of her clothes. And then she crawled up my body, kissing my chest, my neck, slipping her tongue inside my mouth. I gripped her face as she settled on top of me, her knees on either side of my hips. She was so wet, she slid with ease against my cock, and as much as I wanted to reach down and grip my cock, guide myself into her, I didn't. I wanted to see how far she'd go, how long she'd tease us both before finally giving in, knowing the payoff would be all the better for both of us when I finally sank deep inside her.

When she shifted forward, crawling farther up my body, I groaned, wrapping my arms around her thighs as she put her knees on either side of my head. And then I leaned up, licking a straight line up her slit, and pulled her down onto my mouth, sucking her clit between my lips.

She rocked against my face, pressing one hand to the brick wall behind the bed while the other clutched my hair, holding me to her. I ran my hands along the outside of her thighs, over her hips, then clutched her waist before sliding them up to cup her tits, pinching her nipples and tugging. When she ground her pussy harder against my mouth in response, I couldn't stop my groan from reverberating on her. Stroking her with my tongue the way I knew she liked, I lifted my eyes to see her. She was staring down at me, her mouth open, her eyes fuzzy and hazed, but in them I saw everything I'd been feeling. There was no doubting that connection between us in the way she was looking at me.

That connection between us that hadn't ever gone away.

Before I could get her off, make her come on my tongue, she pulled back, breathing hard as she slid down my body until she hovered over my throbbing cock. She reached over to the make-shift nightstand and blindly felt around until she came up with a condom. It seemed like a blink later that she'd rolled it down my length, then she was poised over me and sinking down until our bodies were flush together.

I groaned, wrapping my fingers around her hips, digging them into her flesh. "Jesus Christ, you feel so fucking good."

She leaned forward, resting her face close to mine. She didn't kiss me, didn't trace my lips with her tongue, just leaned so close we were sharing breaths while she rocked over me, while she took me inside her over and over and over again. Needing more, I reached up with one hand and wrapped my fingers around the base of her head, delving into her thick hair, and pulled her against me. Closing my eyes, I kissed her, slipping my tongue against hers and groaning at how good it all felt. Being inside her body, as close to her as I could possibly get.

She pulled back and sat up, taking me all the way inside her, and swiveled her hips, and I thought I'd die. Right there under her, staring up into her face as she drove me out of my fucking mind.

"Jesus, baby." It was hardly more than a whisper, my voice ragged and rough as I closed my eyes against the feel of her surrounding me.

When I blinked my eyes open, she was staring down at me, her hair a curtain around us, making it feel like we were the only two people on earth. I looked up into her eyes, seeing the undeniable connection we had reflected back, and I wanted to stay like this forever. Because when she was here like this, I knew she was safe. And I would do anything to make sure she always was.

EVIE

Riley hadn't been my first partner. Not my second, either. And since my time with him in high school, there had been many others who'd come and gone, mostly nameless, faceless men, but they were there. And while there had been a physical connection, there had never been this all-consuming fire that was always there with me and Riley.

It felt exhilarating and terrifying and freeing, and I didn't know which worried me the most. As much as I wanted to let myself fall into him, into his arms and his smile and his safe harbor, I couldn't. I couldn't let myself get caught up in him, in us, and forget what was chasing me.

Riley reached up, brushing my hair back over my shoulder, and wrapped his fingers around my neck. He slid his thumb along my jawline, and I could barely look into his eyes. Couldn't look away, though, either. I could see everything he was feeling reflecting back at me—the fear for me, the honesty of this connection between us . . . the heartbreak at all the time we'd lost.

And I hated that we'd lost it at all, when in the end, it hadn't mattered. One of the reasons I'd run in the first place was so he could be safe. And now he was here, right in the middle of exactly what I'd tried to keep him out of.

The knowledge that he was still involved with everything, wrapped up in the business that had cost me my life, filled me with so much anger and resentment. I wanted better for him, but more than that, I wanted *him* to want so much better for himself.

"Evie . . . baby . . ." His voice was rough, breathless, and I leaned down and pressed my lips to his. While his tongue slid across mine, I rocked over him, bringing us both closer to the peak. "Fuck, I'm so close," he ground out through clenched teeth, pumping up into me with sure strokes, his hands gripping me, holding me exactly where he wanted me to be. And when he brought one of his hands down, slipping it between us and circling his thumb around my clit as I slid forward and back against him, I couldn't hold back anymore.

At Riley's groan, his body tightening under mine, I came,

head tossed back, body thrumming and pulsing and collapsing against him. His breath was harsh, ragged in my ear, mumbling about how good it felt, how good it always felt with me.

It was little consolation that we felt the same. Little comfort in the fact that while I was thinking about how amazing it always was with him, he was thinking the same thing.

Because there was only one thought that still weighed on my shoulders, one thought echoing in my mind, even while he was inside me . . .

How little time we had left.

Chapter Twenty-One

RILEY

By the time I got up the next morning, Evie was already awake, sitting on the couch and bent over the laptop. I rolled out of the bed and walked over to her, leaning over the back of the couch to peer down at what she was looking at.

"Morning." I bent toward her, pressing my face into her neck and inhaling. Citrus and flowers filled my nose, and I closed my eyes at all the memories that came rushing to me, memories that transported me right back to being eighteen again. Even after five years, she still smelled exactly how I remembered.

"Hey," she mumbled, her fingers constantly moving on the keyboard, her focus intent on the screen in front of her.

"When'd you get up?"

"Hmmm?" she answered distractedly. "Oh, I, um . . ." She trailed off, leaning closer to the screen to read something before swearing under her breath and leaning back. "I didn't sleep very well. I've been up since around five."

"You haven't slept good for days. I guess I need to work harder to wear you out."

She turned her head back to smile at me, but she was distracted, her gaze flitting right back to the computer.

"You find anything?"

"Um . . . maybe . . ." She flew through the data on the screen, switching programs and scrolling through everything faster than I could even comprehend what she was looking at in the first place.

Raising my eyebrows, I asked, "What do you mean, *maybe*?" Maybe was better than nothing, and after all day yesterday of nothing but dead end after dead end, I'd take a maybe.

She pressed a couple keys on the keyboard, then turned her head toward me. "I found a tiny error in the records, so I'm digging into it further, seeing if it leads us to anything." Moving her attention back to the laptop, she started going through the information again. "It's gotta be in here somewhere . . . I know it . . ." She brought her hand up to her mouth, biting on her thumbnail as she searched through Max's accounting records. I had no idea how they'd gotten access to them in the first place, but I wasn't going to ask. Aaron could do just about anything with a computer, and Evie was a fast learner.

Not wanting to distract her, I headed into the kitchen. As I was pouring a cup of coffee, the sound of my cell phone ringing filled the loft. Evie must've had it by her on the couch. She answered it on speakerphone, and Aaron's voice came across the line. "Hey, you find anything?" he asked.

"Yeah, actually. There's a small discrepancy and I'm following that, hoping it leads to what we're looking for. What about you?"

"Not a goddamn thing."

I grabbed my coffee and headed to the couch, sitting down beside her as she rambled on to Aaron about the error she'd managed to uncover. When Evie said, "Holy *shit*," I knew she'd found something.

"What?" I asked, leaning closer.

She was reading from the screen, talking to Aaron and me at

the same time. "Do you see it? All those transfers to Ipsum Technology?"

Aaron hummed on the other end until suddenly he said, "Got it." There was a pause, the sound of keys clacking on his end, then he breathed out a curse. "That company has generic information online, a static front page with nothing else. Probably enough to fool most people who randomly come across it, but what supposed multimillion-dollar company doesn't even have a contact page?"

"It's a front," Evie said.

"That's my guess. Have you added up all the deposits? How far back does it go?"

"I'm tracing it back now and doing the figures," she mumbled as her fingers flew over the number keys, adding up the data she'd found. When she suddenly stopped, I looked over at her, and she was staring at the screen, her mouth open. She turned to me, her eyes wide. "He's been doing it the whole time, skimming in frequent small amounts."

"What's the total?" I asked.

She huffed out a laugh and shook her head, glancing back at the screen. "Twelve point seven million."

"Holy fuck," I said, leaning toward her and seeing the numbers right there in front of me.

"We've finally got the bastard." She relaxed back into the couch cushions, running a hand through her hair. "I can't believe we got him."

"Nice work, Evie," Aaron said.

"Yeah, well, it's not over yet." Evie's relaxed posture disappeared as she leaned toward the phone again, her eyes back on the computer screen. "Not even close. Now we need to figure out what the hell we're going to do with the information. Knowing it and using it to get Max to back off are two different things."

"Well, whatever you do, you need to do it fast," Aaron said. "I was calling this morning for more than just this."

Aaron's voice had gone hard, all business, and I straightened up. "Why, what's happening there?" Even as I asked, I thought about what it'd be like for us if we didn't have someone willing to work both sides like Aaron was. If we didn't have someone there who still had access inside the crew, who had the rank and the expertise—who had the trust of Max to be in on everything he was doing, all the directives he was handing out. Aaron was instrumental in every step we'd taken, from the very first one letting me know Evie had been in trouble until now. I had no idea where we'd be without him.

"Max is having Jade make a visit to Evie's parents."

She stiffened beside me, her back going rigid, every inch of her body freezing at Aaron's words.

"When?" I asked.

"Today . . . later this afternoon."

"Why? What's her directive?"

"Just recon right now. He wants Jade to get a feel for what they know about Evie, *if* they know anything."

"They don't," Evie finally said, her voice hard. "They don't, and they're not going to."

I glanced over at her, remembering how adamant she'd been when we'd first gotten here that they were never to know she was still alive. "Evie . . . Maybe we need to contact them. Warn them what's coming."

"No," she snapped.

Before I could ask her more about it, Aaron cut in. "I have to agree with her, Kid. At least for right now. Jade is just going to get information, posing as an old friend of Evie's, so they shouldn't think anything's up. Not yet, anyway."

Blowing out a breath, I tugged at my hair. "Well, yeah, that's fine for now, but what about when Max gets desperate? I think we should be prepared to warn them."

Evie stood from the couch and spun around so she was facing me, her eyes narrowed. "No one is warning them. None of you are speaking to them, period."

"Evie, I'm not talking about now. I'm talking about when shit starts getting real. When we think Max might go after them just to flush you out."

"Then let him go after them." Her voice was so chilling, so cold, I barely recognized it.

I stared at her, at her set jaw, her rigid shoulders, the clench of her fists, the hard look in her eyes. Shaking my head, I said, "Think about what you're saying . . ."

She didn't even pause as she said, "I don't need to think about it. I've thought about it a hundred times—a *thousand* times over the past five years. No one is going to call and tell them anything, at any time. *Ever,* no matter the circumstances. As far as they know, I died five years ago, and I'm going to stay dead to them. Is that clear to you both?"

"Evie . . ."

"I said *no,* Riley. Now fucking *drop it.*"

EVIE

I stormed into the bathroom, slamming the door behind me, breathing a sigh of relief as I leaned back against it. Thankful that in this loft that had little to no privacy, I at least had this. This small piece of solitude.

And I needed it.

I'd do just about anything to keep Riley from seeing me like this, from seeing me break down. Seeing me crumble. And I knew it was coming, could feel it lurking under my skin, bubbling up until it had nowhere to go but out. I couldn't predict how the flashbacks would come to me. If they'd blindside me during the day, sneak up on me while I was doing something menial and transport me back to the place I never wanted to go. Or if they'd come to me in my sleep, like they so often did. After fighting sleep for so long,

I'd eventually have to succumb to it, and then I was helpless to stop them. And those were the worst ones, when they came to me in my dreams. Because it was like living it all over again . . .

Even though I'd known Riley around the time that everything had changed, it had started happening several months before I'd met him, and he'd never known anything about it. Why I had trouble sleeping. Why I didn't like to be snuck up on. Why I hated bear hugs. Why I liked being in control. He didn't know the reason for any of it. And he'd never questioned it.

He'd known something was off, of course. He would've had to have been blind not to, especially since after we started hooking up, I stayed with him most nights. Anything to escape. The nightmares had been worse back then, near nightly, and I'd been lucky Riley had been a heavy sleeper, unaware of the torment my mind caused me. I could never predict when they'd come on. They were always awful, though, making me a victim all over again, only at that time, when it'd be my dreams holding me hostage, it was my mind to which I'd become a victim, and I hated that I'd had that stolen from me, too.

While I'd never had an idealistic childhood, the kind with Sunday mornings in bed reading the paper and birthday parties in a backyard surrounded by a white picket fence, what I had experienced had been okay. Not great, but okay.

We'd never been very well-off, both my parents working full-time and picking up extra shifts whenever they could in hopes of getting even a little bit ahead. And while initially they had tried to keep it from me, I'd always known we lived paycheck to paycheck. But it had been fine. It'd been a struggle sometimes, sure, embarrassing when I'd have friends over and we didn't have any food in the house or our cable had been shut off because the bill hadn't been paid. But even with the embarrassment, it had been fine.

Until suddenly it wasn't.

Until suddenly the walls felt too close, the rooms too small, the scents and sounds and looks all too much, and I never wanted to be home. Did everything in my power so I wouldn't have to be.

I couldn't even pinpoint one specific thing, because suddenly it was like an avalanche of shit was falling on us, falling on *me*, and I was drowning under it all. I'd started high school, a different one than most of my friends. My dad had lost his job, gotten laid off after seventeen years at the same company. And my mom had to switch to third shift for the higher pay, just so we could afford to stay in our small, shitty house and be able to buy groceries.

It was like one week everything had been normal—not great, not particularly picturesque, but normal for us. And then the next, I was skipping school and getting involved with the crew just so I'd have a place to go, something to do so I wouldn't have to go home.

What I hadn't anticipated finding was the power trip I'd gotten with every job Max had sent me on. And I definitely hadn't anticipated that I'd eventually come to crave that power.

Crave the power that had been stripped from me in the months prior.

It had been the worst time of my life, the dozens of months that shaped the very person I was today, and I hated that I'd let that time mold me, but how could I not? Every decision I'd made, every path I'd taken, had been a direct result of that.

The only good thing that had come out of that time was that I'd met Riley. He'd come into my life, slipped into the dark places casting shadows over me, and been a tiny bit of light. A sunburst on my gray days.

But it was always tainted, because no matter how good Riley made me feel, how safe and secure, how in control, it had always come crashing down when I'd been away from him. When I'd had no choice but to go home. Go back to my house, to the place where my dreams turned into nightmares.

Chapter Twenty-Two

RILEY

By the time Evie came out of the bathroom, I'd long since hung up with Aaron, telling him we'd be in touch later to figure out how we wanted to proceed. And that, for now, to let Jade go to Evie's parents as planned. I'd follow Evie's wishes for the time being, but she was going to tell me what the fuck was going on.

As her footsteps came closer, I asked, "What was that all about?"

Except when she came around the front of the couch to face me, she didn't answer. Instead, she unzipped her hoodie and tossed it on the couch. I raised my eyebrows as she undressed in front of me, slipping off her pants and throwing them next to her sweatshirt, until she was standing there in the outfit that had filled my dreams for three nights now—a thin tank top and those tiny shorts. As sexy as it was, though, I couldn't concentrate on what she was offering, too focused on what the hell was going on with her.

I blew out a sigh and reached up, scratching my jaw. "Look, I get that you're hoping for a distraction, and, baby, you know

I will give it to you. A hundred times. Fucking you isn't exactly a hardship. But before I do, I wanna know why the hell you're so pissed, what it is you're trying to ignore."

"Get up," she said. Ordered, really.

Huffing out a laugh, I just stared at her, thinking she couldn't be serious with this shit.

"Now, Riley. Get up."

It was obvious she was itching for a fight, and after seeing her strip down to next to nothing, it was clear she wanted to spar to work off some of that energy. I stood from the couch, reached back, and tugged my shirt over my head, leaving my running pants on. "Fine. But we're going to talk about this. As soon as you get this out of your system, you're going to tell me what the hell is going on."

She didn't give me any warning, no tell on her face, before she came at me with jabs and kicks, everything in quick succession. It was challenging to keep up with her, her smaller size giving her an advantage, but she still didn't have my strength or my years of training. Despite the fact that she wasn't holding back, I made sure to keep myself in check, giving her enough leeway that she could get this out of her system without getting hurt in the process.

When she came at me with a roundhouse kick to the side— one I barely dodged—I progressed on her, forcing her to move back. "Now you're just pissing me off. Quit trying to attack me, and tell me what the fuck is going on."

She didn't answer in anything but more jabs and kicks, and this time, when she went for a roundhouse kick again, I knew it was coming and dodged it, then spun and grabbed her arm, pulling it behind her as I gripped her with my other arm and held her to my chest, both her arms pinned to her sides. "What the fuck has you so worked up?"

Without answering, she dropped her weight, throwing me off

balance and allowing her room to wiggle from my grasp—the exact move I taught her to get free. The aggression in her face wasn't any less, and I didn't let her get very far before I took the opening she wasn't even aware she gave me and pinned her face-first to the wall, much like I had at her house. We were both breathing heavily, my chest brushing along her back with each inhale, and I used this time to take stock of my body. My ribs ached, my shins, too. She'd managed to get in a few solid kicks. I'd be sore as hell tomorrow. All in all, a great sparring session. If she wasn't pissed as hell and taking that out on me.

"Have you had enough?" I asked in her ear.

EVIE

How could I answer him? I'd thought sparring would help. Feeling that rush of power when I'd gotten out of one of Riley's holds, when I'd managed to surprise him, but it hadn't helped. It hadn't been enough. This need I felt . . . this compulsion to get the control I craved, hadn't yet been satisfied.

And I only knew one way I could rectify that.

Before Riley could ask again, I stood on my tiptoes and pressed my mouth to his, tugging his lip with my teeth. He groaned, easing off me so I could turn, and then his hands were cupping my face, the kiss clumsy and harsh and bruising, and I didn't care. I scratched my nails down his chest, digging into his skin, leaving stripes of red along the way. I wanted to mark him up, remind him—remind myself—that I was the one doing it. That I had the power to.

Riley met me every step of the way, giving back as good as he got, his teeth nipping my lips, his fingers digging into my ass, and I loved it.

"You want it rough?" he asked against my mouth, hauling me up against him and grinding his erection into me. "Is that what this is about? You want me to fuck you hard?"

No. I wanted to fuck *him* hard. I wanted it faster. Rougher. More intense.

I wanted something more than what I had now because it wasn't helping. I needed something, anything, so I could feel in control again. So this helplessness wouldn't eat me alive.

Pressing my hands to his bare chest, I pushed, forcing him backward until his knees hit the couch and he toppled down. He reached out and grabbed my wrist, yanking me down next to him, and then he rolled, pinning me between the arm of the couch and his body. And even though I wasn't really trapped, even though I could easily slip out, that panic inched its way up my chest, cold fingers grappling at my throat. I had to close my eyes and remind myself that this was okay. Everything was okay.

This was Riley. It was just Riley.

And I wanted it. I wanted *him*.

I thought—hoped—that would be enough. That it'd be like the other times I'd felt like this, when I'd been able to gain control and let my memories slip down deep where they belonged. Except it wasn't like every other time, because when he leaned into me, the hard ridges of his body pushing down along mine, pressing me into the arm of the couch, it wasn't his body I felt. It was another one instead. And even though Riley wasn't pinning me until I couldn't move, my mind conjured up the last time I had been pinned down, held in place. Held there so I couldn't struggle . . . couldn't even move.

And I tried so hard to stay present. Did everything I could think of to try and stay in the moment. I breathed through it, pushing back that panic creeping up my spine, but it didn't help. No matter how many times I said it in my mind, how many times I breathed in Riley's scent, knowing it wasn't stale smoke and spicy cologne, that it wasn't the scent that could still manage to make me sick, it didn't matter. None of it mattered because I felt the memory of someone else's hands on my stomach, on my breasts. Someone else's lips on my mouth, my neck, my chest.

Clenching my eyes shut, I repeated to myself a hundred times that this was Riley. This was Riley and this was my choice and everything was fine. But my body and brain weren't communicating, and despite the words repeating over and over in my head, I couldn't stop the images of so long ago from coming back to me. Bombarding me. *Consuming* me. And with each flash in my mind, my breathing got faster. Harsher. Until Riley finally noticed, pulling back.

"Evie?"

"No . . ." I choked out, mangling the single syllable, and then I couldn't manage any words at all. I pressed against his chest with feeble hands, my breaths coming in gasps. Riley's eyes got wide and he pulled back, but it was too late. Even though he wasn't against me anymore, that didn't stop what I knew was coming.

My throat closed up, my chest tightening, and I couldn't get in enough air. Waves of panic rushed over my body, my skin prickling with heat. Riley was talking, but I couldn't understand his words, could only hear the cadence of his voice. I couldn't swallow, couldn't breathe, couldn't control the chattering of my teeth despite my body burning up, and all I could think about, all I could remember was the last time.

All I ever remembered was the last time.

In my tiny little box of a room, no space to move even with only a single twin bed in it. Quiet and pitch-black, always dark. Scratchy sheets under my skin, my throat raw and sore from sobbing, from screaming, and then there was always that feeling of weakness. Complete and utter helplessness. That no matter how hard I struggled, how much I thrashed, how loud I screamed, it wouldn't matter. No one would hear me. No one would come. He'd overpower me anyway.

He always did.

"Baby, *breathe*. Follow what I do. Listen to me, Evie. Listen to my breaths. In and out, in and out. Come on."

I blinked away the memories, the rushing heartbeat in my ears finally receding enough that I could try and focus on not just Riley's voice but also the words he was saying. He was squatting in front of me, his hand a gentle pressure on my back as he murmured bits of encouragement, and I wanted to break down. Right there, on this couch that wasn't mine with a man who wasn't mine, either, I wanted to cry. I'd never allowed myself that, not after I'd left. After I'd run all those years ago, I hadn't broken down. Not once. But now? I wanted to release it all, get rid of it once and for all, because I was so sick of letting it have this hold over me. After so many years, I was still letting this rule my life.

Letting *him* rule my life.

"Listen to my voice, okay? Just focus on me. That's it. When I used to get these as a kid, Gage would talk me out of them. Tell me stupid stories that I don't even remember, but just focusing on his voice, listening to him helped. I want you to do that, okay?"

With the barest move of my head, I nodded, keeping my eyes closed and trying desperately to focus on him, on his words, even through the wheezing rasps of my breaths that echoed as loud as a bullhorn in my ears.

"Did I ever tell you about the first time I saw you?" He laughed, a breathless, self-deprecating sound. "No, I probably wouldn't have, because it'd make me sound like a pussy. I'd seen you in school a couple times, just in the hall, and even before I knew anything about you, I was curious. You were hot as hell and so unapproachable with this . . . fuck-everything-and-everyone attitude. And then one day after school, I went to meet up with my brother, and there you were. Standing over by him and Aaron and the rest of the guys their age, and I hated it. I was pissed as hell that you were already around him, especially when I saw you first. And back then everyone called me Kid, and I'd thought I was fucked. But then you'd looked at me, smiled that smile I love so much—the one where your dimple pops up. Did you know your beauty mark disappears in it when you smile like that?"

As I listened to the soft cadence of his voice and focused on his words, the buzzing in my ears lessened, the awful, crushing weight on my chest easing enough so I could think back to the day he was talking about. The first day I'd followed a sort of friend there, the first day I'd stepped into that life. And hearing it from Riley's perspective was so different from how I remembered it. I wanted to tell him I'd felt like a complete poseur, fumbling my way through shit I had no business being involved in. That I'd thought at any second, someone would call me out for being fake, and that would be it, but I couldn't get my voice to work, couldn't talk past the anxiety still gripping my throat.

"But then you came back the next day and then the next and the next, and it was like I'd won the fucking lottery. But of course I didn't do anything about it. I thought you liked Gage, because you were always hanging around him, but then you asked me to come with you on your first job, and that was it. I was gone. You had me wrapped around your finger from that moment on. I probably shouldn't tell you that—give you more ammunition against me—but there's not really a point in denying it."

Riley didn't stop. He never let up, hardly took a moment to even breathe, it seemed like, as he kept talking about the days back in high school, those early months when we'd first started seeing each other. And through everything, I listened with my eyes closed. Through every story, every memory, I tried to control my breaths, matching each inhale and exhale to the slow circle of his hand on my back, and eventually that tightness in my chest lightened until I could drag in lungfuls of air without struggle. I focused on his words and forgot about everything else. Eventually, my teeth stopped chattering, the cold sweats that had swept over my body passed, and I was left with this overwhelming relief that it was over. That I could breathe again.

And then I was consumed with the shame of having had one in the first place.

I hated these, fucking *hated* that I was reduced to that same weak little girl every time a panic attack came up. That I was transported right back to my childhood bedroom, that even after seven years and hundreds of miles, I still couldn't manage to escape.

Just like always, after the terror passed, I got pissed. At myself, always at myself more than anything—or anyone. Frustrated and angry that I was still chained to this. That even after all this time, there were still shackles on my ankles, chaining me to a life I didn't want to live anymore. Chaining me to memories I wanted to leave forever in the past.

But I knew there was nowhere else for my memories to go. The only way they could manifest, the only way I allowed them to, was in flashbacks and panic attacks. Because I refused to share them, refused to tell anyone anything. It was something I had to keep with me, something I needed to keep inside me, not ever letting it escape.

Because what if I told and someone didn't believe me? I couldn't go through that. Not again.

"There . . . that's it, that's better." Riley heaved a deep sigh, still squatting in front of me, then ducked his head even farther, leaning forward so he was in my line of sight. "You feel better?"

I breathed out an acknowledgment, a squeak of a response, one I hoped he'd take as a yes.

The hand he had resting on my back still rubbed in soft circles, and I realized that this was the shortest attack I'd ever had. Thanks to his touch and his voice and *him*.

"Was that your first panic attack?" he asked.

Not trusting my voice yet, I just shook my head. I couldn't even maintain eye contact with him, too embarrassed at everything that had been unearthed in my mind. Almost as if I was terrified he'd be able to read my thoughts, see the memories that had caused the panic attack, and that urge to push it back, bury it again, was strong.

He wrapped his hand around mine, running his thumb along my wrist. His voice was low, tentative, when he asked, "Was it me? Did I do something?" He swallowed, then asked in a pained voice, "Was I too rough?"

My throat was dry, and no matter how many times I swallowed, I couldn't impart any moisture into my mouth. Still, I croaked, "It wasn't you." It was such a small offering in comparison to everything he'd done for me, but it was all I had.

I wanted to tell him that it wasn't him, it was *me*. It was my fucked-up childhood and a maelstrom of memories that held me hostage—memories that would never let me go unless I did the same.

And I wanted so badly to be strong enough to open my mouth and say the words. Finally say the words that had strangled me for so long.

Maybe, soon, I would be.

Chapter Twenty-Three

RILEY

The loft was still dark when I jolted awake, a sound startling me to consciousness. I tensed, ready for a fight, so desperately afraid Max had found us, but when I listened, I realized the noises were coming from Evie. After her panic attack, she'd asked to be alone—or as alone as she could be in the loft. So I'd let her take the bed, curled up on her side, her eyes glassy and far away, while I'd settled on the couch ten feet away, my body tight and coiled with the overwhelming urge to go to her. To help her. Hold her and talk to her and beg her to tell me what was going on. Protect her like I hadn't been able to protect her five years ago.

I sat up, glancing over the back of the couch and letting my eyes adjust to the darkness. She was on the bed, the covers twisted around her legs. Her head was thrashing back and forth on the pillow, muffled protests leaving her lips. The words spilling from her mouth were unintelligible, but they didn't need to be comprehensible for me to know she was having a nightmare. The sheer terror was coming off her in waves.

I didn't know if this was par for the course for her after a panic attack, if this was something she dealt with all the time. If the attacks had started after she'd left, when she'd moved and changed her name, when she'd first run from Max. I didn't know anything other than the fact that the one last night hadn't been her first.

I pushed off the couch and walked over to her, moving to stand at the side of the bed. Her hair was sprawled out on the pillow, a tangled mess, some strands covering her face, a few caught on her lower lip. She whimpered again, her brow puckered, her face in pure torment. I reached down and brushed my fingers over her shoulder, hoping it would rouse her. When it didn't, I cupped it and shook it gently. "Evie," I whispered.

Just like that, she jolted awake, snapping upright and scrambling to the other side of the bed, her back against the brick wall, her eyes wide as she stared at me.

Whatever she'd seen in her dreams, it was obvious it had terrified her. Softening my voice, I said, "Baby, it's me. It's just me."

She was looking at me like she'd never seen me before, almost staring right through me, and I leaned down, staying on the other side of the bed but resting my hands against the mattress and angling my body toward hers, putting myself directly in her line of vision. "Evie. It's me. It's Riley."

Her eyes came into focus then, and if I hadn't known her so well, I wouldn't have noticed the fear still lingering there. And I sure as hell wouldn't have seen the embarrassment swimming in her eyes, manifesting in the blush blooming on her cheeks. She'd always hated that her emotions showed plain as day on her fair skin, hated that she wasn't able to disguise that from others when she always put up a front when needed. She thought it put her at a disadvantage, made her an easy target. She'd always hated to show any kind of vulnerability at all.

"I'm fine," she said, even though I hadn't asked. Her voice was scratchy and rough, and she cleared her throat and tried again, "I'm fine. Just a bad dream."

Then, as if she didn't have a care in the world, as if she hadn't just woken from a nightmare hours after having an intense and debilitating panic attack, she brushed the hair back from her face, carefully extracted the tangled blankets from around her legs, and got off the bed. With a straight spine, head held high, she headed toward the bathroom with slow, measured steps. The door shut softly behind her, and though this departure was less dramatic than the one from earlier, it was essentially the same. That rectangle of wood might as well have been a brick wall stacked ten feet tall with how effectively she ended any and all conversation about what had just happened.

Except it wasn't going to work quite as well for her this time.

Something was up with her. Something was going on besides what little she was telling me, and while I might've been willing to let it go at one time, that wasn't true anymore.

Not now. Not when I'd seen exactly what keeping this inside had done to her.

EVIE

I splashed some cold water on my face before dabbing it off with a hand towel, then I braced my hands on the vanity and tried to just breathe.

For so long, it felt like I hadn't been able to *breathe*.

I'd known this was coming. After my panic attack, after the talk earlier with Riley and Aaron, I'd known this was what would be awaiting me in my dreams. And yet, try as I might, I hadn't been able to stop sleep from pulling me under.

The nightmare—one so familiar and yet one I hadn't had in a long while—had gripped me by the throat and refused to let me go. And I felt how I always did after one—dirty, sullied, and so sick with the knowledge that what had happened in my nightmare hadn't lived only there, as part of illusions my mind created.

It lived in *me*. Was woven through every thread in my body, in my mind. It was a part of me, a part of who I was, and it always would be. No matter how far I traveled, no matter how much time had passed, it was still with me, buried deep inside.

If the events of today had shown me anything, it was that I was never going to get away from this. Not if I went on like I had been. Not if I continued to let it eat away at me.

When I felt like I was collected as much as I was going to be, I reached for the knob and twisted it softly, carefully pulling open the door. And though I knew it was a futile hope, I wished with everything I had that Riley had fallen back asleep. That somehow after everything that had happened—both now and a few hours ago—he'd let this go.

I should've known better.

The loft was still dark, the barest whispers of dawn brushing over the horizon providing very little light, but I could still see Riley. He was seated on the couch, the breadth of his shoulders so apparent in his white T-shirt, the brightness of it stark against the surroundings.

I crept my way to the bed, hoping he'd let it go. That he'd take all the signs I'd been giving out and just let it *be*. Because though I so desperately wanted to be free of this, I didn't know if I was ready yet.

Once I was at the side of the bed, ready to climb in, Riley turned his head and looked at me over his shoulder. He didn't need to say anything. The look in his eyes, steely determination focused directly on me, said more than he ever could've with words.

"What was that, Evie?" he asked. "Not just this, but earlier, too. The panic attack and now the nightmare. At first, I thought it must've been about Max, especially with how close we're getting, with everything you found today. Or Frankie, maybe? Thinking about when he'd kidnapped you . . . But then I remembered your face when Frankie had broken into your house. Remembered you knocking the fucker out cold, and I realized that couldn't have been it. Because even when you recognized him, you didn't have that look of sheer terror on your face like you had when you'd woken up just now." His eyes didn't let me go, held me captive in their gaze, and I was defenseless to stop the pull I felt—the pull I *still* felt toward him. "That wasn't about Max, was it?"

Closing my eyes, I exhaled, my shoulders slumping. Still, I wasn't giving up so easily. Because even realizing that maybe it was time to finally let this go, denying it was second nature to me. "It was nothing. I just get nightmares sometimes." My voice lacked the conviction it normally held, though, and I knew he could hear it. Even after so long, he'd be able to read me.

"Evie." His voice was soft, gentle, and it broke my heart. Because he was being so careful with me, so reverent, just like he'd been when I'd had the panic attack. Just like he'd been through it all—always. And I wanted so badly to accept it from him, let myself fall into his arms and let him help me carry this burden, but I didn't know how. "C'mere."

Almost without thought, my feet took me over to the couch, and I sat next to him, my head tilted down, my eyes focused on my lap as I picked at my fingernails. Riley reached out, his fingers brushing against my jaw to tilt my face up to look at him, and I couldn't stop the shiver from racking my body at his gentle touch.

After so long filling the void with nameless men, it was a relief to realize that he still had this effect on me. That I still reacted this way to him.

Because it showed I wasn't all broken. Not entirely. That despite the years of torment, the years of lies and secrets, the years of burying everything deep inside, I still *felt*. That after the years of the mask I had to wear, the show I had to put on, the endless pretending and masquerading, I was still here. I was still standing.

And I didn't have to be silent anymore.

Riley sat there, his arm behind me resting atop the couch cushions. Close, but not touching. I could tell he wanted to reach out to me again, touch me in some way, but he held back, both in his actions and his words. After asking me to come over, he'd sat silently for long minutes while I'd taken deep breaths, trying to work up the courage to give voice to the things I'd never spoken before. The words I'd never allowed to leave my lips. Words I'd never truly allowed myself to believe, not really.

And that was the scariest part of it all.

That somehow, if I said it aloud, it made all those years of torment, all those nights of terror, all those days of silence and pain and shame *real*. And that meant I had nothing to hide behind. If I spoke my truth, I was exposed. Completely and utterly bare.

Vulnerable in a way I'd never, ever allowed myself to be.

All this time, I'd held on to the belief that if no one else knew, a small part of me could pretend it hadn't happened. That, maybe, it had all been a product of my subconscious.

Except it wasn't. Deep down, I knew it was real, and it happened. Despite what my mother had told me. Despite the way she'd reacted when I'd tried to tell her something was wrong . . . something was off. Despite her telling me I was confused. That I must've misunderstood the touches, the looks. That none of those things went on. That all those times he'd come into my room when she was at work, all those times he'd held me down, his hand pressed tight against my mouth as tears leaked out of my eyes, dripping down the sides of my face and pooling in my ears hadn't been real. All those times had just been a product of my imagination.

It had taken me more than a year to work up the courage to tell her. To go to her after it'd been happening for a long time— too long—and being certain that she'd help. That finally— *finally*—it'd be better. I hadn't even been able to get everything out before she'd shut me down.

She hadn't believed me.

My stomach churned, the possibility that Riley could say the same thing, that he might think I was a liar, settled heavy on my shoulders.

God, what if he didn't believe me?

"You don't have to tell me anything." Riley's voice cut through the silence as sure as a knife, though it was soft and tentative. "I want to know. I want to help. I don't want to pry, but you know you *can* tell me anything. That's never changed."

I turned my head to look at him, and the pain reflecting back at me in his eyes gave me the courage to finally escape.

Taking a deep breath, I said, "It started when I was fifteen, a few months before I met you."

Riley narrowed his eyes, his shoulders stiffening the slightest bit, but it was the only outward sign he showed. I turned away, focusing on my lap. I couldn't look at him, look into his eyes, too afraid of what I'd see there. Doubt? I couldn't take it. I'd handled my mother's, but coming from him? That would truly break me.

"It started innocently enough. First it was just some looks. Inappropriate, for sure, but I wrote them off. And then there was the first time he touched me. He'd said it was an accident, that he hadn't meant anything by it, and I'd believed him. I mean . . . why wouldn't I? It was my dad, and nothing like that had ever, ever happened before. Not until he lost his job. Started drinking. And then my mom switched shifts, and it was just the two of us at home at night. And then pretty soon those 'accidental' touches weren't enough.

"He . . ." I swallowed that lump of fear in my throat, praying I could say it without actually saying it. But then I realized that I was only giving power to the words by keeping them inside. By refusing to speak them aloud, it was like I was caged all over again, and I was so tired of being behind bars.

"I said no. I pushed him away. I fought. I didn't want it. I never wanted it," I said, because that was so important to me. So important that Riley knew that. I hadn't been able to get away, hadn't been able to stop it, but I'd never wanted it. "But it hadn't mattered."

I didn't realize I'd started crying or that he'd touched me at all until I was suddenly in his lap, his thumbs stroking the wetness from my cheeks. And while I'd been scared of what I'd see in his eyes, terrified he'd think I was lying, when I finally allowed myself to look, when I stared into those bottomless pools, I didn't see the doubt I feared. I saw anger and hurt, confusion and sadness. I saw every emotion currently swarming around inside me reflected back in his eyes.

Seeing all that gave me the reassurance I needed to finally give life to the four little words—five tiny syllables—that had been my shackles for so long.

And, finally, I breathed.

Chapter Twenty-Four

RILEY

I sat on the couch, spine straight as Evie's head lay in my lap, her face turned toward me. I welcomed the cadence of her deep, even breathing, a soothing sound in my cluttered mind. Cluttered with that single sentence she'd uttered as it ran through my head over and over and over again.

My father raped me. My father raped me. My father raped me.

I looked down at her, her eyes fluttering under her lids, her lips parted, and she looked just like the same Evie I'd always known. Resilient and independent and strong. I just had no idea how much each of those descriptors truly fit her. Thinking about what she'd been through, what the past seven years had held for her, had me clenching my teeth, an ache spreading in my chest, filling every inch of my body until it was all I could think about. Until the rage I felt was all I could see.

I wanted someone to pay for this. I wanted redemption. For her, for the childhood she'd lost, for the sleepless nights and terrified days and nightmares that still haunted her. I wanted redemption for her because she'd been denied it. I wanted her asshole scum of a father to pay for what he did to her. And I wanted to be the one who brought the justice right to his fucking door.

I would've, too, would've left this apartment and done it a hundred times if it weren't for Evie. I couldn't leave, not now. Not when she was finally resting in my lap, not after what she'd shared with me.

I didn't want to leave her alone.

In my mind, though, while she lay sleeping, I let myself fantasize. Let it play out a hundred times in my head . . . getting on my bike and driving hours until I pulled up at the door to her childhood home, the one I'd only seen once or twice in the two years we'd been together. The one I'd seen and had no idea what had been happening behind it. In my mind, I knocked on that door, stood in front of that fucker, and beat him until he couldn't see. Until he couldn't *move*. Pounded on him until he was the one huddled in the corner, bleeding and crying and begging for me to stop.

And I knew if I didn't have her head in my lap, if I wasn't running my fingers through her hair, a tangible reminder that she was here with me, in a place he could never get her, that I would. I'd go there, just like in the scenarios running through my mind, and I'd kill him.

I'd kill him.

I wasn't sure that urge would ever lessen. That it'd ever go away.

It'd been hours since I'd pulled her into my lap, wiping away her near-constant tears as she'd recounted the hell she'd lived through. As she'd said the words that had filled me with a rage I'd never known. A rage that couldn't be matched, not even what I'd felt when I'd found out she was dead.

The anger swarming inside me now far surpassed it, because it wasn't just rage at what she'd gone through or who had done it to her. It also was rage directed at myself.

Through those two years we'd been together, the countless nights she'd stayed at my place just so she wouldn't have to go home, I'd never once suspected. And all the while, it'd been happening right under my nose. She'd lived it, day in and day out, and I hadn't done a damn thing. She'd endured *hell*, and I'd done nothing.

EVIE

I woke in the exact position I'd fallen asleep in, on the couch with my head in Riley's lap. He was still playing with my hair, his fingers providing the soothing caresses that had eventually lulled me to sleep in the first place. I didn't know how long I'd slept, but from the soft light coming into the loft, I'd guess I'd managed to crash through most of the day.

And I couldn't remember a time when I'd had such a deep and peaceful sleep.

Was it because I'd been so exhausted, running on empty for days? Or had it been because I'd finally freed myself? I'd exposed all the secrets I'd kept buried deep, and I could finally exhale.

Remembering the words I'd said to him, remembering how I'd opened up and told him everything—that I'd even been able to—was still a shock. And through it all, he'd listened. As I'd recounted my worst nightmare, the nightmare that still haunted me, he hadn't said a word, hadn't interrupted or bombarded me with questions. He hadn't called me a liar, hadn't looked at me like I was someone else, someone he didn't even know. He'd just sat there, stroking my back and listening, and it was the best gift he ever could've given me and he probably didn't even realize it.

I rubbed my eyes, then turned my head to look up at him. He was staring at me, his eyes full of worry and apprehension, and I wanted to erase it. Wanted to reassure him that even after everything, I was okay. I was still me. He was just seeing all of me now, even the parts I'd been trying for so long to hide.

"Hi," I said, my voice scratchy and rough from sleeping for so long and all the tears I'd shed before I'd fallen under.

"Hey. How'd you sleep?" He let his hand slip from my head as I sat up and twisted on the couch so I could face him.

Tucking my hair behind my ear, I looked at his face, trying to get a read on him, on what he saw now when he looked at me. Did he see some broken girl? Someone who was tainted and dirty? Someone who was weak and scared?

Or did he see *me*? Did he see the same Evie he always had?

"Okay," I answered. "How long was I out for?"

"A while . . . most of the day. It's almost five."

I stared at him, my mouth parted, quickly doing the calculations in my head of how long I'd been out. Ten hours. I'd slept, on this uncomfortable couch, a lap serving as my pillow, for ten hours. For longer than I usually slept in three nights combined.

"Do you want me to make you something to eat?" he asked, already pushing up from the couch and heading to the kitchen. "You must be hungry."

He didn't wait for me to answer before he started rummaging around in the cabinets. I stood and walked over to him, reaching up to grab his arm as he pulled out a box of cereal. He froze, looking down at me, and I realized then how tense he was. His shoulders were stiff, the muscles in his arm coiled and tight under my hand, his jaw set.

And while I'd always thought about what it'd mean to *me* to tell him, I hadn't stopped to think about what it must've been like for him to hear it. To hear about it happening to a girl he'd once loved. To know it had been happening while he'd been there and that I hadn't told him. That he hadn't known. Hadn't been able to stop it.

Stepping in front of him, I situated myself between him and the cabinets and leaned back against the counter. Placing my hands on his chest, I ran my fingers in small circles against the soft cotton clinging to his body, wanting to soothe him as much as he'd managed to soothe me earlier.

"I can't imagine how hard that was for you to hear, Riley, but I want you to know that I'm okay."

He gave a jerky nod, but he still studied me, his gaze appraising, and every bit of his body language said he wasn't buying it. The heavy cast of his eyes spoke volumes and said he was worried about me, scared of how to act now, and I hated it. I hated that anything had situated itself between us like this, especially after we'd managed to somehow overcome the five years we'd been apart.

"I'm still me. You don't have to be different around me now."

"I know. I'm just . . ." He shook his head, his eyes closing, and it was clear he wasn't going to say any more.

Wanting that connection back, the connection I'd always been able to feel when I was with him, I stood on my tiptoes and slid my hand up his chest until I rested it against his neck and tugged his face down to mine. He came, reluctantly, and I pressed my mouth to his, keeping my eyes open as I did so, watching him. His eyes were open, too, studying me, but his lips weren't responding like they had . . . before. *He* wasn't responding like he had.

It killed me that there was a possibility he saw me differently. That when he looked at me now, after I'd told him my secrets, he saw someone other than his Evie.

I pulled back, letting my grip loosen on his neck, my eyes darting between his. "You can kiss me, you know."

He swallowed hard. "I know."

"Do you? Because that wasn't a kiss."

He blew out a long breath, then groaned, reaching up and scrubbing a hand over his face. "I . . . I don't know what to do. I don't know how to act."

"I don't want you to act at all. I want you to be Riley and I'll be Evie and that's it."

"It's not that simple," he said in a strained voice.

"Why isn't it?"

"I don't want . . . I mean, what happens if I give you another panic attack?" His eyes darted between mine. "It fucking killed me last night to see you like that."

"Have I ever had a panic attack around you?"

"Just the one."

"So doesn't that say that it's not you? That it wasn't a result of what *you* were doing?"

He breathed out a harsh laugh. "Really? That's hard for me to believe, because I was the one trying to fuck you."

"Riley, how many times have we slept together?" I didn't let him answer, because it didn't matter. "I'm still the same girl I was then. The same one I was yesterday and the day before. The same one you took up against the wall a few days ago." He cringed at that, rubbing his thumb and forefinger over his clenched eyes. I reached up and grabbed his wrist, tugging his arm down. "You can kiss me and touch me. I'm not going to break."

I leaned up again, standing on tiptoes as I rested my lips on his. "I *want* you to kiss me and touch me. I want to know that you don't see me differently. That I'm still Evie to you. That I'm still worthy. I want to know you still think I'm beautiful."

"Jesus, baby, of course I do. I always will. I'd never see you as anything different. I just don't know what will be too much. I don't want . . . I can't cause you pain like that . . . Not again."

"How about I tell you what I want you to do?"

He stared at me for a moment, then swallowed, his Adam's apple bobbing as he nodded.

"Kiss me," I breathed, tugging his face down to mine. It was slower than it usually was with him, more tentative, but it was something. It was more than he'd given me just a minute ago, so I'd take it. I opened my mouth to him, slipping my tongue out and licking against his bottom lip. Reaching down, I grabbed his hand and moved it toward me, guiding it around until it was pressed against the small of my back. And then I added pressure, pushing our lower halves together. "I'm not going to break," I reminded him. "Please don't act like I will."

Chapter Twenty-Five

RILEY

With Evie's hands on me, her lips under mine, soon I forgot to be careful. I forgot to be tentative and hesitant and let myself get lost in the feel of her skin under my hands, her lips against mine. And before long, it wasn't enough. Just kissing her like this wasn't enough. I needed to feel more of her . . . *all* of her.

Reaching down, I cupped her ass in my hands and hauled her up against me. She moaned into my mouth, kissing me harder, deeper, and despite wanting to be careful, I couldn't wait anymore. I held her to me as I walked us over to the bed, then set her on her feet and peeled the clothes from her body before nudging her onto the mattress.

She lay back on the sheets, her hair a chaos of red against the white pillowcase, and I could only stare. She was looking back at me, her eyes open, a hint of vulnerability hidden in their depths. She was bare to me now, in more ways than one. I realized that for the first time in seven years, I was seeing the real Evie. Before, I'd only been given glimpses. But now, I was seeing all of her.

"You've always been gorgeous to me," I said, my voice rough

with my need. "Since that very first day I saw you. But now . . ." I shook my head and let my eyes get their fill of her. I swallowed down my anger, my sadness at her past, and continued, "Knowing what you've gone through and that you're still standing? That you didn't let any of it destroy you? It only makes you more beautiful. You came out on the other side. Strong and resilient and fucking perfect."

"I'm glad you think so." A soft smile tipped her lips, a flush brushing across her cheeks, and then she held her hand out for me, beckoning me closer.

"I *know* so." I reached behind and yanked the neck of my shirt, pulling it over my head and tossing it to the side before I shed my pants and boxer briefs. Then I stood at the foot of the bed and braced my hands on the mattress on either side of her. Starting at her ankles, I let my lips trace every inch of her body, kissing a trail up her legs. Even though what she'd been through had happened so long ago, I had this overwhelming urge to erase the memories from her mind. I wanted them gone forever, and I wanted them replaced with something different, something better, something sweeter.

I wanted them filled with us. Only ever us.

"God, Riley." She moaned when I slid my hands up her inner thighs and pushed her legs apart, running my thumbs along her pussy. And when I bent to her, licking a line straight up her slit, her pleas turned into mumbled snippets of sound, not a word among them. I spread her open with my thumbs, then sucked her clit into my mouth, wanting to drive her crazy. Wanting her out of her mind in pleasure. I wanted to eradicate every bad memory she'd ever had.

When I slipped my fingers inside her, brushing against the part that always made her go off, she arched off the bed, pressing harder against my mouth. I continued to stroke her with my tongue, flicking her clit until her pussy clenched tighter and tighter, and then finally she was coming and moaning and pulsing around my fingers.

I slowed my tongue, stroking her softer, slower, until she was boneless on the bed. As much as I could do this all night, lick her pussy until she'd come a dozen times, I wanted to be inside her. And I wanted it right fucking now. I wanted to feel her skin to skin, wanted to be inside her with nothing between us, but still I reached over and fumbled for a condom, rolling it down my length and protecting us both. When I was fully sheathed, I shifted closer to her, still on my knees, and pulled her legs up and over mine.

She didn't say anything, didn't tell me to stop, didn't utter a word of protest, but still, there was a stiffness in her body and a wariness in her eyes, an uncertainty, and I realized this was the first time she'd ever been under me like this. The first time she'd ever lain prone before me. So giving. So vulnerable.

Last night, when she'd had the panic attack, it'd been when I was pressing her into the couch, sandwiching her between my body and an unmoving object, and I wondered if that was what had set her off. If that had made everything worse. Because in all the times we'd ever been together, I'd never once been on her, holding her down. She'd always managed to make it so she was the one in control. So she was the one guiding, moving, the one deciding how far, how fast . . . deciding *everything*.

And I'd never minded. I'd never even really thought about it, too happy when I'd been a teenager to be getting pussy at all, and now . . . Now I'd been too happy to have *her* again, period.

But I recognized this for what it was. She was telling me without words, showing me with her actions that she trusted me. Even more so than when she'd told me her truth.

I wanted to be worthy of that trust. To do right by her now, like I hadn't been able to before. Twice in her life, I'd let her down, even if she'd never asked for my help. Twice before, she'd been on her own, running scared, and I hadn't been able to do anything about it. Now, though . . . Now I could do something about it. I could, and I would.

I wasn't going to leave her to face anything on her own again.

I gripped my cock, running the head along her slit, and looked into her eyes. Asking her a dozen questions without saying a word. She was so brave, so trusting like this, and I didn't want to take advantage of that. I needed to hear it from her, that this was all right.

"It's okay." Her voice was soft, the barest tremor running through it, and it killed me. It fucking killed me that she had to deal with this. That she'd had this shit done to her in the first place. It killed me, and I'd do anything to help her forget.

"One word, baby. That's it. One word and I'll stop."

"I know you will." She reached out and gripped my thighs, her fingers digging into my flesh, and I took her unspoken request and placed myself at her entrance, then pushed forward.

Her eyes fluttered shut the farther in I got, until our bodies were flush and I was seated as deeply inside her as I could get. I gripped her hips as I slowly pumped into her, dragging my cock out and pushing in deep enough to hear that little gasp leave her lips. She felt so good, so fucking good around me, it took everything in me not to lean over and brace myself on top of her, pound into her until we were both coming. My cock was begging for it, begging to fuck her hard and deep. But more than that, more than the need for pleasure that was coursing through my veins, was the need to make sure she was okay. To make this good for her.

I rocked forward, rolling my hips and guiding her body forward and back over mine, until she was arching against the bed. Her head was pressed into the pillow, her back bowed, her tits like an offering in front of me. And I had to take. I bent over her, leaning down until I could take one of the hard peaks into my mouth. I gently scraped my teeth over it, then captured it between them and tugged just how she liked it, flicking my tongue over the tip at the same time.

"*Shit.*" She moaned and reached up to grip my hair, her fingers digging in and keeping me held tightly to her.

As much as I loved driving her crazy like this, as much as I loved my mouth all over her, I wanted—*needed*—to see her. To watch her reactions . . . know she was okay. That this was still okay. Pulling back, I sat up on my knees again and looked down at her, at her body spread out and offered up to me like a feast. Her eyes were half closed, her lips parted, her skin flushed and beautiful. Her nipples were hard and shiny from my mouth, the gentle slope of her stomach calling to me. I ran my hand over it, then shifted my eyes down and watched where she was taking me into her body, her pussy stretching around my cock. Seeing it, seeing how wet she was, how wet she'd made *me,* reassured me that she was okay. This was as good for her as it was for me.

I dragged my eyes away from the sight before me and looked at her face. She was watching me the same as I was watching her, and seeing the blind trust in her eyes, that open vulnerability that hadn't ever been there before, tore at my fucking heart.

I'd moved on since she'd been gone, moved on as best I could. I'd tried to forget about her, but I never really had. I'd lived my life seeking vengeance for her, and she'd always been with me, by my side with every job I'd taken, every directive I'd carried out. She'd never left.

I'd loved her when I was a stupid sixteen-year-old. I'd loved her at seventeen and eighteen, as our relationship went on, as we'd grown closer. I'd loved her as I grieved for her, as I sought justice for her death. And despite trying hard to forget her, despite trying hard to leave her in the past where I'd thought she belonged, I'd loved her every year since.

And I loved her now.

Even though I was inside her, I needed her closer yet. I wanted her by me, face-to-face, but I didn't want to press her into the mattress. I didn't want to take the chance that it might trigger her, didn't want to ruin whatever progress she was making now, being with me like this. Instead, I leaned forward and slid my hands under her back by her shoulder blades, then lifted her to me, sitting her in my lap and bringing her face right up to mine. As soon as she sank down on my cock, filling her completely, we both moaned. Evie's eyes fluttered closed before she opened them again, bringing her mouth to mine for a kiss.

She wrapped her arms around my shoulders as we rocked together, me on my knees and her in my lap, my hands on her ass as I guided her up and down along my length. Rocked together until our breaths came out in gasps and pants, until all words blended together into unintelligible ramblings, oaths to God and pleas for more and silent promises spoken between our bodies. And through it all, I couldn't get close enough to her. Couldn't get deep enough inside her.

I wanted to consume her.

Because for the past seven years, she'd been consuming me.

When she clenched around me, her pussy squeezing me tight as she came in my arms, I knew that was it for me. *She* was it for me. I went over the edge, spilling inside her, with the thought that whatever fight we had in front of us, whatever challenges we faced at the hands of Max, I'd do everything in my power to make sure this was a fight she'd didn't have to go through on her own.

Chapter Twenty-Six

EVIE

Riley's arms were warm and strong, his heartbeat steady under my ear, and it was all so . . . *normal*. Was this what life could be like? Was this something I could have? Even after everything that had happened, all the shit I'd endured, was this something I could count on? Was *Riley* someone I could count on?

Remembering how he'd touched me, how he'd looked down at me when I'd been lying there, offering absolutely everything I had to him, sent a shiver up my spine, had a warmth settling deep in my heart. Because I knew. I *knew*.

Of course I could count on him.

I didn't know why I'd ever doubted him. I should've known, after all the years, that he wouldn't fail me.

Opening up to him, not just my memories, not just exposing my past to him, but literally laying myself bare before him and allowing myself to be vulnerable to him, had been the scariest thing I'd ever done in my life. I'd let him see into the darkest recesses of my soul, trusting that he wouldn't hurt me. Wouldn't take advantage of what I'd given him.

Even more than the high I got at being in control, the rush I felt at having his complete and utter acceptance was unprecedented.

Riley took a deep breath, his chest rising under my cheek. His arm was around me, his hand settled possessively on my hip. Normally I would've hated it, hated that firm grasp, holding me so tightly to his body. But I couldn't do anything but revel in the feel of it now.

It made me feel . . . protected.

"You doin' okay?" His voice was a quiet rumble vibrating against my ear.

He hadn't said anything after he'd laid us both down on the bed, tugging me into his side. We'd lain there for so long I lost track, nothing but the sounds of the street outside and our breaths filling the loft. I didn't know if he realized I would need some time after, if he was giving me space, or if he'd needed space, too.

"Yeah," I answered, tracing my fingers over the rippled edges of his abdomen. "It was hard, talking about it. The most difficult thing I've ever done. I knew it would be. But I don't regret telling you." I took a deep breath and blew it out, smiling when his muscles tensed under my hand. "It feels like a weight has been lifted off my shoulders. It's . . . I don't know, it's hard to explain." I thought about how it felt like I could finally breathe and said, "It feels like I can finally suck in a lungful of air instead of surviving on only shallow breaths."

He exhaled heavily, and I could almost hear the relief in it. "I was hoping you didn't regret it."

I shook my head and placed a kiss over his heart, grateful that he'd been here with me. Even with my reassurance, his body was still tense under me.

"What has you biting your tongue?" I asked.

Riley froze, then blew out a laugh. "That obvious, huh?"

"To me? Yeah."

He began rubbing circles on my bare hip with his thumb, and
I settled farther into him, draping my leg over the top of one of
his and tracing my fingers over his chest while I waited for him to
tell me what was on his mind.

"You said you tried to tell your mom . . ."

That small handful of words made me stiffen in his arms. I
couldn't help it. It was funny how so few words could transport
me right back to that day, an afternoon seemingly like any other,
except it'd been the day when I'd finally worked up enough
courage to talk to her. Tell her what was happening to me. Or try
to, anyway.

I hadn't even been able to tell her about anything more than
the inappropriate touches and looks before she'd shut me down,
saying I was confused or misreading things. I hadn't corrected
her, hadn't told her the things he'd done to me that could in no
way be misconstrued. Instead, I'd closed up again. All my confi-
dence had vanished, extinguished in the blink of an eye. I'd swallowed it all, kept it locked up tight.

Until Riley.

I cleared my throat, hoping my voice came out sounding
stronger than I felt at this moment. "Yeah."

Riley continued caressing my skin, wherever he could reach.
I didn't know if it was to soothe him or me, but I appreciated the
gesture all the same. "But you never told her more than about
the . . . the looks and the touches?"

"No, she shut me down before I could. And I never tried
again."

"What about . . . I mean, have you ever gone to the cops?
Have you filed a report?"

I closed my eyes, the words my father had said more times
than I could count echoing in my memory. "He told me no one
would believe me, and after my mom . . ." I blew out a shaky
breath. While I'd opened up to Riley, shared my darkest past with

him, that didn't mean this was suddenly easy to talk about. It still clawed at me, my open wound raw and vulnerable, a thousand tiny paper cuts along every inch of my skin. And talking about it was like swimming in salt water.

Riley didn't say anything more, didn't do anything but tug me closer to his side. I relaxed into him, grateful that he'd taken my cues to let it drop. It was a lot to deal with in a short amount of time, and I was still reeling.

We lay there for long minutes before his phone buzzed on the makeshift nightstand, the small black rectangle sliding toward Riley as it vibrated. "Shit," he said, reaching out and grabbing the phone before he glanced at the screen. "Gage called a couple times while you were sleeping. He's gonna be pissed as hell I didn't call back." He blew out a deep breath, then pressed his thumb on the screen and answered the call. "Hey."

I couldn't hear Gage's side of the conversation as Riley held the phone to his ear, just a low, unintelligible rumble, but when Riley's muscles went taut under my roaming hands, I knew something was going on. Propping myself up on my elbow, the sheet clutched to my chest, I looked down at him. His brows were furrowed, his jaw clenched, eyes hard.

What is it? I mouthed. He gave a sharp shake of his head and looked away from me, but I wasn't going to have any of that. I'd been the one to land us in this position—*my* problems, *my* actions—and if anyone was going to be in the know about what the hell was going on, it was going to be me.

With Riley's attention diverted away from me, I quickly reached out and snatched the phone from his hand and pressed the speaker button. As soon as I did so, Gage's voice filled the room. "Aaron confirmed it's at least a dozen more."

"What's at least a dozen more?" I asked.

"Evie," Riley snapped, sitting up and reaching out to try and get the phone from my hand. I held it away from him and scooted farther back on the bed, not caring about my nakedness.

"No way. You don't get to have this conversation in private. This isn't your problem, Riley. It's *mine*. Now tell me what the hell's going on. A dozen more *what*, Gage?"

Riley cursed under his breath, his eyes narrowed on me, at the same time Gage blew out a breath on the other end of the line. Then Gage said, "A dozen guys. Max isn't fucking around anymore. When Frankie didn't contain the . . . situation, Max moved on and sent out runts, just prospects for the crew who wanted to do something for him and ones he knew wouldn't ask questions. Ones who weren't around when you were, Evie, who didn't know you. He's turned the tables, though. Aaron let me know that Max had a meeting with the veterans—the ones who've been there the longest and have the most to lose—and . . . he sold you out. Told them you have evidence to bring down the entire crew and everyone in it. Now Max is mobilizing guys. Plans to send out a dozen more in the next couple of hours."

"Which means we need to move *now*," Riley interjected. He threw off the covers and stood, yanking on the pants he'd shed earlier. His hands were restless, tugging at his hair, the muscles in his back coiled as he paced at the foot of the bed. "Evie's got all the evidence we need. We can get shit in place for a blast, if need be." I knew he meant to have the evidence prepped and ready to send to any and all sources at once, should Max not comply with the threat. He turned to me. "Did you get everything on that flash drive?"

"Hell, yeah, I did. Every last bit of it. Aaron got copies, too."

He gave a short nod. "Good."

"What do you want to do, Ry?" Gage asked. "You want to wait until he comes here, just be ready for him?"

"Fuck, no."

Gage snorted. "Yeah, I didn't think so. If you time it right, wait for the green light from Aaron, you can hit Max in Chicago when all his top guys have been dispatched."

"That's what I was thinking. Catch him alone. I'll probably head out tonight, so I'm in Chicago when I need to be, whenever Aaron gives the go-ahead."

The words he was saying, how he and Gage held the conversation as if I wasn't even in the room, had an uneasiness crawling over my skin. Narrowing my eyes at him, I said, "You mean we. *We'll* head out."

Riley turned to face me, his arms crossed over his bare chest. He was a statue, stoic and unmoving, his eyes hard as he leveled me with a stare. "No, I mean *me*."

I could only sit and stare at him, my heart warring with my mind, because I'd known. Despite how badly my heart wanted to believe that he wouldn't do something like this to me, intentionally strip me of any power I had over myself, my mind—my gut— had counted on it. I huffed out a disbelieving laugh. "You can't be serious."

"Evie," Gage interrupted. "I know you want to be involved, but this is serious shit now. Shit we—"

"Never would've had to deal with if it weren't for me," I interrupted, my voice hard. "You are *not* blocking me on this. This isn't either of your problems. It's *mine*."

"I don't give a fuck if it's your problem or not," Riley said. "It became mine the second I saw you again, the second I got the call from Gage. You're *not going*." His words were hard, delivered like sharp jabs to the stomach.

I climbed out of the bed, jerking on my clothes as I glared at him. "I can't believe you're trying to pull this shit with me. This isn't your decision to make, Riley, and you're not my fucking keeper."

Gage cleared his throat, the sound reminding me we had an audience. I'd forgotten he was on the phone. Riley and I both stared at the illuminated screen lying on the bed, our postures tense. "I'll be by shortly. You guys get this figured out before I get there."

The call disconnected, and Riley and I stared at each other, at a standoff.

Arms crossed, foot tapping on the hardwood floor, I glared at him. "There's nothing to figure out. I'm going."

"You can't seriously think this is a good idea." Riley shook his head, his fingers rough in his hair. "We're talking about your *life*, Evie."

"We're talking about *your* life, too, and I'm not going to stand by and let you risk it because of my choices."

"If you think I'm letting you come with me, you're out of your mind."

I scoffed, breathing out a laugh. "*Let* me? If you think there's anything I need you to *let* me do, then you're out of your mind, too."

Riley's jaw clenched, his eyes narrowed on me. "Well, fortunately, I'm the only one with the transportation."

With that, I could only stare at him, my jaw dropped. He was utterly serious. I couldn't believe he was pulling this, trying to tell me what I could and couldn't do. That prickle that started at the base of my spine spread throughout my body, telling me I was quickly losing control of the situation, that I didn't have a say, and urging me to regain the upper hand. "I'm going to say this one more time: I'm getting on the back of that motorcycle, and I'm going with you."

"You're *not*. I can't have you with me. I can't do that to you. I might not have been able to help you the last times you needed it, but I've got the opportunity to now. I couldn't do a damn thing to save you before, and if you think I'm throwing away the chance I have now to do this for you, you don't know the man I've become very well."

"Then maybe you're right. Maybe I *don't* know who you've become, because the Riley I knew wouldn't tell me what I could and couldn't do. He wouldn't have tried to control me. Certainly not after everything I shared. I had that control stripped from me for *years,* Riley, and I refuse to let it happen again."

"Jesus Christ, Evie, I'm not trying to control you. All I'm trying to do is keep you safe!"

"All you're trying to do is order me around!"

He growled out a frustrated noise, tugging on his hair. Then he dropped his arms and came to stand in front of me, his hands clasping my upper arms. "Baby, listen to me." His voice was soothing now, beseeching, the hard edges he'd spoken with only moments ago softened. He bent his knees to bring us to eye level, and I saw everything he was feeling as I met his gaze— determination, fear, anxiety, and underneath it all, a bubbling undercurrent of anger. "If you go, he'll kill you. He will kill you and he won't think twice about it. He won't see you as enough of a threat. He just *won't.* He's already tried to have you killed *twice,* and you've managed to get away both times. But I'm not taking the chance of it happening on the third try. I'm not going to lose you again. I can't." Then his once-soothing voice turned hard. "You're not going. Period."

That feeling of helplessness was back, clawing at me . . . weighing me down. Because I knew that no matter how hard I fought for this, how much I resisted, how much I argued, the truth was that if Riley didn't want me going with him, there wasn't a damn thing I could do to force him. I couldn't strap myself on the back of the bike. Probably wouldn't even be able to get out of the apartment with Gage no doubt blocking my way. And that thought just sank the dread further into my chest, magnifying every ounce of hopelessness I felt until it was engulfing me.

Despite what I'd come to feel for Riley again after these few days together—despite what I'd felt for him all along—I wouldn't, *couldn't* allow myself to lose control again. Not when I'd finally gained back every bit of myself.

Riley's face had softened in the long moments when I hadn't said anything after his little speech. When he spoke to me now, his voice was more relaxed, like he thought he'd convinced me.

And he had. He'd convinced me. Just not the way he'd wanted.

"You've dealt with too much in your life, Evie. You've had two assholes take everything from you. *Everything.* I can't let that continue. I *won't.*"

With my voice steady and calm, I said, "If you refuse to let me make the choice of whether or not I want to be there with you, we're done. Whatever we had here, whatever sparked between us again, is gone." I ignored the flare of anger in his eyes, that spark of hurt, because my heart was breaking wide open. It was like he hadn't heard anything I'd told him over the last few days. "I can't be with someone who takes my choices away from me. This isn't your fight, Riley. This is *mine.* I'm the one Max is after. I'm the one who has what he wants."

Riley stared at me, his eyes flitting between both of mine, darting all over my face, and I didn't know if he read the truth in my statement or not. I didn't know if he thought I wasn't being serious, if I was bluffing. Or if he just didn't care.

"And I'm the one who's going to make sure you're safe," he said.

I looked into his eyes, bottomless and clear, and I hated that this was what it was coming down to. That after everything, it was coming down to him keeping a choice from me, stealing any ounce of freewill from me. Just like everyone else.

"I was never yours to save."

Chapter Twenty-Seven

I watched from the window as Riley tore out of the alley on his bike, Gage at my back. Riley and I hadn't spoken two words to each other after our blowup. After I told him if he took this choice away from me, we were through.

And he'd gone anyway.

I tried not to focus on the ache that filled up my chest when he'd left, when he'd voluntarily walked away, only after binding my hands. Not literally—not like before—but figuratively. And that was almost worse. I latched on to the anger and frustration I was feeling instead, letting that grow inside me. Letting it fuel me, because if I didn't, if I didn't have something else to hang on to, I'd crumble.

"You got your stuff packed up?" Gage asked.

I turned and looked at him over my shoulder. *What stuff*? I wanted to ask. I had nothing here, not really. Tipping my chin toward the single bag on the couch, I turned back around and stared out the window into the darkening sky. Riley would get to Chicago around three in the morning. And as soon as he got the go-ahead from Aaron, he'd be on Max.

And I'd be here, hundreds of miles away, while Riley fought my battles for me. While Riley risked his life for something that was never his problem in the first place.

Gage walked over to the couch and grabbed the bag. "Come on. Let's move."

Twisting around, I asked, "Where are we going?"

"My place. I don't like leaving Madison alone. Not with this shit going on."

That overprotective bullshit ran in the family, it seemed. Giving a tight nod, I followed him, my movements stilted as we descended the stairs, not taking a backward glance at the loft. At the place where I'd shed so much of my past baggage. Where I'd both found and lost the one and only man I'd ever loved.

Gage was on high alert as he opened the door that led into the alley, his eyes darting to every dark corner, making sure it was clear. He gave a short nod, indicating it was okay, and I dutifully followed him out. It seemed like that was all I ever did—take orders.

Once we were settled in Gage's car, a beat-up old Honda, he drove us toward his and Madison's place, his body tense. Probably anxious to get back to Madison.

After long moments of silence, he finally said, "It's better this way."

I rolled my eyes, crossing my arms as I turned my head to look out the window. Because yeah, I'd be safe here, locked away. Protected. But if I wasn't ever given the opportunity to fight for myself, how would I know if I could? I'd run scared twice before, not just from Max but also from my father. I'd stayed away, hadn't thought twice about ever going back to my old life, because I needed to leave all that shit behind. Just forget it like it'd never happened.

Except no matter how far I ran, I couldn't escape. It was

melded to my very soul, and there was no running from the skel-etons in my closet.

And now, after everything I'd done, after all the steps I'd taken, I wanted the chance to do this. To finally take a step to seize that control once and for all. To prove I wasn't scared anymore.

"He cares about you. Loves you. He just wants to keep you safe."

I turned to Gage then, looked at the strong outline of his jaw covered in stubble, the slope of his nose, those eyelashes that went on for miles. He looked so much like Riley, I ached. Ached for the man I loved. The man who'd voluntarily walked right out of my life. "I want to be able to keep myself safe."

"Then you're dumber than I ever thought you were."

"Fuck off, Gage."

"No, you've got nowhere to go now but to sit here and listen to me. You've always been a smart girl, Evie. You've always used your head, and you were good when you were with the crew. I don't know if being away from it for so long has fucked with your memories of it, but this meeting with Max isn't going to happen over fucking cookies and tea. He has no qualms about taking lives, and it doesn't matter if you're a woman. He doesn't give a shit. He has no honor, no morals. He's not doing this for a greater purpose. He's not secretly a good guy caught up in a bad situa-tion. He's bad to the core. That's how he's held control of the crew for so long. And he won't think twice, won't even blink, be-fore killing you."

"I'm not stupid," I snapped. "I know exactly what he'd do. I *know* what this meeting will entail. Which is exactly why *I* wanted to go. Riley doesn't deserve this. He did nothing, had no hand in any of this, except to get me away after you called him. Why should he suffer for my mistakes? And what makes him my keeper?

The person who tells me what kind of decisions I can or can't make about *my* life?"

Gage blew out a deep breath. "Look, I get that you're pissed. But cut him some slack. In the past week, he found out that everything he's done in the past five years, the whole reason he really got involved in the crew, wasn't reality. That every job he took . . . it was all for nothing. Not only that, but he found out that the very guy he worked for was the one who ripped you away from him. He's owed his vengeance."

"And I'm not? I was the one hiding away for five years, Gage. *Me.*"

"I know that. I'm not saying otherwise. And I get that you're angry he didn't want you with him. I get why you'd want to go, I do, but I also get where he's coming from. I agreed not to tell him you were alive, and it ate at me for years. I wanted to protect him and respect your choice, but it killed me to watch my kid brother suffer for years, grieving for you. Especially when I knew the whole time you weren't dead. Now that he knows the truth, we need to give him this. He doesn't want to lose you again, Evie."

Gage's voice was gruff, his focus on the road, and I knew how much this was costing him to talk about. Gage didn't do feelings. He didn't do talking, either, not really. And I got what he was saying. I did. I just wished he could get what *I* was saying. It wasn't like I'd planned to walk into Max's place by myself. I had no illusion of the outcome of something like that. What I'd wanted, what I'd counted on, was doing it *with* Riley. I'd wanted to be by his side. This was my fight, but I'd wanted us to face it together as a team.

The apartment was dark when we arrived. Gage had called Madison on the way over, making sure everything was okay. She'd confirmed it had been quiet there, so he didn't hesitate as he walked in ahead of me, flipping on a light before tossing my bag on the couch and his keys on the tiny circle of a dining table.

"You can crash out here tonight." He gestured with his head toward the already made-up sofa. "I'll keep you in the loop, let you know when I hear from him. I don't expect anything for a couple hours, so you might want to try and get some sleep."

I gave a distracted nod as he mumbled something about going down the hallway to check on Madison, but all I could focus on was that set of keys he'd tossed without a second thought. Gage's car was a stick shift, something I'd never driven, but I bet I could figure it out pretty damn fast if I had to.

If I was running.

I listened as the door down the hall opened, then came the muffled voice of Madison before the soft snick of the door closing behind Gage.

My heart was pounding a staccato rhythm in my chest, my lips thrumming along at the same erratic beat. I crept over so I could peek down the hallway to make sure their bedroom door was still closed, the soft carpet masking the sounds of my footfalls. Seeing nothing but darkness down the hall, I glanced again at the small ring of keys and swallowed. I had to make this decision now, without consideration. Because I knew every second I wasted contemplating whether or not I should do it was a second I'd never get back. And Gage could waltz back out here any minute, snatching the opportunity right from under me.

I took a quick look at the clock on the microwave, seeing that Riley had taken off less than thirty minutes ago. If I left right now, I still had the possibility of catching him. Of confronting Max with him. Of claiming back all those years that had been stolen from me.

Without thinking another second on it, I tiptoed over to the table, gripping my purse before snatching his keys. The dead bolt was silent as I unlocked it, the door barely a whisper as I pulled it open. And then before I could look back, before I could think twice, I was gone.

Not knowing how much lead time I'd have before Gage figured out I was gone, I ran down the stairs, through the entryway, and out the front door, into the dark night. The moon was full but partially covered by passing clouds, just like the setting of a hundred different horror movies. I swallowed my nerves as I rushed to where Gage had parked the car, looking behind me toward the front of the apartment building to make sure he wasn't on my heels.

I was so preoccupied worrying about Gage coming after me that I didn't consider who else might be outside waiting, didn't bother checking my surroundings for other threats.

The sound of footsteps directly behind me startled me, but it was too late to even turn around. "Gotcha now, bitch."

A rough hand covered my mouth as an arm held me back against a chest, then there was a tiny prick on the side of my neck.

And those three words were the last I heard before everything went dark.

Chapter Twenty-Eight

RILEY

My head had swum with Evie's words the entirety of the ride back to Chicago. Over every mile that had passed under my tires, I'd remembered the look on her face when I'd told her she wasn't going with me. Her eyes had sparked, her lips thinning into a straight line. In that moment, she'd absolutely loathed me. That look of anger was the last thing I'd seen before I left.

And if she'd been telling the truth, if those last words she'd said to me had been honest—and I had no doubt she'd meant them—then it was going to be the last look I'd ever see on her beautiful face.

It gutted me, ripped me apart inside—the thought that I might never have her in my life again. But so long as she was safe, it didn't matter. Not my feelings. Not hers.

I knew she thought I hadn't heard her, hadn't listened, but I had. I'd heard what she was saying, knew how much it would cost her to give in on this, but in the end, it hadn't mattered. I couldn't let it, because it wasn't just her feelings that were at stake. It was her life. And I didn't care that I was keeping this choice from her if it meant she'd be alive.

Even if that life wasn't with me.

My phone had buzzed in my pocket more times than I could count while I'd been riding, but I hadn't pulled over. Hadn't even taken the thirty seconds to check it when I'd stopped to fill up, too focused on getting back on the road as quickly as fucking possible. I was anxious, uneasy, and I wanted to get this over with *now*.

While I'd been driving here, Gage had been dealing with all the back-end stuff—setting shit up with Aaron and making sure we had the fail-safes in place, if the unthinkable happened . . . if I didn't come out of there alive. If they sent someone after Evie.

I wasn't going to let it come to that, though. I needed to convince Max that he didn't have any other options than to call off all the guys he'd sent after her. And once I got that confirmation, heard it from his mouth, I'd call Gage and give him the go-ahead to give Evie back her freedom.

I had no idea what she intended to do when this was all over. I didn't know if she planned to go back to Eric, planned to go back to being Genevieve, and I couldn't think about it. The thought of her falling right back into her false life ripped my fucking heart apart. Thinking about her doing it despite everything that had happened in the days we'd been together. Despite everything that had happened between us . . .

I couldn't focus on that shit now. Couldn't bog my mind down with what-ifs and possibilities for the future. I needed to focus on the here and now, get my head in the game if we had a chance of pulling this off.

Needing to call Aaron to get a read on when he'd be ready for me, I pulled into a deserted parking lot close to my neighborhood. He was taking a major risk, staying behind and acting as

Max's right hand during the confrontation, but I knew that if anything went bad, he'd have my back.

I hoped he would, anyway.

Slipping my phone from my front pocket, I pressed the button at the top, illuminating the screen. Fourteen missed calls, all from Gage. I reached up and scratched my jaw, my brow furrowed. What the hell was going on? My mind immediately conjured up every possible situation. Had he spotted other guys in town already? Did something happen on Aaron's end to make it so he couldn't be there tonight? Even if that were the case, it wouldn't stop me . . . not when I was this close. Not when it was Evie's life on the line.

I thumbed my way to his number, then hit Send and waited as it rang. When his voice mail picked up, I blew out a long breath, then hung up and tried Aaron's number. Once again, I waited as the phone rang, and then was subjected to the same generic recording. I hung up and cursed under my breath. Knowing Gage would get a text faster than listening to a voice mail, I opened up the screen to send him a message.

Status?

The minutes I stood there waiting for a response were the longest of my life. I tried Aaron once more, to no avail. I'd just thumbed my way to the screen to call Gage again when a text came through from him.

Plans changed. Move now. Get your ass to Max.

My heart stopped, my blood running cold. Gage never switched the plans unless something fucked up was going down.

I tried calling him one last time only to have his goddamn voice mail pick up again. If he was able to text but not pick up his phone, I assumed that meant he was on a call with someone . . . I just didn't know who.

I could barely bring myself to type the four little letters, but I needed to know.

Evie?

His response was immediate. *Now, Riley. MOVE NOW.*

"Jesus Christ," I breathed, and started the ignition on my bike before I pocketed my phone and revved the engine, then took off. My instincts had been right, knowing now something was wrong. Gage hadn't answered the question on Evie, and I couldn't think about what that meant.

I sped toward the old warehouse on the South Side where Max did all of his business, figuring it was my best bet. I was supposed to have gotten confirmation from Aaron on where Max was stationed, but with nothing from him to go on and only a few urgent texts from Gage, I had to wing it.

It seemed like forever before I pulled up outside the dark building. There was only one other car here that I could see—Max's—and I took a quick survey of the surroundings when I dismounted my bike. Pulling out my phone, I typed out a short text to both Gage and Aaron, letting them know I'd arrived and I was going in. I only hoped Aaron would get the message in time.

The perimeter was clear, no one keeping guard, which meant the time was right. Everyone had cleared out, just like we'd planned. Normally, Max would have two guys posted at each door for security. You didn't do his line of work without having some protection. He didn't allow just anyone to walk into his place.

The back door wasn't locked, wasn't chained, which reassured me that Aaron had come through, making it easy for me to slip inside. My boots were silent on the concrete floor as I headed toward one of the rooms in the back where Max spent most of his time. I slipped my hand in my pocket, wrapping my fingers around the knife I'd slid in there. It was smaller than the one secured to my boot, but it was handy in a fight. As nice as it was having backups just in case Max made Aaron do a search of me, neither of those blades reassured me as much as the cool metal of the gun at my back, tucked into the waistband of my jeans.

Sporadic lights illuminated my path as I walked toward the back corner, which held one of only two rooms in the entire place that didn't have an open ceiling. The door was ajar, two masculine voices trailing out from it. I had no way of knowing if that was Aaron in there with Max, but I hoped like hell he was. I slipped closer on silent feet, my back against the wall, keeping an eye on my surroundings, just in case the cleared security had been a ruse.

When I was a couple feet away from the open doorway, I could make out one of the voices as Max's. His tone was level, almost bored. "What's the situation?"

"Secured and restrained." That was definitely Aaron, and I felt the barest hint of relief that at least that part of the plan was in place.

I knew there'd never be a perfect time to walk in, that Aaron wouldn't be able to give me a signal for when I should walk through that door, and the longer I spent out here, the farther the guys Max had sent out for Evie got. I took the two steps to the door, then walked into the poorly lit room in which Max took care of business. He was sitting at his desk, leaning back in his chair, his body turned away from the doorway. Aaron was standing in front of the desk, his back to me, but from the stiff set of his shoulders, I knew he heard me come in. Very little was done in Aaron's presence without him knowing about it.

"Max." I forced the single syllable out, just barely restraining myself from leaping over the solid piece of wood furniture that stood between us and killing him with my bare hands. All I could think about was the orders he'd given to end Evie's life. I'd feel nothing but pure pleasure if I snuffed out his pulse.

He turned his chair to face me. His poker face was exceptional, and if it wasn't for the brief flicker of surprise in his eyes, I would've thought he'd almost expected this. "Well, well, well. I should've fucking known." His posture was relaxed,

his elbows braced loosely on the arms of his chair, showing me he
didn't find me a threat at all. Didn't matter that he wasn't surrounded with his normal level of security. Didn't matter that it
was only Aaron—who now stood off to the side, facing me—in
the room.

Taking a couple steps closer to him, I said, "We need to have
a little talk."

He hummed and nodded, interlocking his fingers as they
rested over his stomach. "Yeah, I think we do." Then he flicked
his eyes to Aaron and addressed him, "Pat him down and take
his gun."

I cursed internally, having hoped he wouldn't order Aaron to
do it, yet knowing he would. I could only hope Aaron wouldn't
strip me of the knives I had, too.

Aaron made quick work, patting me down efficiently, making a big show of pulling the gun out of my waistband, but not
going for either of the knives I had on me.

"You know, I have to say I'm surprised by you," Max said.
"We figured someone was helping our little Evie, someone within
the ranks. And with you disappearing over the last few days, all
clues pointed straight to you. And yet even with all that, I gotta
tell ya, Kid . . . I was sure it wasn't you. Honestly didn't think you
had the stones for something like this. Going up against the head
of the whole fucking crew? Your brother's gotten stupid since he
walked away if he sent you on this suicide mission."

"Not going to be a suicide mission at all."

"Oh, yeah? What makes you say that?"

"Because it would only be a suicide mission if you want all
the evidence of you embezzling twelve point seven million to
get sent to every major news outlet and the fucking cops. But
you know what? It'd almost be worth it just to see you go down
like that."

He laughed then, a cold, chilling sound, and reached down

to open his drawer. I tensed, ready to go for my bigger knife if forced to.

What he held up, though, wasn't a gun. But it was something equally chilling.

"This evidence, you mean?" Between his thumb and forefinger, he twisted a tiny black tube back and forth. One I wouldn't have taken a second glance at merely a week ago. But now, today, seeing it had my face draining of color, my heart thudding against my chest, my skin burning up. Because Evie had shown me that same little black object a couple days ago. The one she'd managed to hide for five years. The one that had been tucked safely away in her purse when I'd left her with Gage.

Every possibility went through my mind as to how he'd have that here, each worse than the last. I wanted to glance at Aaron, see if I could read anything in his expression, but I didn't dare. "Where'd you get that?"

Max hummed and flipped the object between his fingers, back and forth, back and forth. "It wasn't easy, I can tell you that. Your Evie is a tricky one. And, of course, with her working with two guys who were once in the crew, well . . . Made shit difficult for me. Speaking of, do I have you to thank for sending Frankie back to me looking like a goddamn MMA fighter?"

When we'd left Frankie at Evie's house all those days ago, I hadn't bothered to pay any attention at all to what kind of damage I'd done, too focused on getting Evie out of there. Couldn't say I was devastated to hear he'd taken a beating, especially when it was delivered by my hands. "He's lucky I didn't send him back looking like a fucking corpse."

Max let a smile creep over his face. "See, that's what I liked about you, Kid. You always did enjoy the physical aspect of the job, didn't you? And you were damn good at it. But you never had the heart for it. Not like Frankie. He's a complete fuckup, can't get his head out of his ass, could never stand against guys like you or Ghost, but he's a sick son of a bitch who loves doing the kind of fucked-up shit I have no problem sending his way."

"I don't need a history lesson on Frankie. I know the asshole."

"Do you?" he asked with a chilling smile on his face. "Do you know what he's been up to the last twenty-four hours, then? Seems he redeemed himself a little for that botch on the boat five years ago. And not managing to get her at her house." Max's hands clenched on the desk, the only sign that he was well and truly pissed off about those hiccups. "Even with two guys helping her, she was bound to slip up sooner or later. I just didn't think she'd practically fall right into our laps." He tipped his chin toward Aaron as he leaned forward, his forearms braced on the desk. I wanted to turn and lock eyes with Aaron as he walked by, wanted to get a read on what the hell was going on, but I didn't dare look away from Max. I couldn't understand what he was saying, what he was going on about. And what it meant that he had something of Evie's here with him.

There was a scuffle then, the sound of muffled grunts, and my heart stopped at what I saw coming through that doorway when I turned. Aaron followed behind as Frankie dragged Evie in, one fist wrapped tightly around her hair, the other on the hands bound behind her back. Her mouth was duct-taped, her hair was matted with a dark red stain on her hairline, and there was a bruise blooming on her cheek.

"She wouldn't give any information, so I had to rough her up a bit. She's a mouthy little bitch, isn't she?" Frankie said with a smile.

I didn't even need my knife. I was going to kill him with my bare hands.

I took half a step toward them before Max cut in, saying, "Uh-uh," at the same time Frankie's hand tightened on her hair, yanking her head back. She tried not to make any noise, tried not to show how it was affecting her, but I heard a muffled grunt with each tug of Frankie's fist against her hair.

Darting my eyes to every inch of her body, I took stock of everything else, noticing the wide rip in the neckline of her sweatshirt, part of the top of her bra showing. She had bruises on her neck in the shape of fingers, and my nostrils flared, my hands clenching into fists at my sides. It took everything in me to stay where I was, not to move forward, not to help her . . . get her to safety.

"Notice those bruises on her neck, did you?" Max asked. "Seems Frankie's got a little pent-up aggression in him. Especially after your little bitch head-butted him. That got him a bit more worked up than he already was."

Frankie's nose was darkening at the top, the skin below his left eye a deep purple, and it nearly brought a smile to my face because that was my girl.

"Now that I've showed my hand, Kid, I think you can see why I said this was a suicide mission for you. You're both here and we have the evidence. You don't have a lot of leverage."

It was my turn to laugh then, not taking my eyes off Evie. There was no fucking way I was turning my back on Frankie. Even with Aaron there. I wasn't sure I could trust him. Not now. Not after seeing he'd let Frankie alone with Evie. Part of me wondered if something had happened. If something had changed along the way. If maybe Max had promised him a cut of that twelve million he'd stolen in exchange for getting information from us. I'd known Aaron for a long time—he was the only guy in the entire crew besides me who Gage trusted, but money made people do a lot of fucked-up shit. And when that money was in the millions . . .

Still watching Evie, I said to Max, "If you think that's the only copy, you're a fucking idiot."

"Of course I know that's not the only copy." He must have

made a gesture because suddenly Aaron stepped over to grab a chair from the wall and placed it next to where Evie and Frankie were.

"Go stand guard at the front," Aaron said to Frankie as he reached for Evie.

Frankie's mouth drew back in a snarl, and his hand tightened in her hair, drawing her head back until her neck was taut and her eyes were wide. "What? No fucking way. I was promised I'd get to kill this cunt."

"You also told Max that you'd already killed her. That she was dead and he didn't have anything to worry about. And now look at the mess you've got us in. I said to go to the fucking front unless you want to join her on your knees in front of me with a gun pointed at your head." Aaron's voice was steady and calm, with no inflection, but he radiated authority. I didn't think anyone in the room doubted just how serious he was, and I almost wished Frankie was stupid enough to spout off more. I'd love nothing more than to see him bleeding out at my feet. The only regretful part would be me not having a hand in it.

Frankie shoved Evie toward Aaron, then stalked off, flipping the bird as he went. Aaron's eyes lifted to mine for the briefest moment as he pushed on Evie's shoulder and guided her to sit in the chair. It took everything in me not to run after Frankie. Not to take him by surprise and make him sorry for every finger he'd ever laid on Evie. The only thing that held me glued to this spot was Evie herself. I wasn't leaving her alone. I couldn't.

"Now," Max's voice cut in, "I'm going to ask you one more time where the rest of the evidence is. Or you get to watch while she gets a bullet put through that pretty little head."

Chapter Twenty-Nine

I watched with horror as Aaron took a gun from the waistband of his jeans and pressed it against Evie's head. Her eyes went wide then, frantic, as she stared at me. She was breathing rapidly, her chest heaving as she tried to pull in deep breaths through her nose. A million things danced in her eyes, a thousand unasked questions, and I didn't have any answers. I didn't know a fucking thing. Nothing was going according to plan, nothing was how we'd talked about it, and now her life was on the line. Now she was in danger, and I wasn't going to be able to do a damn thing to help her. Again.

Every time she'd ever needed me, needed someone there to help her, I'd failed her, and this was no different.

"It's okay, baby. It's okay," I said, trying to soothe her, trying to keep my voice even and calm, but by the fearful gleam that still shone in her eyes, I wasn't successful in convincing her.

Max laughed again. "Aww, that's sweet. I hate to be the bearer of bad news, but nothing is going to be okay until you tell me where the rest of the evidence is."

Swallowing my fear, I leveled my voice and spoke to Max,

though I kept my eyes on Evie, on the point of the gun nestled in her hair, on the finger Aaron had wrapped around the trigger. "It's too late. Everything's already been put into place. If Evie and I don't come out of here, evidence gets mailed off to every major news outlet and to Chicago's finest."

I heard the creak of his office chair and caught movement out of the corner of my eye as he leaned forward. "Well, that's not the answer I was hoping for, Kid. Seems we've got a bit of a problem. Because I'm not letting either of you walk out of here. And it would be very bad for business if anyone got wind of the twelve-million-dollar nest egg I'm sitting on, courtesy of Chicago's favorite businessman, Blaine Pruitt. I've been doing this for six goddamn years, and if you think I'm going to let you two lackeys fuck this up for me, you haven't learned a damn thing from me."

"I don't think they're the ones who are going to fuck this up for you, Max. I think you did that all on your own." The voice came from the doorway, and I slid my gaze from Evie for a split second to watch as three guys filled the frame of the door. The one in front was dressed impeccably in a well-tailored suit, the two guys flanking him at the back in dark shirts and jeans, much like Aaron, their bulk blocking out the light from the open warehouse behind them.

It took me a minute to place the guy in front, but as I stared at his dark hair peppered with gray, his aristocratic nose and clean-shaven face, a spark of recognition flared, and this was either the best possible outcome or the worst, because it seemed that Blaine had decided to pay Max a visit.

"Hope that piece of garbage at the front wasn't anyone important," he said as he walked farther into the room, glancing to the left at where Evie sat in the chair in front of Aaron, then to the gun pointed at her head. When he turned to look at me, his eyes settled on my face for a couple of seconds before he turned to Max. He unbuttoned his suit coat and tucked his hand into the front pocket of his pants, casual as you please. "This is quite the shit hole you have here. You'd think with twelve million and some change you'd be able to afford a nicer headquarters for your crew."

Max's face turned red with rage as he stood from his chair, leaning over his desk. "You fucking bitch! You sold me out."

Though her mouth was covered, Evie's eyes sparkled like she was smiling, and then she moved the arms from behind her back, sliding her hands free of the rope and letting it fall to her feet, and reached up to peel the tape from her mouth. "I didn't, but I sure as hell wish I had."

"What the fuck . . ." Max breathed. And then before I could move, before I could blink, before I could even really consider how Evie'd been able to get out of her restraints, I watched in horror as Max reached under his desk and pulled out a gun, pointing it right at her. "Should've done this myself five years ago."

I didn't think before I dove toward her a split second before a shot rang out.

EVIE

It all happened so fast. The blink of an eye, really. One minute Aaron had his gun pointed at me, and the next he was using the distraction of Blaine to loosen my ropes enough so I was able to slip free of them. Then there was shouting, the angry look Max fixed on me as he pointed a gun straight at my chest. Riley crashed into me from the side, knocking me off the chair and onto the floor at the same time the earsplitting sound of a gunshot rang in the small room, followed almost immediately by another. His full weight settled harshly on top of me as I slammed into the cool concrete floor, the force of which knocked the wind out of me.

There was so much commotion, so many voices, none of which I could focus on. All I could do was stare at the ceiling and wonder why Riley hadn't gotten off me yet. And then I felt the wetness at my shoulder a moment before Aaron was above us, rolling Riley to the side as Riley's loud groan filled my ear.

"Jesus, Kid," Aaron said, kneeling next to us, his focus on Riley. "Can you hear me?"

Was he asking that because the shots had been so loud in the tiny room? My ears were ringing, but I could still make out everything he was saying, could still hear movement from elsewhere in the room, other voices, too. Once again noticing the wetness seeping through my sweater onto my skin, I reached up to press my fingers to it. Red-stained fingertips met my gaze when I brought my hand in front of my face.

"Is Evie okay?" Riley asked, his voice frantic and strained. "Did she get hit?"

Even as I heard Aaron say, "She's fine, man. You did good," I still took stock of my body, thinking I'd somehow gotten shot in the commotion, that my body had gone numb from the shock. But Aaron was leaning over Riley, all his focus on him, and everything clicked into place. The gunshot. Riley knocking into me from the side. The bloodstain on my shirt.

It wasn't my blood. It was his.

"No . . ." I breathed, scrambling up on my knees to look down at Riley. Dark red pooled under his shoulder, the stain spreading. Someone was calling my name, but I couldn't focus on anything but the sight of Riley lying in front of me and his bloodstained shirt.

I reached out, running my hands over his face, over as much of his body as I could reach, making sure he was okay. His eyes were focused on me, blinking up at me, and I wanted to drown in them. I didn't realize I was crying until Riley reached up with his good arm and wiped the flow of tears with his thumb.

"It's okay. I'm okay," he said.

"Evie!" Aaron snapped, shaking my shoulder to finally get my attention. "I need you to put pressure on the wound so I can help him sit up. Can you do that?" He grabbed my hands and placed them on either side of Riley's shoulder, then used both of his to apply pressure to mine, showing me what to do.

I nodded and looked over at him, realizing that he'd stripped off his shirt at some point, the warm cotton material now under my hands and helping to stop the blood flow from Riley's bullet wound.

"Okay?" Aaron asked again. "The bullet went straight through, but it managed to miss all his main arteries. He's gonna be fine."

"You can't know that! He needs to get to a hospital."

"Evie." Aaron's voice was low but commanding, and I looked over at him, my eyes wide and frantic, hands hovering helplessly above Riley's body. "This isn't the first gunshot wound I've seen. I've got Doc coming in, but we can't bring him to the ER. You know that."

Because if Riley went to the hospital with a gunshot wound, the police would be called. Doc had been the one Gage and Aaron had called to patch me up all those years ago, so I trusted him. Nodding once again, I swallowed and pressed down with both hands while Aaron helped Riley sit up.

Aaron moved to stand, but before he could get far, Riley asked, "Gage? Does he know?"

Aaron was stoic, had always been a blank slate, his poker face impeccable, but I swore the side of his mouth tipped up on one side. "Who do you think called Blaine? As soon as he realized Evie'd been taken, he was getting shit lined up."

Riley blew out a sigh of relief as Aaron walked to another part of the room, his voice mixing with a couple others, but I couldn't focus on what they were saying. Couldn't focus on anything but Riley's pale face, his forehead beaded with sweat, as his eyes darted to every inch of me that he could see.

"You're not hurt?" he asked.

"No," I said, the single word coming out in a croak.

As if he didn't take my word for it, he swept his eyes along my body, his brows creasing when he got to my chest. Reaching out with his good arm, Riley tugged up the neck of my shirt, the part that Frankie had ripped earlier. When I'd been conscious enough to start fighting. He hadn't been with me long before Aaron had come in, but it'd been long enough. Long enough for him to backhand me. Long enough for me to break his nose.

"You can show me that pretty bra later," Riley said. "The rest of these assholes don't need to see it."

It was such a Riley thing to say, even as he was sitting there with a fresh bullet wound, that I couldn't stop the choked laughter from spilling forth.

Riley's eyes darted down to my mouth, then his lips kicked up at the sides, a small smile forming. "There it is." He brought his hand up to my face, his thumb running along my cheek. "I've been waiting this whole week for you to smile for me like that. If I'd known all it took was a gunshot wound, I might've made it happen sooner."

The smile dropped from my face, thoughts of everything that had happened over the last few hours bombarding me. I didn't attempt to stop the tears as they welled up and spilled over. "Don't say that."

"Hey, it's okay. I'm okay." He reached up again, his hand cradling my face as his thumb tried to catch every tear rolling down my cheeks.

"No you're not! You're shot, and it's my fault. Because I got it in my head that I couldn't be strong and still stay behind. I'm sorry, Riley. I should've listened to what you were saying instead of holding so tightly to what I thought I needed to do. I was so worried about you taking any power I had away from me that I couldn't see past it."

"Come here," he said, his voice gruff as he tugged me forward until our noses were mere inches apart. "I don't ever want to make you feel powerless, Evie. It wasn't about taking the choice away from you, but about making sure you were out of harm's way. Making sure you were safe. I didn't want you anywhere near Max or Frankie again."

I nodded, closing my eyes as fresh tears ran down my face. I couldn't stop them, didn't even try to. I was too relieved that Riley was okay.

"You don't need to prove your strength to anyone, baby. Least of all me. I *know* how strong you are. You've been through more in your life than everyone else in this room combined. And you're still standing. That's pretty strong. That's pretty fucking amazing."

I allowed his words to seep into me, letting them wash over my insecurities. I heard him, heard everything he was saying.

I just had to start believing.

Chapter Thirty

Riley's apartment was so familiar, even though I'd never been here before. It was reminiscent of the place he and Gage had had when we were in high school. The walls were white, stained yellow with age, the carpet a dark brown, no doubt hiding years of stains. A beat-up couch and a giant TV were the only things in the living room.

It was so strange that I felt more at home here, stepping into this space I'd never been, than I had the entire time I'd lived in a beautiful house with Eric.

Riley led the way down the hall, our hands linked between us. He hadn't let me out of his sight since everything had gone down with Max. Not when Aaron was making calls, barking orders to everyone in the crew who'd been sent out to find me. Not when Aaron had come over to talk to Riley as Doc had patched him up. Not when Blaine offered his gratitude to me for finding the evidence about Max's embezzlement. Not when we'd crammed in the backseat of Aaron's car so he could drop us off, since Riley wasn't going to be able to drive his bike for some time, at least not until his bullet wound healed.

He didn't say anything as he flipped on the light in his bedroom. His bed was unmade and rumpled, a few pairs of jeans lying on the floor. The room was bare, much like the rest of his place. Riley's grunt pulled me out of my appraisal of his space, and I turned to see him attempting to tug his shirt over his head.

"What are you doing?" I asked, the reprimand in my tone apparent.

"I'm getting undressed so *we* can get in the shower." His eyes flitted up to mine, then focused on the place to the right of my eyes, the place I knew was a matted mess with dried blood. When Frankie had backhanded me earlier, the force had sent me flying, my head glancing off the corner of a table. It still hurt like a bitch. "I can't stand to look at that on you and think about what he did to you."

His voice was filled with so much emotion, so much agony, that I couldn't do anything but nod and follow him into the bathroom. We undressed carefully, our movements only focused on inciting the least amount of pain. Riley's arm was contained mostly to his side, the barest movement causing his teeth to clench, his wound wrapped in a waterproof bandage at Riley's request, with more supplies given to us so I could play nurse later.

Once we were under the warm spray, I grabbed the bar of soap and sudsed up my hands then ran them over his chest and arms, giving the area around his bandage a wide berth so I didn't accidentally get it wet. When I let my hands wander over his abdomen and lower, he grabbed my wrist before I could get to where he was hard for me. He took the soap from me and scrubbed the rest of himself in under a minute.

Then his attention was focused directly on me, and I couldn't look away.

He switched our positions so my head was under the spray, and I closed my eyes as I let the hot water beat down on me.

Using his good arm, he reached up and brushed the hair back from my face, then grabbed the shampoo and poured some directly on my hair before he started working it into a lather. I tried to reach up and help him, knowing how difficult it probably was to do one-handed.

"Let me," he said, his voice low and gritty. His eyes were concentrated on me, on the wound at my hairline—the one that looked worse than it felt. "If he wasn't already dead, I'd kill him myself for hurting you."

And he would, too. Of that I had no doubt. The conviction in his voice just reiterated how much he would do for me. Reiterated that he'd always be there to make sure I was safe. That he'd do anything to see me happy. That I'd never have to go through anything on my own again. Not if I didn't want to.

His fingers were gentle, delicate, as they brushed over the place where my throat was sore, where Frankie had choked me. Then he trailed them over the rest of my body. There was nothing sexual about it, despite the fact that his cock was straining toward me. He washed me, cleansed me of not only the dirt and grime that had accumulated on my body, but the emotional weight that I'd carried with me as well.

When the soap was rinsed from both of us, Riley turned off the shower and reached out to grab a towel for me. He tried as best he could to dry me off with one arm, trying so hard to take care of me, even though he was the one with the bullet wound. Once I was able to wrest it from him, he grabbed one for himself, quickly and efficiently drying off.

"Shit, I can't even wrap a goddamn towel around myself."

I knew he was frustrated, knew how hard it must be for him not to be able to do everything for himself when he'd done so for so long. But even knowing that, I couldn't help but chuckle as I stared at his naked backside.

He looked at me over his shoulder, his eyes darting down to take in the towel I'd covered up with. "You find that funny, do you?"

Trying to suppress a smile, I shrugged. "A little."

Before I could stop him, he reached out and snatched the towel from around my chest, letting it pool at my feet. He mimicked my shrug, then said, "Fair's fair."

I didn't protest, standing in front of him naked as I tended to his wound, getting a clean bandage on him. Once he had a fresh dressing on the wound and he'd slipped one of his shirts over my head, he pulled me into his bed, tucking me into his good side. We lay together, much like we had right before we'd gotten the call from Gage. The call that had set everything in motion. And even though it hadn't gone ideally, hadn't gone how any of us had initially planned, I couldn't regret it. Because Max was dead and Riley was safe and I was in his arms.

We were quiet for a while as Riley ran his hand up and down my arm, his fingers slowing down until eventually they stopped and I knew sleep would come for him any second. Instead of succumbing to it, he asked, "What now?" His voice was heavy, just a whispered breath between us.

Running my hand over his stomach, I said, "Now you need to get some sleep. It's not every day you get shot."

He squeezed my hip, turning his head toward mine, his nose nestled in my damp hair as he inhaled deeply. "I don't mean tonight. I mean tomorrow and the day after and the day after that." His once-relaxed body was now tight under my caressing hand. "You can do whatever you want. You don't have to be hidden away as Genevieve anymore."

I could do anything. Go anywhere. Be anyone. I could move to Phoenix or Portland or stay right here in Chicago. I could utilize the degree I'd gotten and actually do something I liked with my life . . . I could go into investigative journalism like I'd always wanted.

I could be with Riley.

"Just sleep. Don't worry about it right now. We can talk about it more tomorrow."

But as Riley's breathing evened out, his body going lax, I knew I wouldn't need till tomorrow to make a decision. Because there wasn't one to make. There'd never been one to make.

I only wanted to be one place with one person, and while I was there, I wanted to be the version of myself he brought out in me. The version he reminded me I could be.

Thinking about my life in Minneapolis, the one waiting for me, the one I'd set up so perfectly, only filled me with a sense of dread. Because it wasn't there I wanted to be. It wasn't Eric's arm I wanted to be attached to for the rest of my life. My home wasn't a fancy house, living there while attending fundraisers and brushing elbows with some of the wealthiest people around.

It was wherever Riley was.

After Riley's breaths had evened out enough that I was certain he was asleep, I slipped out from under his arm and crept into the living room, looking for his phone. I found it on the counter by his keys and picked it up. I stared at the small rectangle, thinking about what I was about to do. What making this call would mean. There was no going back after this. No do-overs. If I did this, it was final.

I brushed my thumb up and down the screen, then powered it up. After navigating to the call screen, I took a deep breath as I dialed the number I'd memorized.

Three rings later, a deep voice answered. "Hello?"

I paused, closing my eyes. Then I said, "It's me."

"Gen?" Eric asked immediately. "Are you all right? What's happened?"

I blew out a huff of laughter and shook my head. What *hadn't* happened? Since I'd last spoken to Eric, I'd been on a roller coaster, my entire world flipping and spinning and dropping into a free fall. Instead of saying any of that, I settled simply on, "It's done. We're not in danger anymore. Riley made sure I was okay."

"And you're still not going to tell me what's going on?"

"I can't, Eric. I don't want you involved any more than you absolutely have to be. I never wanted you to get caught up in the crossfire, and it's safer if you don't know any details, even if I don't have any reason to believe it'd ever come back to haunt either of us. I just want to keep you as safe as I can."

He hummed in acknowledgment, then was quiet for a moment before he asked, "Is this good-bye then?"

"Eric . . ."

"No, Gen, don't. Don't feel guilty. Is this what you want? Is Riley the life you want?"

Without hesitation, I answered, "Yes."

"Then that's all I need to know—that this is what you want. That *he's* what you want. I'd never want to keep you from that. I just want you to be happy."

"I want you to be happy, too." My voice was wobbly when I said it, but this was breaking my heart. Eric had been my only friend for so long. And he *had* been a friend. My best friend, one who may not have known the true person I was, but who accepted the bits I'd shown him.

He sighed heavily, and I could picture him in his fancy hotel suite in London, pacing the floor with his hand in the pocket of his suit pants. Looking like he had the weight of the world on his shoulders. "Me, too. And I'm working on it. Figured if you can be brave, maybe I can, too."

I smiled at that, his words warming my heart. Then I thought about everything that was paid for and in place: the wedding dress that I'd already purchased, the vendors who'd already been paid, the reception hall that had already been reserved. And he was going to have to deal with it entirely on his own. "What'll you tell your parents?"

"Don't worry about that. I'll figure it out. You just focus on yourself, okay?"

I swallowed the lump that was suddenly filling my throat. I tried to stop my voice from quavering, but didn't quite manage. "Will I talk to you again?"

"If you want to."

"I do."

"Then we will. Whenever you want. You know how to reach me, Gen."

I was quiet for a moment, then I said good-bye once and for all to the manufactured me. The one who hid from her troubles instead of facing them. "It's actually Evie."

He hummed, and I could hear the smile in his voice. "Suits you."

I smiled at that, feeling lighter than I had in longer than I could remember. "I'll talk to you soon, Eric."

"Good-bye, Evie."

I hung up and placed Riley's phone back on the counter, then walked down the hall and into his bedroom. He was still sound asleep on his back, his head turned to where I'd been lying before I'd slipped out. I crawled onto the bed and slid under the covers, tucking myself up against his side. As soon as I was close enough, his arm settled around me, holding me tightly to him. He dipped his head until his lips rested against my forehead. I felt his mouth move against my skin as he breathed, "Stay with me."

I ran my hands over his smooth skin, tracing the parts of him I'd memorized so long ago. He was my past, the tiny flicker of light in a sea of darkness. He was my present, when everything was jumbled and uncertain, but where I'd be able to figure it out if I was with him. And I knew, with utter certainty, he was my future.

Pressing my lips over his chest, I answered his plea. "I will."

Epilogue

RILEY

I paced the length of the apartment as I waited for Evie to get back. She'd been gone all afternoon, hours spent without me, discussing things I knew she'd rather never mention again. But she did. She was so fucking brave, so strong. She amazed me.

She'd called awhile ago when she'd finished up at the courthouse, letting me know she was done and on her way. She'd sounded exhausted, her voice scratchy and rough, no doubt from crying, and I wished so fucking much that she'd let me be by her side when she had to do shit like this. That she'd let me go with her when she'd gone to the police station the very first time. Or any of the dozens of times she'd met with her lawyer. But I could understand her reasoning for wanting to do it on her own.

She wanted to know she could be strong even without me by her side.

A key slid into the lock, and then the doorknob was turning. Evie walked through the door and shut it behind her as she leaned back against the heavy wood, her head bowed and eyes closed.

Her hair was pulled away from her face, secured in a ponytail at the base of her head, not hiding any bit of her from me. She looked absolutely exhausted, purple bruises marring the skin beneath her eyes.

I walked over until I stood in front of her, then reached for her hands. Running my thumbs back and forth against the backs of them, I waited until she lifted her eyes to mine. When she did, there was the undeniable exhaustion I knew would be there, but there was also pride shining through.

She tipped her chin up and said, "I did it."

I bent my knees until we were eye level, and a smile spread across my face. "Yeah, you did, baby." Wrapping my arms around her, I lifted her off her feet as her arms encircled my neck. "I knew you could." I turned my face to her neck and inhaled, then pressed a kiss to her skin. "You wanna talk about it?"

She shook her head against me.

I asked every time, though her answer was always the same. After every step of the way—when she'd gone to the police station, after her first meeting with the lawyer—she'd come back emotionally exhausted, without the desire to expend any more energy talking about what happened. In time, she always told me. Sometimes in bits, sprinkled throughout several days or even longer, and other times in a waterfall of information all in one sitting. However it was, however she was most comfortable sharing, I'd take. I'd take it and I'd sit there and be the shoulder she needed to lean on.

Setting her down on her feet, I pulled back enough to look in her eyes. "What do you want to do? Name it."

She answered the same as she always did. "Movies and ice cream."

With a nod, I said, "Done." I leaned in and captured her lips between mine, pressing several kisses to her mouth. Then I wrapped my hands over her shoulders and turned her around

before giving her ass a slap. "Go change. Meet you on the couch
in five."

While she was in the bedroom, I grabbed a carton of her favorite flavor out of the freezer and a spoon, then set them on the
coffee table—an addition Evie'd said we had to have when we'd
moved into this new apartment in a better area of the city to make
movie nights more comfortable. I went back into the kitchen and
opened the cabinet over the fridge. It was too high for her to
reach, so I knew I wouldn't have to worry about her accidentally
coming across the long rectangular box I'd slipped in there a
couple weeks ago. The box that had been sitting there waiting.
For the perfect time. For today.

Her footfalls echoed down the hallway as she made her way
into the living room, then she shuffled through the collection of
movies we had until she settled on what she wanted. "How was
work last night?" she asked.

I'd gotten home late, after three in the morning, and she'd
left midmorning, waking me long enough for a good-bye kiss before she went to the courthouse.

I grabbed a beer out of the fridge, mostly so I didn't walk
out there empty-handed. "It was okay. I actually had a visitor."

"Oh, yeah? Who?"

"Aaron."

Her head whipped around from where she stood by the TV,
her eyes wide and panicked.

"No, it's okay. It was nothing wrong. Well, not really."

"What was it, then?" she asked as she walked over to the
couch, kneeling on the cushions and bracing her arms on the back
as she looked at me still in the kitchen.

"He wanted me back."

"Running jobs?"

"Yeah. Said I could pick and choose which ones I take. That
I'd have seniority over all the other guys there."

I studied her face as I said everything, watching for a hint of apprehension. And I found it. Even though she didn't hold it against Aaron for stepping up to run the crew after Max's death, she didn't agree with it. It held such bad memories for her—first the place she'd run to when she'd needed an escape from her life, then the place she'd run *from*.

"What'd you tell him?"

I twisted the cap off my beer and shrugged. "That I'm happy bouncing at the club, and I have no intentions of ever going back."

I didn't, either. The years I'd spent running with the crew seemed like a lifetime ago, though in reality it'd only been months since I'd been in that life. I'd done it initially because it was all I'd known. And then, even when I didn't have to stay in it, when I could've done a dozen other things, I'd let myself get pulled deeper because it'd been the only way I knew to obtain justice for the murder of the girl I loved. But the only guys who needed to pay for that were both six feet under.

Slipping the box into the pocket of my hoodie, I walked over to her and sat on the couch, settling my beer on the table. She turned toward me, then sat down, her legs tucked under her.

"You're sure? I don't want you to feel like you have to stop for me."

"Baby . . ." I reached out, tugging her face to mine for a kiss. "I started for you, and it was for all the wrong reasons. I'm stopping for you for all the right ones. And I'm not sorry about it."

She stared at me for long moments, her hand resting on my chest as her eyes flitted back and forth between mine, then she gave a little nod of acceptance. Glancing over at the table, she asked, "Where's your popcorn?"

"Forgot to make it." I moved to get up, but she pressed the hand on my chest harder.

"I got it. Get the movie started."

She walked into the kitchen and soon the microwave was

going, the kernels popping and masking the sound of me moving around. I slipped the box out of my pocket and set it on top of the ice cream container, then settled back against the cushions as she came back around and handed me a bowl before she sat down next to me.

Without looking down from the movie already playing on the screen, she reached for the carton on the table, knocking the box off in the process.

Glancing at it, she asked, "What's that?"

"Looks like a box."

She rolled her eyes and reached over to grab it, setting it in her lap. "I can see it's a box, but what's in it?"

"Should probably open it and find out."

Narrowing her eyes, she stared at me for a minute before she looked down as she pulled the lid off. It wasn't even a second later before recognition struck and she gasped, her eyes already filling as they looked up at me.

"Riley . . ."

I reached for the box, gripping the thick silver chain-link necklace as I pulled it out. With steady hands, I unclasped the hook, then gestured for Evie to turn her back to me. I slipped the necklace over her head, placing it on her neck and hooking it in place.

"How long have you had this?" Her voice was barely over a whisper.

"A while." She glanced back at me, and I said, "The whole time. Gage had gotten it for me after the story of the boat went through the ranks in the crew. It's been sitting in a drawer, broken, for five years. But you deserved to have it back. A couple months ago, you told me it always made you feel safe whenever you wore it, and I want you to feel like that all the time."

With her head bowed, she reached up and touched the heart-shaped locket that hung in the center, right at the dip of her collarbones. She turned then and climbed into my lap, her hands settled on my jaw. "I love it. More than anything. And I'm glad you gave it back to me. But I don't need it anymore to feel safe. Not when I know you're here. That you're by my side no matter what."

I leaned forward and pressed my lips to hers. She melted into me, brushing her tongue against mine, and I didn't think this would ever grow old. Holding her in my arms, waking up next to her every morning, having her be the last thing I saw before falling asleep. Five years ago, I'd lost the girl I'd loved more than anything. And then I'd found a woman who I loved more than I thought was possible.

I pulled back and whispered the only word that mattered. "Always."

A Note from the Author

Dear Reader,

This story was a hard one to tell. And one, to be honest, that I fought in the early stages with every ounce of my being. For authors, our characters are sort of like our children, and the thought of them going through something so horrific is hard to accept. It killed me to think that something this horrendous happened to one of my characters. More than that, though, it kills me to know that it happens to hundreds of thousands of others every year. But the truth of the matter is, it does, and it's not anything to turn a blind eye to, not anything to turn our backs on. When I stopped trying to find every excuse in the world for the path Evie took and finally listened to what she had to say, I understood. Her history, as awful as it was, is something that makes her who she is—not something that defines her, but something that's a part of her, just like her tenacity and strength.

If you found a kindred spirit in Evie, I hope you've found the strength to share your story. If you haven't, there are people who are there to help and to listen. You don't have to be silent anymore.

RAINN (Rape, Abuse and Incest National Network)

www.rainn.org

National Sexual Assault Hotline

1-800-656-HOPE

National Sexual Violence Resource Center

www.nsvrc.org

Acknowledgments

Sometimes, thank you isn't enough, and I found that to be the case many times while writing this book. Alas, all I have is *thank you*, so I'll say it a thousand times.

To Christina, I think this all the time, but I rarely say it, so I'm saying it now: your strength and resilience is amazing and awe inspiring. Thank you for giving me the courage and the push needed to stop trying to find excuses for Evie's character and truly listen to her, allow her to speak. Thank you for holding my hand while I wrote the hardest thing I've ever written, and for offering your wisdom and encouragement and support while I traversed the difficult path of her character. You're amazing, and I'm so very grateful I get to call you not only my Plot Whisperer but my friend.

To every single survivor I spoke to who willingly shared their experiences with me, thank you. It doesn't suffice, but it's all I have to give. Thank you a million times for your insight and for trusting me enough to share your stories with me.

To my editor, Rose Hilliard, for brainstorming with me in the early stages and helping me grow this into the idea that eventually became Riley and Evie. Thank you for helping me develop this book into the best it could be.

To my agent, Mandy Hubbard, for always being an e-mail away when I need you. And for being a total rock star. To the various people who helped with various aspects of this book. Now that we have Twitter, it's become so easy to have experts at our fingertips and get help when we need it. I'm so very grateful to Shari Slade, Elenna H., Sara Taylor Woods, Sarah Henson, Kristin W., Tara Wyatt, and Elisabeth H. for your insights and suggestions on everything from analogies to bullet wound cleaning to sparring techniques. You all rock.

To the readers who enjoyed *Captive* and were excited to get Riley's story, thank you for your support and for reading! Your excitement over my work only makes me want to produce it faster.

To all the girls in Brighton's Brigade on Facebook, you all rock so hard. Thank you for your friendship, your support, and your experiences and opinions that you freely offer me when I ask!

And last but not least, to my family and friends who have supported me so much more than I ever imagined. If I could, I'd thank each and every one of you by name, but then the acknowledgments would rival the length of the book. If you're reading this, and you know me, know I count you among this group. Thank you, from the bottom of my heart. I love you all.